COME ABOUT FOR MURDER

A MELLINGHAM MYSTERY

SUSAN OLEKSIW

Hale Street Press ◆ Prides Crossing, MA ◆ 01965

Copyright (c) 2016 by Susan Prince Oleksiw

ISBN 978-0-9973520-2-3

Other books by Susan Oleksiw

The Mellingham Series
Murder in Mellingham
Double Take
Family Album
Friends and Enemies
A Murderous Innocence

The Anita Ray Series
Under the Eye of Kali
The Wrath of Shiva
For the Love of Parvati
When Krishna Calls

DEDICATION

David Scott Allen and Mark J. Sammons

* * * * *

Acknowledgments

Elenita Lodge and Harry S. Lodge read earlier versions of this book and offered valuable suggestions on the story as well as technical aspects of sailing.

Come About for Murder

CHAPTER ONE

In his last will and testament, Commodore Charles Jeremiah Winslow, one of the greatest yachting enthusiasts in the history of Mellingham Yacht Club, asked to be wrapped in a mainsail and cremated, with his ashes left to sink into Mellingham Bay. His family argued for six days and six nights over whether or not to comply with his wishes, but when they understood how much money was riding on this, they agreed to do as he wanted.

Annie Beckwith, only a teenager at the time, thought it was a terrible waste of a good sail. But she agreed one hundred percent with his longing to remain in the sea for eternity and his equally strong desire to stay out of the family mausoleum. Her sister had achieved this two weeks earlier by falling off a sailboat and disappearing below the waves, but her sister's husband, Randall Connolly, had died on land only two days later, early on Sunday morning. So here Annie was, on a Friday morning in August, standing outside the family mausoleum and all she could think about was that it was a perfect day for a sail.

If the day had been gray and rainy, that would make Randall's funeral all so much easier. Funerals required a certain backdrop—dark gloomy weather, people in black leaning on each other as their umbrellas flapped in the rain, the cold wind sending sharp tendrils around bare ankles. The weather should make everyone miserable. Instead, she got men and women in casual clothes, khakis and summer dresses, and a sunny day with perfect air.

The clouds were just the right size, the right shape, little puffs to move a boat along, sending it cutting through the waves, lifting the spindrift to the bow and the faces of the crew. The sky was just the right hue to shade into the ocean, merging sea and sky into one magnificent world that animated her soul.

Annie's thoughts went to the Lady Mistral, which should have been riding at anchor as the light breeze sent waves rippling along her water line. Annie imagined the halyards slapping the top of the mast, the creak of floorboards and the coaming. But the boat wasn't at one with the sea and the wind. It was dry-docked at Mellingham Marina by order of Chief Joe Silva and various other authorities, including the Coast Guard. Annie winced at the thought. It was bad enough that she had to shut her eyes against the image of her sister slipping into the ocean. But to have the chief of police of quiet little Mellingham suspecting something more than an accident made her stomach clench and her knees go weak. She couldn't even bring herself to look at him, though she knew he stood among the other mourners, his uniform exchanged for a dark suit.

Annie felt a gentle tug on her elbow as Max Hasden, family friend and attorney, pulled her to the side and six men carried her brother-in-law's casket into the mausoleum. She had known Max for years; he was a constant at summer parties and holiday gatherings. He was Randall's closest friend, and she seemed to have inherited him, or his professional interest, after Randall's death. He did all the things a good lawyer is supposed to do, including urging her to draw up a last will and testament after Randall's death, review the family bills and commitments, and go through all the documents scattered around the house.

Annie had to laugh at that. Neither Deb nor Randall was the type to scatter anything anywhere—they were tidy not just as a matter of character but also as a result of not collecting stuff. They owned what they needed and liked, but neither one was the shopping kind. Deb and Randall kept impeccable records, and Annie's eyes glazed over whenever they fell into a discussion of the best filing system for photographs or the best storage materials for tax records, or whatever it was they loved talking about over wine on the back deck. Annie fell asleep in a nanosecond as soon as they started. But she had admired them and their ability to manage life, and promised them both she would take their advice—eventually. As a result Annie had no will, all legal papers looked the same to her, and she thought the best place for paper records was the recycling bin.

The cemetery was small, one of the oldest in Mellingham. The Beckwiths had a family plot that dated from the early eighteenth century, as well as the carved granite mausoleum from the nineteenth. Annie might not have Deb's body to honor with a service and a salute as she set sail for another life, with the wind at her back, but Randall's body would be the anchor for Annie's grief. When the episcopal priest objected to the service, on the grounds of how Randall had died, Annie threatened to withhold the funds that came from the Beckwith family trust for the cemetery upkeep. He acquiesced, and she lapsed into the semiconscious state that had been her norm since her sister's death.

The minister spoke to her, a whisper that sounded kind though the words made little sense, and she could hear people murmuring to each other behind her. She heard the rustling of paper as mourners put away the order of service, the occasional word as they began speaking to each other again. Car doors slammed, a truck started to drive into the cemetery and was sent back, a gaggle of boys on bicycles careened by on a side street. Annie counted the minutes until the entire ordeal was over.

Later that afternoon, after the funeral meats, Max Hasden drove Annie back to the Agawam Inn, which stood almost directly across the street from Deb and Randall's house. She had rented a room there the day after Randall's death, preparing herself for the day when she would have to walk into her sister's home alone. She had hired a HazMat team, but left it to Chief Silva to pass along keys and instructions.

Max offered to stay with her for the rest of the day after the funeral, or longer, but she sent him away. She had to get her bearings, and she had to do it on her own. Chief Silva had returned the house keys to her after the service, reported the HazMat team had been and gone, and she was free to occupy the house when she was ready. When Max's car had turned the corner, driving out of sight, she looked across the road at the shingled house standing quiet and empty in the afternoon sun.

With a twist of her shoulders, perhaps to shake loose more self-confidence than she felt, she crossed the road to her sister and brother-in-law's home.

Annie walked through the house like an interloper—afraid to touch things because they belonged to someone else, afraid to open closet doors because it felt like prying, afraid to talk to Max about Deb and Randall's estate because it seemed so tacky. The first floor was excessively clean and tidy, the result of the HazMat workers who had descended on the property after the police gave the go-ahead.

Barely a week after the loss of her sister, Deb, in a freak boating accident, Annie struggled to absorb the death of her sister's husband. His death had been ultimately recorded as a suicide by the state police. At first Annie avoided looking at the sofa where his body had been found, but an hour later she couldn't stop staring at it. How could two people, who had lived such a charmed life together, who had their best years ahead of them, come to such sudden and violent ends?

CHAPTER TWO

On Tuesday, four days after Randall's funeral, Annie leaned on the railing at the Mellingham Yacht Club and watched the club launch travel from boat to boat, delivering sailors one after the other. Tuesday in the summer was never a slack day, but she didn't recall it being this busy either. A horn tooted and Lincoln Walsh, the club captain and the only full-time employee of the yacht club, raised his head and swiveled around, checking for the call. He saw the source, and turned the launch toward it. He provided the yacht club's private ferry service, among other things.

The mooring float and flag for the Lady Mistral bobbed in the outer harbor. Twenty years ago, when Annie was still a teenager, the Lady Mistral, the Beckwith family boat, had been one of at least half a dozen 210s making up a fleet whose skippers raced at least once a week in the summer, sometimes three times a week, and met throughout the year to plan events for the coming season. The Lady Mistral was a member of the Beckwith family, just as all the other 210s were members of other skippers' families. The Lady Mistral was dark blue, with a gray deck fore and aft, and plain white sails.

Annie waved to Lincoln as he swung between boats heading for the float. She turned around and crossed the deck to the storage area and small kitchen. The yacht club sat on a deck built on pilings, the thick boards unfazed by the highest storm surge any time of year. In the kitchen she unrolled the posters she was carrying. She tacked one onto the bulletin board, next to an announcement that MYC races scheduled for August 21 to 23 would be rescheduled at a later date. She glanced at the dates, and then crossed the deck to the clubroom.

With three walls of French doors and a fourth wall with a wide stone fireplace, the clubroom was the preferred location for meetings no matter the time of year. Since the room had no heat, a roaring fire and blankets greeted the club Board members as they arrived for their meetings in the off season. Annie's father described many a session in which members had to be unburied from within their blankets so their votes could be heard. Annie tacked up another poster below a photograph of the late Commodore Winslow.

The idea of selling the Lady Mistral gnawed at Annie after her sister died. She had toyed with the idea of letting Randall keep it and coming out to sail occasionally. But when he died, Annie knew she'd had enough. You could love something to the point of its suffocating you, and she knew that would happen with this boat. Sailors are a superstitious lot, but they're also eager to save the precious. She was counting on someone to want the Lady Mistral, even though its skipper had fallen overboard and drowned.

With one poster left, Annie crossed to the club office at the outer edge of the deck. This was Lincoln's refuge, with large windows on two sides, and a smaller one beside the door. The notice board on the back wall was covered with flyers from the Coast Guard and NOAA, the National Oceanic and Atmospheric Administration, which seemed a cross between the IRS and the Gestapo to people with lives tied to the sea.

At the very back of the small office a door opened into a tiny room with a cot and a small desk, where Lincoln could rest or keep up with paper work. The computer pinged, and Annie glanced at the blinking cursor. A breeze lifted papers on the desk, and she moved the mouse to hold them in place. The screen woke up and a list of names appeared with what looked like a schedule for the month of August. When more papers fluttered Annie slapped them down on the desk with the palm of her hand and grabbed a book for a paperweight.

The best spot for her poster was occupied by the newest directive from NOAA. She moved the government notice and tacked up her own flyer. There was something about seeing the Lady Mistral on a For Sale poster that made her throat constrict. The blue boat was pictured coming toward the photographer, in full sail, its spinnaker out and lifted by the wind. The boat was a stunner, for those who loved to sail, and Annie sat down on a stool just to admire it.

Annie wasn't so naïve that she thought she could take risks and never face danger. The first lesson for the neophyte sailor was safety—watch the boom, watch the wind, watch the sheets. A good sailboat was a powerful device but also a dangerous one. It was full of traps for the unwary, the untrained, the unsuspecting. But this was true for anyone. Nature was not one-hundred percent predictable, no matter how much experience someone had on the water.

The number on the sail, announcing when it was built among the total, wasn't visible behind the spinnaker, so Annie had included it in the specs on the poster. It wasn't a low number, which might have enticed collectors, but even in the 400s a 210 was still a good buy. The numbers didn't go above 500, so they would become exceedingly rare soon enough, perhaps by the time she was too old to sail.

She had considered the possibility that she might regret selling the boat, that she might discover at age sixty that the only thing she wanted was a sailboat from her childhood. Possible but unlikely, she decided. And if she was wrong, well, then, she was wrong. She'd have to find something else to compensate for not having a 210. It might be the boat she knew best, but it certainly wasn't the only one she could love.

A man in his fifties with thick brown hair and a deep tan on skin as rippled as waves on a lake came into the office. Lincoln Walsh dropped the launch keys on the counter that ran the length of the office, just below the front window. The board served as desk and storage for a variety of logs and binders.

Annie greeted him and nodded to the poster. "I just put these up—one in the kitchen, one in the club room, and one here. Hope that's okay."

Lincoln walked over to the bulletin board, rested his hands on his hips, and read the poster, leaning in and squinting as he read through the specs. "I'm sure it wasn't an easy decision."

Annie shrugged. "Nothing's been easy since Deb died."

"I know you two were very close." He had sent Annie a kind note about her sister and husband a few days ago, remarking on Deb's skill with a tiller.

"I wouldn't even have been here that day if she hadn't called me specifically to come out," Annie said, standing up. She pushed the tall stool back against the wall, out of the way. "She called me the Friday before, said she had something she wanted to talk about. I told her I'd come out next week and she said that was soon enough. And then . . ." She made a short turn in the small office, as if to clear her head.

"Did she tell you what she wanted to talk about?" He turned away from the flyer.

Annie shook her head, pushing her hands into her pockets. Outside a horn tooted. Lincoln reached for the keys, but didn't take a step towards the door. "What?" she said. "Oh, sorry, no, she didn't tell me, and now I'll never know what she wanted." She glanced again at the poster. "It's better to let it go, don't you think?"

"Yes," Lincoln said, turning to look at the photograph of the boat under sail. "Yes, I do." He followed her out of the office to the middle of the deck.

"Why're the races canceled that weekend?" Annie asked.

"Don't really know," Lincoln said. "The commodore called a week ago and said we had to postpone, something about the Priestlys having a special visitor and wanting quiet. No canons going off at the start of a race to disturb the afternoon lunch or early cocktails."

"Oh, that'll just be the senator," Annie said. "Ellen Priestly tells everyone she meets that her husband and the senator were in the same class at Harvard, along with a few hundred other people."

"Including Randall?"

"Not quite. Wrong year." Annie grinned.

"I guess the town wants to avoid what happened last summer," Lincoln said.

"Probably," Annie agreed. "Ellen was furious when she saw that flotilla of boats protesting the senator's position on the new luxury tax."

"Well, that issue died."

"I guess so. This year the senator's all about peace in the Middle East." Annie pulled her car keys out of her pocket. "Thanks for letting me post the flyers here. I'll email an ad to use on the club website if that's okay." Lincoln nodded.

"Shall I call the marina and have them put it out so people can get a look at it if they're interested?" Lincoln paused with a cell phone in his hand. "Glad to do it."

"Hmm, no thanks. Chief Silva still has it dry-docked."

"It's still down there?" Lincoln said, turning to study her.

"Two deaths in one family in a matter of days," Annie said, her voice catching on the last word. She took a deep breath to steady herself. "And Cecily was so distraught that I guess the chief wants to wait before he talks to her one last time, or something like that." She addressed this information to the dark oiled planks of the club deck, staring as though she didn't quite understand them. "He wants her to be calm enough to remember everything that happened while she and Deb were out there on the water."

"He'll probably release the boat soon," Lincoln said. "I haven't heard anything from anyone down at the marina, so I think it's just a matter of time."

"I hope so. Anyway, if no one expresses an interest in buying it, I may just leave it there for the winter. I'm not sure how I feel about getting too close to it right now."

"Not many want a 210 these days," Lincoln said. "Our fleet is almost gone—you and the Harrises are the last ones." He turned to the boats in the outer harbor. "I suppose you've already considered the idea of staying out here?" This was put delicately, in a casual tone, since he was an employee of the Mellingham Yacht Club, not a member. Asking personal questions of members would be considered going too far by some. Lincoln came on board just a year earlier and caught on at once to the nuances of his position. He was well liked.

Annie crossed her arms, but she was smiling. She liked Lincoln. They weren't so far apart in years, both of them hovering around forty, and they shared a devotion to sailing, even if neither of them got much of a chance to do it. He might work at this yacht club in the summer, and another one in Florida in the winter, but that didn't mean he got to sail. Annie shook her head. She had been devastated at the loss of her sister—she and Deb had always been close—but losing the Lady Mistral was hard in a different way.

This was the boat she and Deb had learned to sail in, had loved and cared for devotedly throughout their childhood, had raced with their father at the helm. Just shy of thirty feet, the 210 was meant to be fast on the water, and it was. Together Annie and her dad had won the fleet championship in their class twice. Even now, when Annie recalled the ceremony when the silver platter was handed out, she couldn't hold back a smile and a silly feeling. Her dad had sent her up to receive the award. She tried to stand still, be dignified and nonchalant, so important to a teenager, but she was so excited she was bouncing on her toes. But that was then and this was now.

With a final glance at the boats in the outer harbor, Annie left the club.

CHAPTER THREE

Annie thought about the Harrises as she drove out of the parking lot of the yacht club. Cecily and Leo Harris had attended the funeral, and it didn't bother her that Cecily had barely acknowledged her. Annie hardly blamed her. The woman was terrified of the water but determined to conquer her fear. Annie admired that, but in the end her fear had been the warning that this wasn't the world for her. Cecily had been alone on the Mistral for hours after Deb fell overboard, and she'd been unable to get the boat under control and sail back in. Deb had kept the boat in conformity with racing protocols, so there were no electronic devices at all, though a basic radio would have passed muster. With no working cell phone and no radio, Cecily had no way to tell anyone what had happened. And it did something to her—Annie could see that. Everyone could see that.

"One minute she was there, and the next minute she was gone." Cecily had said the same thing over and over and over again to anyone who questioned her about what happened to Deb—the town police, the state police, the coast guard. Annie guessed she was in shock, unable to absorb what had happened right in front of her, afraid perhaps of the regret and feeling of helplessness she knew she would have to live with for the rest of her life. "She was there and then she was gone."

"Did she call out?"

Cecily shook her head.

On Friday afternoon, when Annie arrived at the yacht club to pick up her sister as Deb had asked her to do a week earlier during a regular phone call, she leaned on the railing and waited for Deb and Cecily to sail into the harbor. They were very late but Annie wasn't worried. She knew Deb often lost track of time. But instead of seeing Deb slicing cleanly past the channel markers, Annie had found herself watching the familiar blue boat swing awkwardly through the outer harbor. Annie knew Deb was teaching Cecily to sail, but she kept wondering why Deb didn't take the tiller as they entered the harbor area. It was soon obvious something was terribly wrong.

Annie still couldn't help wondering what had happened. The International 210, which was meant as an improvement on the then ubiquitous 110, was unsinkable. If asked, she probably couldn't have said why she was so confident about the boat, since the Lady Mistral was all wood—wood frame covered with mahogany plywood and a Sitka spruce mast. The blocks of white Styrofoam in the bow had been such a comfort to her as a child that she had never questioned how they might work; it was wonderful to take something for granted, to live without doubt and with complete confidence in what you were told. But something had gone wrong. Annie could only sit quietly and listen as the policeman questioned the other woman.

"Did you see her?" he asked

"I heard the boom. I heard something hit." Cecily's voice was so soft that everyone had to lean in to hear her.

"Where were you?"

"Pulling in the jib. The sheet got loose and I had to go up on deck and get hold of the sail to bring it in and catch the sheet."

"Are you a good sailor, ma'am?"

Deb's sudden fall off the boat had terrified Cecily. "Accidents happen," Randall said later, trying to conceal the effort required to be compassionate and understanding. "Deb—" He didn't seem to know how to end the sentence. "She was a good sailor." He said this in many different ways, but no change in intonation helped him accept the accident.

But it was more than an accident. It was a seminal moment in the life of the yacht club. Fewer couples signed up for weekly races, the number of youngsters enrolled in sailing classes went down, and even though people still laughed and told stories at the club when they got together, the atmosphere remained subdued, as though everyone was waiting for news, and expected it to be bad. When Leo tried to talk to Randall a day later, Leo said Randall growled at him.

It was generally agreed Randall Connolly took his wife's death hard, and even though he never said anything, many suspected he blamed Cecily. She wasn't much of a sailor, and she came across as a timid sort of person, too ready to stand on the sidelines and watch things develop instead of stepping in and doing what was necessary, even if that meant diving overboard to save a friend or at least throwing a line or her own life vest. No one stated the obvious—Deb hadn't been wearing a vest and should have been. But then no one wanted to place blame and each person who got so far as to notice the question of a vest being donned was quick to pull back; after all, it was a small town and an even smaller yacht club and neither could afford the kind of schism that resulted from inchoate suspicion or ill will or blame.

The odd thoughts swirled through Annie's brain, but she stumbled no closer to a resolution of her feelings. She wanted to acknowledge to Cecily the anguish she must have endured while watching her friend float away, and her fear of sailing alone into the harbor. If she hadn't taken the tiller and tried her best, she might have sailed off into the ocean and never been found. Without some control over the tiller, she too was in danger of being lost at sea.

CHAPTER FOUR

In the late afternoon on the Wednesday after Randall's funeral, the Mellingham Chief of Police Joe Silva followed a teenage boy along the dock to the end, where his stepson, Philip, knelt alongside a small boat tied up. Philip jumped up at the sight of Joe. He looked to be bursting with excitement, and Joe felt a surprising frisson of anticipation as well. This summer he had promised himself he would teach Philip to sail, even if the boy had been initially lukewarm about it. No one could live so close to the water and not know how to cope with it. But to Joe's delight, Philip was tumbling all over himself to get out on the water.

"Hinkie's been going over some stuff for me," Philip said. Joe frowned for a second until he realized Hinkie must be the teenager standing beside him.

"My dad and I spent part of the winter working on it," Hinkie said, smiling and nodding at the small boat. "It's a wooden Penguin, one of the older ones, but still a great sail, especially to begin with. You catch on fast." Hinkie continued with his sales pitch, or testimonial, with Philip matching him nod for nod.

Joe thanked him and tossed the sail bag into the boat along with two life vests.

Hinkie headed back up the dock, bouncing on his toes and swinging his shoulders. He stopped abruptly and hurried back down. "Oh, I almost forgot. My dad said could you stop by afterwards. He wants to talk to you about something. I think it has to do with Annie Beckwith's boat, the Lady Mistral." The boy blanched when he realized what he was saying, and took a step back. "I said I'd tell you."

Hinkie sometimes lisped, and his scrawny but hard limbs looked like they couldn't possibly belong to a teenager, but on the water he was a different person. Joe was quietly glad that he and Philip hit it off, and that one was introducing the other to the water before Joe became the teacher.

With Joe's direction rather than help, Philip checked the tension on the stays and raised the mainsail. He managed the downhaul, which pulled the sail tight on the mast. He had a little trouble measuring the distance of the outhaul, which pulled the sail taut at the far end of the boom, but tightened it within the necessary distance, about six inches.

"Suppose the span of my hand is more than eight inches?" Philip asked after Joe said to spread his fingers to get the right distance between sail and end of boom.

"You'd know that before you started," Joe said, then wondered if that was true. He took so much for granted, and Philip's questions reminded him of that almost every day. Joe had set aside the idea of fatherhood some time ago, and now that he was stepfather to two, he found himself ill prepared for the questions and surprises children seemed to bring every day. He worried about failing them, and found unexpected comfort in the idea of teaching the boy to sail. He felt safe on the water. He threaded the sheet for the mainsail through the Cunningham and tied it fast to a cleat.

"What about that?" Philip said, pointing to a block near the mast.

"That's for a vang, a set of lines that holds the boom in strong wind. We're not using that today. Light air this afternoon." Joe watched as Philip set the rudder against the stern and dropped in the pins. He slipped in the tiller and pins and pulled on the tiller, feeling the pressure of the water against the rudder.

"That's it?" Philip looked skeptical.

Joe knew what he meant. This eleven-foot wooden structure was going to carry two men out onto the water where anything could happen, and only a large piece of nylon was going to help them. "That's it, except for the centerboard." Joe unhooked the raised centerboard and pushed it gently to get it to sink into the water.

"How much room do we have, Pae?" Philip could see the beach grass waving below, in the shallow water. Joe paused before answering. Philip had recently switched to calling him father in Portuguese, which both startled and warmed Joe. It told more about how the boy was feeling that anything else ever could.

"Depends," Joe said, reaching up to untie the bowline on a cleat on the dock. "With the two of us, it's probably at maximum draw. Two people are about it for a Penguin. But with you alone, or someone else about your size and weight, you might draw less than two feet. So, between two and four feet."

"Oh." Philip looked over the side.

"We need to balance, so you shift forward a foot or so until we get out of the marina's working area, and then we'll head out so you can take the tiller." Joe worked his way back and settled on the bottom. There were no benches in the Penguin except the center one where the centerboard and sheets came through and the cross piece for stepping the mast, which wasn't enough to really sit on. He was glad he hadn't waited any longer for this lesson. Another year and he might not be able to get in or out of the little dinghy.

Joe pulled the tiller toward him, then back and forth a few times until the bow headed away from the dock and the sail caught a light breeze, just enough to give the sail shape. "Lesson one, for this part of the world anyway," Joe said. "When you want to change directions, you come about. You don't jibe." And then Joe had to explain both terms. "When you want to come about, point the bow into the wind, pull in the sail, and give your passengers warning. Ready to come about, hard to lee, meaning the leeward side of the boat. Jibing is the opposite and it's dangerous. The boom will swing too fast and hard."

"Is there a speed limit for sailboats?" the boy asked as a motorboat passed sluggishly, its small wake barely rocking the little sailboat. Joe shook his head.

"But around here you also have to watch out for paddle boarders." Joe nodded to the three people standing up and paddling on boards, weaving among the moored boats. Philip swung around and peered at them, then called out a greeting.

"You know them?"

Philip nodded enthusiastically. "I'm surprised to see Aaron Whipple out here now. He usually goes out late at night because he works for his dad during the summer, so he must have today off. I don't know the other two very well. They're not in my class." The teens waved to each other, and Joe made a note of the names of the three paddle boarders. He was glad to see Philip experiencing the camaraderie of the water.

"Is this a good sailing day?" Philip asked later. They had reached the channel and were now sailing among moored boats, which grew larger and longer as they closed in on the outer harbor.

"Hmm, a quiet one. Light breeze. No white caps." Joe scanned the area. "Here, take the sheet." He handed over the line and looked up at the sail. "You play with the sheet to keep the sail taut. See those bulges along the mast? That's luffing. It means you're losing wind, so pull the sail in tighter. There, tighter now."

For the next several minutes, the little boat tacked through the outer harbor, and after half an hour headed out into the bay. The wind began to pick up, and Joe pointed out the still shallow waves. They headed across the water to the rocky shore of a small island. By now, Joe had handed over the tiller and changed places with Philip, and was wishing he weighed less or the teenager weighed more. He'd forgotten how small these little boats were.

"If there's so little wind, how come there are waves over there?" Philip asked, nodding to a spot in the water on the starboard side.

Joe craned his neck to get a look. "That's Hidden Rock. There's supposed to be a marker. It used to be a tall metal rod, but there was some damage a few years back and it hasn't been repaired. It's hard to see from this angle, but there's still a metal pole there, just a shorter one. You want to sail well clear of that on the ebb tide." Joe caught Philip's look of confusion. "The waves tell you it's there, and the higher they are, the lower the water. But it's a big hazard, even if you can't see it, so you don't want to get close to it." He turned forward and gave the tiller a gentle push.

"So even this boat couldn't sail near it?" Under Joe's guidance, Philip pulled in the mainsail, and sailed close hauled farther out into the harbor.

"If you pulled up the centerboard, you could probably sail over most of it at close to high tide," Joe said. He turned around to face Philip. "But there's no playing chicken out here."

"No, sir." Philip sat up straight and studied the sail.

"Let's tack over there." Joe pointed across the bay, and Philip practiced bringing the little boat about. As they sailed across the water, the wind picking up as it does in the late afternoon, Joe scanned the scenery.

"Whose place is that?" Philip said.

"That's the Priestly house." Joe studied the early twentieth century mansion perched at the end of the peninsula. Every year the Priestlys brought someone important to their idyllic home on the coast, and every year the local authorities, Joe included, scrambled to make sure adequate security was in place. He was glad the state police and the authorities in DC had taken over the headache.

"Do they own the island too?" Philip pointed to the tall rocky island that sat as a sentinel at the mouth of Mellingham Bay.

"They do, but it's useless. Almost sheer rock, despite all the pines growing on it." He peered at the shore. "Sail along there. Can you see the causeway?"

Philip brought the boat closer to shore, where the ebbing tide revealed a sandbar stretching between mainland and island.

"That's where people find out they draw more than they realized. They sail right into the sand, and they have to wait for the tide to come back in and release them," Joe said. "Hitting that bar can be quite a jolt."

"Is this where Annie Beckwith's sister drowned?"

Joe had wondered when this question would come up. He had arranged the sailing lesson weeks ago, asking Hinkie's dad to find a boat they could borrow off and on during the summer. Finding the boat had been easy, getting time to sail had been hard. When Deb Connolly had disappeared off her boat and been presumed drowned, Joe had worried that Philip's enthusiasm would wane, but had said nothing—until now.

"I don't think so," Joe said. "From what Cecily Harris said, they were much farther out, on open ocean. And Deb was a good sailor. She'd sailed her entire life. She wouldn't do anything so foolish as to take that kind of risk." He nodded to the water eddying around coastal rocks, knowing that there were plenty of good sailors who liked to gamble. He dismissed the latent worry, confident that Philip, though young, was sensible.

"Stay this side of the red marker," Joe said. "Green on right heading out, Red on right returning."

"Oh, okay," Philip said, glancing back at the markers.

"This boat has a shallow draft, so you could probably safely sail on the other side of the channel marker and get a look at how shallow the water is over there." Joe pointed to the grass just visible below the water line.

"But we sailed over grass on the way out," Philip said, nodding to the shore near the yacht club.

"Depth is deceptive out here," Joe said, "until you get to know the area or you have a chart, you need to be cautious. I'll get a paper chart for you to study. But if you get stuck out here," he said, nodding to the beach, "you can walk in at low tide or swim and explain to Hinkie's dad what happened."

Philip pulled a face. "Yes, sir, I get it." He glanced, perhaps wistfully, at the shoreline. "Sort of like driving a car—safety rules."

CHAPTER FIVE

Joe could see Hinkie working on the dock well before he and Philip reached it. The chief was glad to leave the two teenagers to take in the little boat. As he walked up to the marina Joe listened to the bantering. It was easy to guess what this evening's dinner conversation would be about. Philip was not going to live with a dinghy named Princess, and Hinkie was already offering suggestions.

"How did it go?" Hugh Trask stepped out of a workroom brushing sawdust from his shirt front and sleeves. The two men shook hands.

"Philip catches on quick," Joe said. "And like a kid of his age, he did a good job of not showing how excited he was. Sailing is completely new to him and he did well. I think he felt competent, really competent, in a new way. Plus he likes having a lot to think about, otherwise he gets bored."

Trask threw his head back and barked. "He'll love it out there. Wind, water, sails, hazards, other boats. He'll have plenty to watch out for." The two men crossed the paved yard and entered the large open shed. At the far end the Lady Mistral sat high in its cradle, surrounded by wooden saw horses and rope marking the area off limits. "I told my guys to stay away from it, and to make sure no one else goes near either. And then I called the investigator with the state police. He gave me his card, but he said they already had noticed that and taken it into consideration and they don't think it played a role."

"I appreciate your letting me know," Joe said. Hugh Trask was normally a calm, quiet man, soft spoken and thoughtful, but today his step was bouncy and his words clipped.

Trask walked to the back of the shed and pushed out a standing ladder on wheels. He maneuvered it to the side of the boat and locked it in place. "I thought you should see this." He climbed up and pulled back the canvas covering, and then climbed down. "Go ahead and take a look."

Joe climbed up and peered in at the boat. The International 210 had benches running along both sides, with a seat that lifted up for a storage compartment on one section at the far end, near the tiller. This was the only fully enclosed area. Sail bags and other items were stored under the covered stern, beneath the tiller. The bow offered some storage space as well but far less; here, under the deck, the Styrofoam blocks were tied in place. Near the blocks were a spinnaker pole and a sail bag, which Joe took to be the spinnaker. Joe noted the battens neatly stacked along the benches. The mainsail had been rolled and tied on the boom instead of being taken down and stowed in its bag. The jib had been dropped but not unhooked from the stay; the sail had been rolled and tied with its sheets on the bow. None of this was unexpected. But the lines in the center of the cockpit were.

Joe climbed up another rung of the ladder and sat on the gunwale, to better study the mass of lines and blocks covering the fore cockpit floor. The lines were attached to the vang, but the vang was no longer attached to the boom. He looked down at Hugh, who was resting one hand on the ladder and one foot on the lowest rung.

"I gave Philip a basic lesson in using the vang, but we didn't try it. I figured he had enough to learn without adding that." He glanced at the cockpit before continuing. "It's pretty simple. Just clip the vang onto the boom and the mast. Easy to adjust. But that's not what I'm seeing here."

Hugh shook his head. "You're seeing a couple of things. First, the Lady Mistral had what's called a cascaded fiddle. That's a fancy term for an extra line to take off some of the stress on the lines running through the tackle, so increasing the purchase of the vang. The load on the blocks is halved, so it's a stronger system." Hugh waited while Joe gave the equipment another look.

"And yet it looks like it failed." Joe swung his legs into the boat and sat on the port side bench. In the quiet of late afternoon, with the marina all but closed for the day, few voices traveled to him inside the boat. Someone spoke to Hugh, and Joe heard a soft reply, but he wasn't listening too hard. His mind was on the fitting of the vang that should have been in the underside of the boom but was instead lying on the floor of the cockpit. Joe ran his fingers lightly over the fitting screws. He knelt down and peered up at the boom and ran his fingers along the wood, checking the depth of the screw hole with his index finger. The crumbly beige material floated to the deck and he rubbed a few bits between his fingers.

"So, I guess you saw what I saw." Hugh Trask looked up as Joe again sat on the gunwale and looked down at the other man. He looked sick, his face taking on an ashen color.

Joe held out his fingers, which were still covered with the little particles. "Unless I'm mistaken that's some kind of plastic wood."

"Can you look under the deck?" Hugh called up. "One of my men was just being his thorough self and looking for any problems before hoisting her up and he found something. I told him to leave it exactly where he found it. So he did. Don't know if you can get to it."

"What am I looking for?"

"A tin can. Nothing else in there."

Joe crawled along the cockpit floor and underneath the stern deck. Near the back he saw the tin can. He reached for a batten and used this to pull the can toward him. He tipped the can so he could see and moved it so it caught the light. He didn't need to do more. "Has anyone else been up here?" He leaned over the port side and looked down at Hugh. Hugh shook his head.

Joe slipped on plastic gloves and pulled out a crushed piece of paper, and this he slid into a plastic envelope. He studied the interior of the can another moment and then left it in the boat.

"I didn't think anything of it until I got a look at the vang and the mast, and that was this morning." Hugh rested his hands on his hips. "Should've looked sooner."

Joe climbed down the stairs. "No reason you should have been looking for anything. No one had any reason to doubt Cecily Harris's explanation, and the boat was left here until the family could decide what to do with it. And that means waiting for Annie Beckwith."

"I didn't want to call her," Hugh said. "She's got enough on her plate right now. I heard she's thinking of selling the boat, so I figured I'd just wait." He paused and studied the stern. "And then this."

"Is this normal?" Joe asked.

Hugh pressed his lips shut, but they wiggled as though he were fighting to control himself. He could barely conceal his disgust. "You know as well as I do no one in their right mind would use plastic wood to secure the bolts for a vang system, no matter how small or light the boat."

"I have to ask, Hugh."

"Of course, of course, I understand. Anything you need, just ask." He grew calmer, though he struggled to conceal the horror of finding plastic wood relied on for something like a vang.

"Is there any way to tell how long it's been like that?" Joe asked.

Hugh shook his head. "We readied the boat for the water in May, and put it out on the mooring in early June. It would have to be after that."

"What kind of check do you do before you take a boat out?"

"Thorough, Joe, thorough. Even if it's been sitting for a while in the cradle, we check it over, 90 some points, before we head for the water." Hugh leaned his outstretched arm against the ladder, but not for support. He was stiff with distress and struggling to hold back his anger.

"Would you have noticed then if someone had tampered with the bolt holes?"

"We check everything," Trask said. "I'm a demon about the outhaul and the stays especially but we check everything that could fail. We check the bolt on the deck and then on the boom. You can't be too careful."

His distress at the thought of this kind of failure happening in his marina was obvious, and Joe guessed he was imaging what else could have gone wrong.

"I'll need to talk to your people," Joe said.

"I understand." Trask's shoulders tightened as he shoved his hands into his pockets. "This took time, Joe. If it happened here in the yard we would have known. But that boat was perfect when we put her out in June."

"That means it had to have been done sometime after it went into the water," Joe said. "Is that possible?"

Trask looked up at the boat, at the crusty water line and the paint beginning to peel near the bow. "Yes, it's possible, but it wouldn't be easy. You'd have to have a small battery-powered drill and a wrench and a few other tools. It would be awkward."

"But doable."

Trask followed the lines of the Lady Mistral, his expression growing sadder and sadder as he came to the balloon at the end of the keel. "Yes, doable. Jeez. What a thing to do." He ran his hand over the bottom, feeling the roughing of the paint beneath his fingers. "What a thing to do."

"It might have been done recently," Joe said. "It's not as hard deeper into the holes. Like it hasn't fully dried." But he was talking to himself, working out the little he had discovered, while Trask alternated between sorrow and outrage. "I'm going to get a technician down here to take a look, but I'd appreciate it if you kept this to yourself."

Hugh's eyes widened and then narrowed. "Joe, I don't want to even think it."

"What kind of security do you have here?"

"State of the art. We had a boat that belonged to one of the skippers in an America's Cup race stored here for a while and he insisted we upgrade. Even paid for part of it." Hugh glanced up at the camera not quite visible. "If anyone comes near the shed, or any other part of the marina, we know about it."

"Who's on the other end?"

Hugh named the security company, and described the rest of the system. "Joe, I don't want to think this could be . . ."

Joe dusted the flakes and specks from his fingers, and rubbed the pad of his index finger one more time. "No, I don't either. It may be nothing, but I want to be sure."

Joe and Trask studied each other for a moment. Joe knew it wasn't nothing, and he knew Trask felt the same way.

CHAPTER SIX

Gwen shook out the green and white flowered tablecloth, and let it float down over the garden table. For a moment the fabric blocked out the setting sun, and Gwen felt like a little girl hiding in a tent in the back yard. It was one of those moments of unexpected delight that seemed to dapple her life with Joe just as the sun sprinkled polka dots onto the lawn.

"Explorer," Gwen said. She glanced at Joe, who held a bottle of beer halfway to his lips. "That's the name he chose this afternoon, after he got back from your sail. Explorer." She leaned over the table and ran her flat palms over the cloth, brushing away the ripples and smoothing out the creases. "Explorer." She rested her hands on her hips as she repeated the name, as though testing it for suitableness. "Not terribly original but I like it."

Joe watched her, knowing that Gwen was a little afraid of the name, of what it implied. Just as he was. He reached across the table and ran his knuckles down her arm, rubbing gently. "It'll do, until he's older and decides it's too ordinary." He took a pull of his beer and turned his attention to the table, where Gwen was now setting out cutlery and plates. "Just the two of us?"

Gwen nodded. "I promised Jennie and Philip they could stay late for the barbecue on the beach."

"Well, it'll give him a chance to crow about his afternoon on the water. I'd forgotten about that."

"The club did get a permit, didn't they?" Gwen asked. Joe nodded. "Good. So, they'll be home around eight. Only another hour, but they certainly won't want anything to eat. They'll be full of marshmallows and hot dogs."

"When do they develop taste buds?"

"When they have to buy their own food."

Gwen handed Joe a pair of skewers piercing a number of vegetables. He put down the beer, took the skewers, and went to stand in front of a small grill, placing the skewers next to two pieces of grilling chicken. He brushed a marinade over the chicken and stepped back when a plume of smoke dashed up at him. Half an hour later he and Gwen admired the results and settled themselves at the table to enjoy their meal. Joe poured Gwen a glass of wine.

Beyond the foot of the yard a small brook crept beneath overhanging branches on its way to the harbor, where it would pass under the street and fall with surprising force over a culvert into the salt water of the cove. Joe could watch the spate of water change during the day, depending on the weather, through his office window. During a recent drought he had caught himself repeatedly swinging towards the window, unsettled by the quiet, when the brook fell too low to do anything more than send a trickle over the cement.

"Am I allowed to ask what's on your mind?" Gwen said.

When they had at last decided to marry, soon after Joe's family reunion, they had also decided to buy a house and face the practical realities of a future together. They had chosen an old colonial rehabbed by a much younger couple whose daughter had taken a bad fall during the renovations and never quite recovered. The sadness of the house had at first repelled both Joe and Gwen, until the wife had taken Gwen aside and admitted that she longed for a family with children to buy it. She wanted to know there would be laughter in the house again. She needed that. They'd been happy here, she said, and she hoped others would find they could be happy here too. Gwen and Joe loved the old house and the young architect's design that linked the back of the house with the small garage/office by a brick terrace running the length of both and enclosed by a wall of windows and skylights above.

"Sorry if I haven't been paying attention," Joe said. "It's nothing."

"It's never nothing, Jose." Gwen removed the plates and left them on a tray nearby. "But I understand if you don't want to talk."

Joe listened to voices in the distance. Even though the street ran within a few feet of the front of the house and children played on a side street nearby, the back yard afforded near perfect privacy. Condos in a brick building on the other side of the brook were screened in warmer weather by thick maples and shrubbery.

"Hugh Trask found something in the Lady Mistral," Joe said.

"Found something?"

Joe glanced at her, feeling once again the ambivalence of sharing confidential information but Gwen had become the only person he felt thoroughly comfortable with when he needed to talk things through.

Gwen slid lower in her seat and rested her chin on her steepled fingers. "So, what does that mean exactly? Found something?"

"Nothing so far except maybe Cecily Harris was very lucky." Joe reached for his beer. "But I'm taking another look at the participants and the entire sequence of events—the sailing, Cecily, Deb's disappearance, Randall's death."

"So you think the investigators missed something?" Gwen tipped her head to study Joe. She felt she learned more from watching him think through what he would say than from what he did in fact say. Right now he was hesitating to commit himself.

"We know about the accident and Cecily's fear of the water. The preliminary report on Randall Connolly confirmed probable suicide." Joe rubbed a hand over his face.

"That's a lot of iffiness," Gwen said. "And you didn't like the results before." Joe lifted an eyebrow and gave her a quizzical smile. "Don't look at me like that. When you think something is really settled, like cut in stone, and you're satisfied with how things are, you clean out the garage and then you take us all out to a new restaurant. On the day you decide that whatever it is, it's finished, we have to cancel whatever we're doing and go off with you. Jennie pointed that out to me."

"Jennie?"

"The canceling part. She has earned a reputation among her friends, but they forgive her because they think they're in on the big news before anyone else. It's like a secret code she has going with her BFFs." Gwen sat up and draped an arm over Joe's shoulder and gave him a gentle tug. "She's been waiting for you to take us out somewhere. She's onto you, Joe."

"Those two are going to grow up to be dangerous," he said. "All right. All right. Yes, I'm worried. I knew something about this wasn't right but I couldn't get at it and the others didn't see anything amiss."

"So, now you get to do all the work." Gwen stood up and picked up the tray. "Let's go for ice cream. I feel like a walk."

CHAPTER SEVEN

Early the next morning, Joe walked across the parking lot behind Town Hall and shook hands with a stocky middle-aged man. Tango Brockelman, the harbormaster, looked as if he would sink like an anchor if he fell into the ocean but like many who are overweight, he was remarkably light on his feet. His mother-in-law had nicknamed him Tango when they first met, at a mutual friend's wedding.

Tango had come with a friend of the groom, and he took over the dance floor, dancing with every woman over fifty, not because he was a ladies' man but because he guessed, correctly, that they knew the older dance steps—the Lindy, samba, mambo, waltz, foxtrot, and more. He managed to dance with a few younger women, including the one who later became his wife. The bride and groom had to be forced into their car to head off on their honeymoon because the party was too much fun to leave. A down-to-earth guy who built go-carts every year for the local fundraiser for youth sports, Tango never smiled when anyone asked about his dancing days. "Done and gone" was all he would say before changing the subject. It wasn't quite true, but Joe knew Tango was a private person.

The town's thirty-foot launch motored under the train trestle and past the two marinas on the point. It was barely six o'clock, but already the town was abustle with commuters heading to the train station or onto the highway. The early morning light made it seem later in the day, as though everyone should be wide awake instead of raising window shades and turning on coffee makers.

Chief Joe Silva stood beside Tango, and felt the old tug that had drawn his father and brothers down to the docks in the early hours. As the harbormaster's launch approached the Mellingham Marina, Joe could see his stepson, Philip, and Hinkie Trask readying the Penguin for a day on the water. After he and Jennie had returned from the barbecue on the beach, Philip had asked to meet Hinkie at the marina, where they would repaint the name on the Penguin. It was late, really too late for that, but Joe understood the twinge of embarrassment for a young teen sailing a boat named Princess. He agreed, and had collected Philip at close to midnight when he'd called to say he and Hinkie had finished painting the new name on the boat, Explorer. He'd ride home but his bike had a flat tire. The bike in question was still in the back of Joe's SUV. Joe was surprised the boy had managed to get himself up and out so early—the lure of the sea, it seemed, defied all borders.

"Hey, Pae!" Philip stood up in the small boat and waved both arms as though he were signaling. Hinkie looked up from where he knelt on the dock, lifted a hand in greeting, and grinned at his fellow crew.

"You're lucky," the stocky man at the wheel said. "Pretty soon he won't even admit he knows you." Tango gave a casual wave to the boys but kept his attention on the water and boats.

"How do you handle it?" Joe took a position beside the helm, holding the handle on the dashboard. He knew Tango had a large brood but he couldn't remember how many.

"I don't ask them to acknowledge me. I just tell them what to do and expect them to do it." He pulled a face. "Works out most of the time. I think the wife has something to do with it." He throttled back to give himself time to scan the opposite shore. "So, what're we doing out here? Other than enjoying a near perfect day in Mellingham."

Joe stepped back enough to see around the windscreen and take in the inland shore. The homes along the peninsula rarely had private docks because of the marsh but it was still possible to launch a dinghy from that side. The water was accessible from either side of the harbor to anyone determined to get out on it. He turned to Tango and explained what Hugh Trask had found on the Lady Mistral.

"Cecily Harris is lucky she didn't get killed herself," Tango said. "That's a lot of line to go wrong—the jib and the vang." He turned the launch towards the small park and scanned the coastline.

"She was pretty scared," Joe said. "But she doesn't know much about sailing. She only knew things were flapping around, I guess."

"So this trip through the harbor," Tango began. "You're looking for what?"

"I guess a way for someone to get to the Lady Mistral." Joe leaned back against the dash. "I don't know this coastline from the water at all, so I have a hard time imagining what is possible."

"You think the vang tampering could have been done while the boat was on the mooring?" Tango said.

"It seems the most likely explanation," Joe said. "Trask was pretty definite it couldn't have happened at the marina."

Tango slowed to take a better look at two people in a day sailer, a man and woman in their thirties, perhaps, but they waved easily when they saw him slowing near them. He waved and continued on. "But you have doubts?"

"I don't know about having doubts one way or the other," Joe said. "I just want to get a better idea of the waterways out here and how it might have been done."

"You're thinking not daytime." Tango turned to port and threaded between the moored boats. The harbor had been dredged within the last three years and fifty-foot sloops often anchored here, in view of a small beach sitting in the embrace of bright green grass on the edge of an inlet. The logic of moorings wasn't obvious to an outsider, but these larger sailboats also had motors and could motor out of the harbor. They didn't need to be closer to the bay. The larger racing boats had no motors and were grouped at the outer harbor. Joe studied the shore along the peninsula, with its alternating coast of rocks and marsh, as the launch drew closer to the Mellingham Yacht Club on the opposite shore.

"If anyone did go out, they'd have to time it just right, with the tides," Tango said. "That shore line looks close but between here and there is mostly mud and marsh. You couldn't walk through it to get to a dinghy or raft." Tango turned away from the peninsula and headed out towards the mouth of the harbor.

"It's less marshy out here," Joe said. They passed between the peninsula and a point jutting out from the other shore.

"It would be more possible here," Tango said. "It's deeper here at high tide, so maybe three good hours of time for getting in and out."

"On a dinghy or paddle board?"

Tango pulled a face. "Possible."

"But noticeable?"

"There's a lot of ambient light along here." Tango nodded towards the houses visible through the trees. They approached the yacht club, with its floats hosting overturned dinghies for the junior sailing classes.

"How obvious would it be at night? Would anyone notice? I don't see anyone taking one of those dinghies and putting it into the water and rowing out," Joe said, nodding to the yacht club float.

"Whoever it was would have to bring his own oars. They lock up tight at night." Tango nodded to the offices and shed. At the edge of the moorings, beyond which lay Mellingham Bay, the land rose sharply, and the homes sitting on the shore had terrific views, but no easy access to the water. No one even tried to build a dock in this area.

"So not boats from the yacht club," Joe said. "What is possible?"

"Possible? A stand-up paddleboard, or a surfboard. Maybe a rubber dinghy or even something like your Penguin," Tango said. "Possibly a motorboat."

"Wouldn't that attract attention?"

Tango tipped his head from side to side. "People are surprisingly trusting on the water. They have to be. They have to trust and be trustworthy. Someone might notice but not think much of it. A smaller boat going in or out of the harbor wouldn't attract much attention, especially if they cut the engine and drifted much of the time. People come in late from excursions all the time in the summer."

"How about lights?"

"Easy enough to rig a canvas over the boom and work underneath it, hiding light and maybe some of the noise." He motored around a pair of bobbing moorings. "If there were two of them, one could be playing a radio on shore while the other worked."

"How much noise would a battery-operated tool make out here?"

Tango studied Joe for a moment before speaking. "Hard to say. Some nights every single sound travels across town, but some sounds don't leave the yard. The noise of the tool operating could be mistaken for something else. Not many people would think first of something happening on a boat in the harbor even if they did hear it."

"We're coming up to the mooring for the Lady Mistral," Joe said.

"The 210 fleet always had the outermost moorings. Don't know why," Tango said. "I've seen some of the younger ones cutting through the harbor down near the park like it was a private highway. Great skills some of those kids have."

Almost parallel with the end of the moorings for the yacht club was the tip of the shore where the Harrises lived and beyond that a private beach arcing to the southeast and the rest of the peninsula. The peninsula extended farther into the bay, ending at the rocks and a causeway leading to Sutter Island, a bit of useless property. In another few days the area would be swarming with security boats in response to the senator's visit but for now it was quiet, an early morning promising to be a perfect day for a sail. At Joe's request, Tango skirted the shore, beginning with the beach and Leo Harris's property.

"Maybe whoever you're looking for didn't come from the shore," Tango said.

"How so?" Joe turned to regard him.

"Could have been staying on one of these yachts that come in for a few nights and then sail on." Tango slowed the boat and reached over the side to pull up some floating trash. He tossed it into a metal box he kept for the purpose. "I'm thinking of asking for funds to hire a few kids in the summer months to help with a cleanup. This harbor is pretty clean but sometimes a trash bag goes over the side and stuff starts washing ashore and it stays there until someone gets sick of it and picks it up."

"Do visitors have to check in with you?" Joe asked.

"Not with me," Tango said, shaking his head. "The town doesn't have any moorings to loan anyone or rent out. Anyone can stop for a few hours at the town docks, pick up some provisions at the grocery store there, but they couldn't stay over night. No, I was thinking about the Mellingham Yacht Club. If one of their members is gone for a few days, the owner might allow his mooring to be used. The clubs have reciprocal agreements, especially for races and those exchange weeks they run."

"Exchange weeks?"

"Yeah, we send a fleet down there and they send a fleet up here. Socializing and sailing, and then everyone goes home."

"I'll check on that," Joe said.

"Take a look over there," Tango said. "There are two empty moorings at least, both for 210s. The Lady Mistral and Leo Harris's boat."

"How do you know that?" Joe asked.

"You get to know boats and where they are," Tango said. "It's like walking the dog every night. You know who has one and where and if you don't run into the other animals you wonder where they are or if anything's happened to them."

"Like knowing where you set your lobster traps," Joe said.

"Yeah, but without the buoys." He spun the wheel. "Now, closer in, for the ones with motors, there are a couple of open moorings. The owners are sailing up in Canada, I heard. So we'll see some visitors there probably. And there's another one out there, near the point." He nodded again. "That one has changed hands a few times in the last ten years, sort of unusual."

"I'll ask Lincoln Walsh about them," Joe said. "Has Mr. Harris's boat been out at all this summer?"

Tango shook his head. "It wasn't put out this spring, his regular time. He likes to get out in May, get onto the water early, though anything earlier than that is a little risky. I've been expecting to see his boat on the mooring, but it never showed. Don't know if he offered his mooring for rent or not."

The idea of a visitor renting a mooring was a possibility; Tango was right about that. But it seemed unlikely to Joe. Counting on getting a guest spot in a timely manner could be too unreliable to do the job that the tamperer clearly wanted done. "There's a dock down there," Joe said, pointing deeper into the harbor towards the town.

"That's an old one, hardly usable anymore. Belongs to one of the homes along there," Tango said, turning around to look at Joe before he added, "the Eaton family."

CHAPTER EIGHT

The time spent touring the harbor with Tango Brockelman changed Joe's thinking about the tampering with the Lady Mistral. He felt like he was facing an entirely new investigation, standing at the beginning. But he also felt he had a free hand. Hugh Trask had been very clear that the state police considered the investigation into Deb's drowning and Randall's shooting closed. The deaths were tragic events, one an accident and the other a suicide, but nothing more. Joe essentially had a free hand, and he intended to use it.

Joe drove to the other side of the harbor and along the old paved road almost to the end of the peninsula. Just before he turned into the driveway to Leo and Cecily Harris's home overlooking the mouth of the harbor, he caught a glimpse of the outer bay where he and Philip had tacked contentedly along the shore. He wondered how long before he'd be able to get out on the water again with Philip. If he continued on this road, he'd come to the private beach he'd pointed out to Philip, one that was rarely occupied because of its rocky shore and seaweed, which stank at low tide.

The driveway curved along the ridge to an old summer home at the point, looking over the outer harbor and the Mellingham Yacht Club on the other side. Joe parked in the circle. The front door was open, leaving the screen door on the latch, and Joe pressed the old buzzer. He could hear its screech jolting through the house. A moment later the housekeeper, in a pale blue cotton dress with a white apron, led the way to the back patio.

Settled with a glass of iced tea under an umbrella blocking out the late afternoon sun, Joe waited for Cecily Harris to finish with her version of proper hostess behavior. She was nervous, that was obvious, and her references to Leo not yet being home seemed like a sign of insecurity. She paused, as if hearing Joe's thoughts.

"I babble, I know." She lowered her voice, glanced in the direction of the house and then across the water to the yacht club. "It's beautiful, isn't it?"

"Did you grow up here?" Joe asked.

She shook her head. Her heavy blond curls shivered a little, but otherwise her hair stayed in place. The curls had sagged in the heat, but her hair was thick and held its place. "I grew up inland, in the Midwest, in a small town in Michigan. I came here for school." She smiled, the first genuine and relaxed expression Joe had seen on her. "I'm a graphic designer. When Leo and I got married, he said I'd have a chance to work for him, do his company's graphic design work, but . . ." She seemed lost at the end of her sentence.

Cecily Harris was different from the other women who lived in this part of town, where families had spent their summers for the last hundred or so years, driving down in May to open up old shingled homes, the husband traveling to the office in Boston every day on the train, though perhaps on a reduced schedule. The peninsula, with its private road, served as a gated community, and the Mellingham police rarely had reason to visit.

"It's the accident, isn't it?" Cecily said. She rested her clenched hands on her knees, leaning forward. "I dream about it every night. It was so unfair."

"Unfair?"

Cecily's green eyes widened. "Yes, unfair. She could swim and do all sorts of things on the water. I should have been knocked out and she could have rescued me. It would have been easy for her."

Joe had expected Cecily Harris to feel guilty over surviving the sailing accident, but this was a different sort of reaction, and he couldn't quite put his finger on it. She was young, barely into her thirties, and half the age of her husband, Leo. This was his third marriage, and everyone thought her an acceptable version of the trophy wife, the kind of joke that is meant to be flattering among men but is in fact cruel. Cecily exuded all the innocence of good character, and it had landed her here in Mellingham, where Joe guessed she had few real friends.

"Could you take me through the afternoon again," Joe said.

Cecily sat up straighter, like a good student, and began. Deb had picked her up at the house and they'd driven over to the yacht club.

"You didn't row across?" Joe knew that some of the sailors on this side of the harbor rowed the short distance to the club. Cecily stiffened and shook her head. "Go on."

She explained meticulously the ride on the launch, how friendly Lincoln was with Deb and her, readying the boat, and setting off. "She was pleased. The boat looked good and felt good."

"Did she say that?" Joe said.

"Not exactly." Cecily frowned and pursed her lips. A seagull landed on a rock near the lawn, studied them for a minute, and lifted off, landing on the roof of the club. It squawked and another joined it. Then both flew off deeper into the harbor, where a small lobster boat was slowly returning to a town-owned dock, to offload its catch. The birds' squawking faded. When they had disappeared from sight, Cecily returned her attention to Joe.

"Can you remember what she did say?"

"We had the mainsail up and she was about to pull in the sheet—that's right, isn't it? —and I know she was going to tell me to drop the mooring buoy. I said, it looks good, doesn't it? And she said, yes, and she looked surprised. It looks very good, she said, as though it looked better than she expected."

"Looks very good," Joe repeated. "Can you be more specific?"

"I don't know," Cecily said. "Clean, maybe? It did look sort of shiny, but Deb and Annie always take good care of that boat. They love it like most people love their pets." She leaned forward expectantly, her shoulders relaxed but her hands still balled on her knees.

"So tell me what happened next," Joe said.

They set out to sail around the larger island, tacking through the bay and waving congenially to the other boats. It was, according to Cecily, one of the most pleasant afternoons she'd spent here since her marriage. She thought people were different on the water, as though they accepted the leveling that came with the challenge of the ocean and its unpredictable ways. Once they left the safety of the bay, however, the wind picked up and Deb thought it a good time for a lesson. She adjusted the sheets, and got ready to come about. But the wind was stronger than they thought and the jib sheet flew loose. Cecily had been the one to tie a knot at the end, to keep it from slipping free of the block. She had to climb onto the bow to grab the flapping sail to pull in the sheet.

"I'll wait till you get the sheet," Deb said, calling over the wind and standing in the cockpit, the tiller in one hand and the mainsail sheet in the other. She didn't seem to be bothered by the sudden squall, according to Cecily.

The next thing Cecily heard was a sound she didn't recognize. The boat lurched and Cecily fell flat on the deck, holding onto the sides for dear life. She worked her way back into the cockpit with the sheet in one hand, but when she turned around, Deb wasn't there and the boat was lurching more deeply, side to side, swinging erratically. Cecily was terrified.

"I can't really swim," she said.

"Did Deb know that?" Joe asked.

Cecily nodded. The silence settled on them. A motorboat cut its engine and puttered into the harbor at the required speed limit, its earlier wake spreading to shore and crashing against the rocks. "It was my fault. She taught me to tie knots and I tied the knot in the end of the jib sheet and that's the one that came apart so the sheet flew through. It wouldn't have happened if I'd done a better job."

She wouldn't cry. That was obvious to Joe. But she would believe she had done this to a woman who had befriended her in a town that had ignored her at best and ridiculed her behind her back. She took a deep breath and described the harrowing, to her, sail back to the harbor. Lincoln had seen her coming, knew something was wrong, and was the first to reach her, with another motorboat close behind.

"Did you do anything to the boat while you were sailing back in?" Joe asked. "Did you tidy anything up? Did you undo anything?"

Cecily shook her head. "I just left everything. It happened just when Deb said she was going to teach me about vangs." She paused. "I think that's right. But first I had to get the sheet for the jib, and then she'd show me how to work the vang. She had started to hook it up, so I went for the sheet."

"Did you hear anything?" Joe said. "Did she cry out?"

Cecily shook her head and almost smiled. "Deb didn't cry out. She banged her toe once very badly and didn't make a sound. I saw her and I knew it hurt because it bled. But she made a face, and she held it till the pain went away. Most people yell or say something but she didn't."

"When you came back to the cockpit what did you see?"

The question seemed to surprise Cecily, and she leaned forward just a bit more and stared at the chief. She blinked and turned away, staring now at the water in the outer harbor. When she turned back she studied him a moment longer. "I just saw the cockpit."

"Did you notice the lines on the floor?"

She shook her head, but very slowly, from side to side, as though unsure. "I just knew I didn't see Deb. I don't remember thinking about anything else."

"Did you see anything in the water?"

Again she shook her head, but more easily now. "She was just gone." She repeated what she'd told the authorities on the fateful afternoon: she was there one minute, and then she was gone.

CHAPTER NINE

At the end of the Harris driveway Joe let his car idle as he watched a pair of gulls fight over a scrap. The larger one flew at the other, smaller bird, flapping its wings and driving the little one inland to the rocks. The wings were powerful, and the little bird was stymied by them, moving backwards and sideways, trying to save its morsel. The scrap fell from its beak and the larger bird dove for it. But the smaller one recovered and flew beneath the other one, scooped up the prize and swerved out over the water. The larger bird was left to tumble under its own weight and speed. Once on its feet on the sand, the bird looked up and down the beach, as though something else might be worth its interest. And then it was airborne, heading out over the bay. Just like people, Joe thought, fighting over scraps.

Joe had spent much of the previous evening distracted by the idea of a boatyard worker so careless that he'd jeopardize a sailor's safety. But Hugh Trask knew his employees, and was ready to vouch for all of them. He had his own security and review systems to back up his claims of the boat's seaworthiness when it was towed to the mooring at the beginning of the season. Joe knew the marina's reputation and had no reason to question Hugh Trask.

The next possibility was that Deb and Randall had tried to undertake a repair on their own. But there was no logic to this. After talking with Hugh Trask, it was clear that neither one had ever undertaken their own repairs before, so why would they start now, and with something so important as the vang system?

The next question was obvious. Who wanted to injure Deb or Randall or both? And why now, in the summer and in this way? Joe glanced at the plastic bag on the seat next to him and headed into town.

Soon after leaving Cecily Harris, Joe pulled into the Town Hardware parking area in the small mall by the Community Center. Town Hardware had been a part of Mellingham for as long as anyone could remember, passing from Grandfather Sarebian to son to grandson, every generation moving to a new location until they found themselves in a spiffy new building next to a coffee shop, computer repair shop (the width of a shoe box), and knitting shop. Anyone walking in could be excused for thinking it a brand new store, but anyone who got past the Employees Only sign in the back could be excused for thinking they'd fallen through the proverbial rabbit hole into another century. Whenever the store relocated, the family moved all their stock with them, and recreated the storeroom from the original building right down to the floorboards and walls (because this was how they could get the shelving to fit together, and without the original shelving they had no idea where anything was stashed).

Joe had once inquired about a screw for a 1928 Vintage Electro Dental Portable Floor Fan, owned by his parents, and the older Mr. Sarebian wandered into the back room and drifted past the shelves until he came to the small dirty paper box he wanted. He opened it, sniffed it, and poked around till he found the screw he wanted. He charged Joe twenty-five cents. The store philosophy seemed to be, "If you know about it, we have it."

The current Mr. Sarebian, now in his sixties and grandson of the original owner, was a wiry, congenial and perpetually cheerful looking man with thick gray hair, a long narrow face and sharp chin, and hands ready to spring forward and examine whatever item was held out towards him. Joe offered him the plastic envelope with the yellow receipt from the coffee can found on the Lady Mistral, the receipt for the plastic wood. Mr. Sarebian took it with both hands and peered at it.

"I see," he said. He wore a brown leather belt pulled to the last hole, which bunched up his khaki pants around the waist. It was possible he was losing weight for reasons to do with health, but it was more likely that he had failed to grasp the essentials of fashion. His wife was still wearing full-skirted shirtwaist dresses from the 1960s. The family was frugal, but more by accident than design. They merely lacked interest in keeping up with the world around them. "You need another tube?" He began to turn around in order to scan the shelves before Joe could stop him.

"I don't need another tube, thanks," Joe said. "I need information."

Mr. Sarebian's eyebrows went up, making a solid line of thick white hair across his forehead. But then his head jerked back and the feathery gray hair flipped away from his forehead. "I have little information on this material, but I can get everything you need to know. We have very good relations with our suppliers and I do know some chemists who have worked on this kind of thing. Just tell me exactly what you need to know, and I am pretty sure I can get it for you." He squinted as he scanned the horizon, and Joe could see he was already running through his mental Rolodex, looking for the best source.

"It's nothing to do with the product in that sense, Mr. Sarebian," Joe said. "I'd like to know when it was purchased and by whom. Can you track that information?"

Once again the eyebrows went up, but this time the black eyes were on the plastic sleeve and the receipt. He pursed his lips and studied the form. "Yes, I think I can help. Come with me."

Mr. Sarebian led Joe through the store, nodding to customers as they went, sharing a few words about the weather, the changing season, climate change, and the beginning of the school year. The two men passed a colorful display of backpacks, pens and pencils, notebooks, t-shirts, and a few other items, on their way into a narrow office. This room looked like it had been transported with the storeroom—the floors were made of old wood, the shelves were wood, and an old roll-top desk stood against one wall. Stacks of paper leaned against a computer, and a box of two penny nails sat on the mouse pad.

"I do try to keep track of such details," he said. He settled himself on a cushioned stool and rolled it up to the computer. In a moment he was running down a row of numbers, which Joe recognized as close to the number on the receipt. "Ah, here it is." He clicked on the number and a line of text appeared, repeating what Joe already knew—one tube of plastic wood with attached spreader was purchased for the grand sum of $5.99 plus tax.

Joe bent over his shoulder. "Is there a date?"

"Here it is," he said, "last Sunday in June."

"June," Joe repeated. That leaves out anyone at the marina, he thought. "Can you tell who the purchaser is?" Joe asked. "Perhaps it was a charge?"

"No, not a charge," he said, "but let's see. Sometimes we make a note just in case it's an ongoing project and the customer might want follow-up, perhaps a special order to finish the job." He scanned the information on the screen, glanced at the receipt in the plastic envelope, and finally shook his head. "I guess not."

"How about the salesman," Joe said. "Can you tell who sold it? They might remember who the purchaser was."

"Hmm. Possible." Once again Mr. Sarebian studied the computer screen, but in the end he shook his head. "No, not here."

Joe stepped back, and leaned against another desk, this one also piled high with papers and boxes. "Is there any way to tell who was working that day? Perhaps he might remember."

"Or she," he said.

"Hm?"

He spun around on the stool, and smiled. "My granddaughter works here sometimes, Joe. Friend of your boy, I think. I'll take a look." He walked over to a shelf with a row of metal files, studied the card slots in front, and pulled one out. He carried it to the other desk, propped it on top of a box, and opened it. Inside were hundreds of small timecards. He began rifling through them until he came to a section. He fingered a group of cards and pulled them out.

After reviewing the cards, he said, "It would appear we had three people on that Sunday afternoon. My granddaughter was one of them, along with Jim, who's been working here longer than I have, and Jim's cousin. So, we can ask." He replaced the cards and the file, and led the way back into the store. But the questions went nowhere. Jim, tall and straight and well into his seventies, didn't recognize the receipt, or the item purchased, and the granddaughter stared hard at it for a while, then shrugged and pulled a face of apology. She didn't remember it either. A phone call to the cousin was also a dead end.

"Sorry I couldn't be more help," Mr. Sarebian said. "Something to do with the Princess?" He leaned closer, his excitement brightening his eyes. "I saw you and your boy going out in the little boat yesterday. You ever need anything along those lines, you let me know." He bobbed his head in enthusiasm. "My granddaughter's a good crew too."

CHAPTER TEN

Joe walked out of Town Hardware satisfied that the Mellingham Marina and Hugh Trask's work had been vindicated. If the plastic wood had been purchased in June, after the Lady Mistral had been towed to its mooring, someone else had to have tampered with the vang. If Deb and Randall had tried an amateur repair, Deb's death was a tragic lesson and might have led to Randall's suicide. But nothing like that had come out during the initial interviews. Joe had never heard anything negative about the young couple, but then he had never looked.

Every town has a central site where news spreads like germs, some good, some bad, but either way swirling in the air and settling on the furniture, caught on a dog's wagging tail or blow into an open car window, coming to rest on a warm cheek. In Mellingham this place was the Community Center, located at the far end of the parking lot between the train station on one side and a small row of shops on the other. Joe turned from his car, parked in front of the hardware store, and headed for the Community Center, a one-story white clapboard building that consisted of one large open room with designated corners for different activities, and a row of small offices and meeting rooms along the rear wall.

The director, Denny Clark, had faced a number of troubles over the years, but Joe had come to regard him with reserved respect. No one had yet asked Denny to join the biweekly poker game the chief was dedicated to, but he was spoken of kindly when the men around the table talked about

53

anything other than sports and town doings. If Deb was as much a part of the town as Joe had been told she was, this was the place to learn more. Joe climbed the steps to the center, steeling himself for the assaultive noise of myriad activities.

The center was divided into four unequal parts, with each quadrant set aside for a different purpose. One front section focused on children's activities, and the back two quadrants were a wide open space that could be united for a large exercise class, an AA meeting, or a traveling exhibit of handmade goods from a third-world country. And beyond the open space were offices, where Joe expected to find Denny.

"Hello, Chief. Need help finding anything?" The question came from a woman wiping her face with a towel. Her black exercise outfit revealed a near perfect body, and perspiration glistened on her limbs. Patches of black hair stuck to her forehead and neck, and her gray eyes gleamed. She was one of those who derived physical pleasure from a workout.

Joe recognized Peg from some of Gwen's activities. Over the last few years Gwen had taken to hosting book groups and a few other groups on weeknights on a rotating schedule, and Joe's idea of what made the town hum had changed a bit. "The schedule's been changed, so there's no class today."

"Gwen probably mentioned it."

"And as a man you filed it away and forgot about it." Peg propped her hands on her hips. "Gwen's taking the yoga class on Saturdays."

Gwen takes a class in just about everything, Joe thought, but he decided not to say that. Peg turned to say goodbye and offer a few words of encouragement as the women from the class just ended packed up to leave. "This is the advanced class. Deb was in it, and we wanted to spend some time sharing our feelings about losing her."

"Did you know her well?" Joe asked.

"I guess." Peg frowned as she thought about this, her professional facade showing signs of weakening. "She was pretty good at it, yoga I mean, and she was always enthusiastic." She pressed her lips together, gazing out the window. "She was always on time, ready to start. But, you know, she didn't mind waiting if someone was late. She wasn't like a lot of people who are punctual. They get kind of antsy while they're waiting for the rest of the class. But Deb was relaxed about it and waited and never complained. I like to start on time." She turned away, a half-smile on her lips. "I'll miss her, I really will." She swung her arms out, took a deep breath. "This week, the other people in the class just wanted to talk, to process the shock of her dying, so we talked for almost half an hour. So we're a little late ending." She glanced up at the large clock on the wall over the main entry.

"Did she seem any different lately?"

Peg tipped her head and looked at him. "That's an odd question. I don't think so, but you know today we all said the same thing. It was so sad that she drowned. She grew up here and she loved the water, sailing, swimming, kayaking—all of it." Peg clasped the ends of the towel hanging around her neck.

"Did she talk about swimming?" Joe hadn't been the only one to think it odd that Deb had drowned. But if she'd been knocked unconscious by a wildly swinging boom before falling into the water, it was understandable.

"No, but I ran into her regularly up at the 4 Square Fitness Center. I work there too, and Deb came every week for a while." Peg paused to refold the towel and drape it over her left shoulder. "She was teaching a friend to swim."

Joe couldn't help noticing the sudden change in Peg's expression. The cheerful, confident exercise maven grew serious and seemed uncomfortable, but she took a deep breath and continued. "She was great to Cecily. It's too bad it ended the way it did."

"What do you mean, she was great to Cecily?"

"Oh! Didn't you know? No, of course not," Peg said, answering her own question. She looked around as though about to reveal a secret. "She was teaching Cecily Harris to swim. Cecily couldn't swim and apparently she was terrified of the water, so Deb offered to teach her."

"When was this? Recently?"

"This spring, early summer. I used to see them all the time."

"So, Cecily and Deb were good friends, very close."

Peg twisted her shoulders back and forth, as though unsure which direction to take. She pulled the towel from her shoulder and gave it a shake before folding it and holding it against her chest, wrapping her arms around her. "I think it was something of a secret." She lowered her head so she was talking down to Joe's shoes. "They came at the slowest possible time, and sometimes Deb asked if I'd just let them stay in the pool an hour or so after closing, while I was working in the office." Peg shrugged. "I wasn't supposed to do something like that but Deb was a great person. I always said yes, even when I knew I shouldn't have."

"What was the big secret? Only that Cecily couldn't swim?"

"It was more than that. I think it had something to do with Cecily's marriage." Peg made a disapproving face. "I think she didn't want her husband to know. Leo can be, well, a real piece of work. I shouldn't say that. But, this is his third marriage, after all, and he's been something of a serial dater too. The man gets around."

Joe nodded; he had taken note of Leo's serial marriages and relationships.

"Deb was an awesome teacher," Peg said, swinging out her arms and shaking out the towel. "Cecily caught on fast. I wish my students would turn out to be that good."

CHAPTER ELEVEN

Joe found Denny Clark, the director of the community center, folded into his office chair with a telephone cord twisted around his knees. The director had extended his phone cord when he began working at the center, to allow him to wander around as the spirit, or conversation, moved him. Now, it more often meant he ended up so entangled that he spent minutes extracting his limbs from the phone line. Joe pulled up a chair to watch.

"Don't know what's wrong with this thing," Denny said, his long limbs flailing. The sandy-haired director loved chatting with the members of the center and anyone else who wandered in. His personality, despite its flaws, had made the center notably welcoming and a town success. He gathered up the cord and dropped it into the wastebasket, usually empty as it was now, and turned to his guest, blinking and gathering himself as he did so.

"Maybe you should ask for a cell phone next year, when you submit your budget to the town," Joe suggested.

The director looked aghast. "What a horrible idea, Joe. What would I hold onto when I got excited?" His head gave a little spasm of dismay and he rolled his chair back a few feet. "So, what's with you these days?"

Denny made Joe wonder if teachers used to talking to young children all day turned the same tone of voice to adults when they left the school and went out into the adult world. "This is unofficial. I'm trying to get some clarification on Deb and Randall Connolly's last few days." Denny's eyebrows rose to his hairline. "Did you notice anything different about either of them?"

"Hmm. Either of them." Denny frowned and turned to stare out the window. He had an excellent view of the train tracks and the end of the platform. "I only saw Deb in here, never Randall, though I sometimes ran into him at Town Meeting or something else. Nice fellow. Deb? Hmm. Anything different." He closed his eyes and leaned back, tipping up his chin.

"Anything different or unexpected or at all unusual," Joe said, trying to clarify.

"Not really. She seemed quieter than usual the week before she died, and I figured that was just the way the heat was hitting her. Some people don't do well in the summer heat, and I figured she might be one."

"Quieter," Joe repeated. "Do you mean withdrawn?"

"We have a great group of programs for women here— lots of yoga, Tai Chi, some other things. And then we have all the crafts. Some of these gals, Joe, I tell you, they have talent like you wouldn't believe. None of this using a sewing machine or an extension on one to put in all that design on the final quilting. No, sir. They do this work by hand, and it's perfect. Really. Perfect."

"Did Deb do handwork?"

"Oh, no." Denny leaned forward and bounced back. "I didn't mean that exactly. Just that we have so many programs and courses and people like Deb just flow through from one course to the next, trying this or that, setting up another group because the first one got too big. I mean, people get really involved and they're like a community within a community. They all know each other. I mean, well, somebody did mention something about Deb, about whether or not she was okay. She was always in the center of things but for a week there she was kind of quiet, on the periphery."

"When was this? Do you recall?"

Denny winced and leaned over, as though in pain. "Her last week." He straightened up suddenly. "But no one thought it was serious. I mean, she was just quiet, more thoughtful, as though she had something on her mind."

"Do you recall who mentioned it?"

He shook his head. "I was going to ask her if she was unwell, if maybe, I don't know, something wasn't right." He rested his arms on the chair arms and leaned forward. "I can do that. I can ask if the air conditioning is too high or not high enough and that usually gets someone to say no, they have a cold or a headache or they're worrying about something." He leaned back and crossed his legs, glanced out the window and turned back. A train gave a short toot farther down the line and he waited for quiet to return as the cars trundled past, gathering speed. "Something was bothering her. You could see it in her face. She had something on her mind. Not something big. At least I didn't think it was something big." He leaned forward and back again, the chair squeaking.

"Any idea about what it could have been?"

Denny shook his head again. "Only I knew it wasn't anything here at the center. She was as gracious as always when I talked to her, just as nice to everyone else, but something was bothering her."

Joe thanked him and stood up.

"Are you thinking there's more to that accident than everyone assumes?"

"I'm not thinking anything yet, Denny. Just looking into things a bit."

Denny nodded, and Joe knew he hadn't fooled him. No one asks about a death after it's been investigated and closed.

CHAPTER TWELVE

The last few months had been relatively easy ones for Joe. Gwen made him happier than he ever thought he would be, his stepchildren were turning into young adults any parent would be proud of, and the Mellingham Police Department ran like a Maserati, smooth, powerful, and quiet. He should have known there was a bump in the road ahead. Joe pushed aside the files on his desk and set down a fresh cup of coffee, the swirl of the cream spreading outward until it reached the rim, its pace slowing as it slithered against the rim.

The bag holding the receipt for the plastic wood occupied the center of his desk. He sat down and stared at it. When he had first listened to Cecily Harris's story, he had admired the gentle but efficient interrogation by both the State Police and the Coast Guard personnel. He had come away with no doubt that she was telling the truth. But after Hugh Trask discovered the condition of the vang, that truth came to be only a superficial or abbreviated view of the incident.

At first Joe had been willing to consider the possibility that a poorly trained employee at Mellingham Marina had repaired the vang attachments with plastic wood. But if that was so, then the Lady Mistral was in dangerous condition in early June, when it was first put out on the mooring. The vang wouldn't have held in any kind of wind, so any accident would have happened much sooner if any of the skippers—Deb, Randall, or Annie—had chosen to use it. And there had been plenty of windy days in June and July when sailors most likely would have pulled out the device and hooked it up. This made it likely that the tampering was carried out later, perhaps even as late as in August, just before Deb and Cecily went out. This was actually likely, since Joe felt the material deeper in the bolt holes had not fully dried.

Joe reached for his coffee. The mug was still hot beneath his fingers. The cream had cooled it some, but it was still hot coffee. After Deb's accident came Randall's suicide, and Joe had the feeling that each one distracted from the other.

Mindy Dodge leaned in the doorway. "Sir, that call to Boston is on the line."

Joe thanked her and swung his chair around to the phone. Mindy was the newest addition to the Mellingham Police Department. She began as a general office secretary, and decided she liked the environment, and began taking courses in criminal justice. She probed discreetly and tactfully into the thinking of Joe and the other men on the force, perhaps to determine if their ways of looking at the world would be congenial. When Joe asked her if she was thinking of applying to the police academy, she mumbled about not being sure where she wanted to go, but she definitely wanted to stay in the office and work.

Joe picked up the handset and thanked Max Hasden for returning his call. They had spoken only once before, when Joe had not been able to reach Annie Beckwith after her brother-in-law's death.

"As far as I know," Max Hasden said in reply to Joe's question, "no one but the marina ever worked on that boat. I never heard either Deb or Annie talk about working on the boat themselves, other that getting new battens or a new bailer or something like that."

"Any chance that Randall could have tried a repair?"

"Randall? Not a chance. I used to tease Randall about not knowing the difference between a drill and a bread mixer." Max's voice softened.

"Who would have hired someone to work on the boat if not the marina?"

"Both would have been involved in that kind of decision," Max said, and his voice was firm. "Deb owned the boat on paper, but she and her sister were co-owners in a sense.

One never made a decision without consulting the other. After it went into the water this summer, they never had any trouble that I ever heard about."

"Have you sailed on it this summer?"

"Not this summer." He paused. "I was planning a visit for late August, my usual time out there."

"You knew both sisters fairly well?"

"I knew them through Randall, but I knew Deb better than Annie. I saw Deb and Randall a few times a year, and I talked to Randall at least once a month." Joe could hear the sound of papers chafing against each other. "There is a point to all this, I assume."

Joe explained the plastic wood and the conclusions from Hugh Trask. Max fell silent and then swore softly.

"What do you make of it, Chief Silva?"

"I'm not drawing any conclusions just yet," Joe said. "It's possible someone tried to help Deb and Randall with a minor repair and didn't know what they were doing."

Joe listened to the silence on the other end of the line. It was obvious, at least to Joe, that Max didn't believe a word of this. "I'm aware that you can't answer certain questions, but perhaps you can help me out here."

"I will if I can, Chief." Max's voice thinned with skepticism and caution.

"Were there any financial difficulties for anyone in the family?" Joe asked.

Max's laugh was quiet, the sound of a man confident in his position in life. "None whatsoever. I was Randall's attorney, but also a general advisor. Actually, we advised each other on various things. I can say with confidence that Deb and Randall had no money worries whatsoever."

"And for Ms Beckwith? Can you say the same for her?"

The silence lengthened, and Joe felt that familiar feeling in his stomach when he had stumbled on something that would open unexpected doors.

"I can't say specifically, but in general Annie hasn't had a lot of money. She chose a different life, nonprofit—artists, social services, that sort of thing—and made enough to live on, very modestly, but that's all. She spent her inheritance from her parents."

"Will she inherit anything from her sister?"

Joe felt the nature of the silence shifting as Max Hasden decided what he could or should pass along to the police. Joe waited.

"Randall was an only child, and he left everything to his wife, as is appropriate. After that, he had a few legacies. In the event of his wife's death, he made Annie his legatee. The bulk of his estate goes to Annie, his sister-in-law. Both Deb and Randall wanted it that way intentionally. They helped Annie out a few times, but they were confident she'd use the money wisely."

There's more to this, Joe thought. "Any particular reason they considered whether or not she'd use the money wisely?"

"Yes. You'd probably figure this out for yourself, so I'll save you the trouble. I will, of course, tell Annie we've had this conversation." He paused, apparently deciding what to say and how to say it. "She inherited a substantial sum from her parents at a young age, as did her sister, but Deb's was held in trust for a few years because of her age, which gave her time to think. Annie is older and her inheritance came to her directly. She spent it. She gambled some—mostly cheap lottery tickets and slots— and traveled some and gave away some, and it was gone. For a while it seemed she had a gambling problem, but she faced up to it and dealt with it. That no longer seems to be a concern, and Deb and Randall changed their wills accordingly."

"Can you give me a rough estimate of her inheritance?"

"She gets the bulk of seven million dollars." His voice changed again. "This is not a surprise to her or anyone else," he added quickly. "And the sisters were close. I don't know how Deb's accident happened, but I'd bet my life Annie had nothing to do with it."

"Or with Randall's death?"

Joe heard a quick hard hm.

"Or with Randall's death." Max was emphatic, and Joe didn't press him.

CHAPTER THIRTEEN

The medical examiner's office had released Randall Connolly's
body almost immediately, declaring it a suicide and finding
nothing suspicious in the death. Joe clicked on the computer file
and reviewed the photographs of Randall's body, and he had to
agree that on the face of it Randall's death did indeed appear to
be a suicide—one shot to the forehead with an old pistol. The
state police had sent the crime scene photographs to Joe, largely
in part because of his friendship with a certain detective. The file
included a close-up photograph of Randall's hand holding the
weapon. The photos weren't pleasant to look at, but then such
things never were.

He leaned back in his chair and let his mind drift to the
scene of the cove outside his window. When Philip had first
asked about learning to sail, Joe had thought he'd find a small
dinghy, leave from the small dock along the public ramp, and
sail around the cove before going out under the train trestle. But
he reminded himself that Philip was not a child anymore, and he,
as a stepfather, had to recognize that. Philip would have been
hurt and disappointed if Joe had acted as though he were too
young and inexperienced to take on a real boat on a real sail.
Assumptions and expectations, Joe thought. He had learned to let
Philip push him forward, and was rewarded with a teenager who
trusted him.

Assumptions and expectations.

Deb's unexpected death had knocked everyone off
balance. That was obvious. When Randall, her husband of over

ten years, died by an apparently self-inflicted gunshot, no one thought to question it. Joe didn't know either Deb or Randall well, and listened to those who did for signs that something might be wrong. Their devotion to each other was acknowledged, and the only note of caution was the usual one. "I never thought Randall would go that far," a neighbor said, "but they were inseparable. You never know what grief will lead to." The investigators didn't find anything to challenge that view. Not even the discovery of the plastic wood on the Lady Mistral moved the other authorities from their final positions.

A white-painted lobster boat, its open stern piled high with new yellow traps, pulled away from the dock and motored through the cove into the inner harbor, the sun glinting on the aluminum frames, the wake barely noticeable as the water rippled under the moored boats. Lobstering seemed so safe to those on land, with its traps set close to shore from easily maneuverable boats. But every year Joe recorded at least one death by drowning of a lobsterman in the area. It was too easy for a man to suddenly feel a line wrapped around his ankles jerk him into the water, the trap pulling him down, his slicker overalls filling with water, holding him down. When he realized his carelessness it was too late.

Joe watched the lobster boat enter the shadows of the train trestle and fade into darkness, but he could hear it emerge on the other side. Randall's death had to be the echo of Deb's, but Joe didn't know what it meant. Did Randall repair the Lady Mistral, recognize his mistake, and kill himself out of remorse? Did Randall mean to kill Deb and then himself? Did Randall know Deb was murdered, and was then himself murdered to cover it up? Were Deb and Randall killed by the same person for the same reason? Was Randall the intended victim of the Lady Mistral's repair? Or were both Randall and Deb meant to die on the boat? Or, was the intended victim neither Randall nor Deb but Annie Beckwith, who was known to sail the boat alone as often as possible?

Joe pulled out the HazMat report. Annie Beckwith had hired them but asked him to hand over the keys to the workers without ever stepping foot inside the house. Joe could hardly blame her. She showed all the signs of shock though she tried to conceal it. At least, that had been Joe's take until he talked to Max Hasden, and now he wondered how much more there was to Annie Beckwith. What had he missed? There were so many questions bumping along in his head that he didn't know where to begin. Maybe he should think about retiring. But first he needed more information on the main parties to this event.

Joe walked out to Mindy Dodge's desk and handed her a slip of paper. "See what you can find out about these residents."

"Leo and Cecily Harris." Mindy read out the names. "I know where they live. What do you want to know?"

"What Leo wouldn't want other people to know," Joe said.

"Got it." Mindy smiled the smile of a puppy discovering a sneaker under the sofa. "And Mrs. Harris?"

"What's her background. She told me she was from the Midwest, Michigan. She came here to go to school. That's all I know about her."

"Right. Got it."

"And this one also." Joe pointed to another name. "See if she has any debts or if she's been seen in any of the casinos."

"Sure thing." Mindy's eyes sparkled with the excitement of digging into the hidden world.

CHAPTER FOURTEEN

Joe stepped out into the outer office, also used as a waiting room, and regarded Sergeant Ken Dupoulis. The younger man sported his most professional expression as he listened to Carl Manderson complain, and Joe thought for a brief moment of simply walking back into his own office and leaving him to it. But Mr. Manderson's earlier phone call had been nearly hysterical and certainly irate, so despite Joe's complete faith in his sergeant's abilities, he headed into the waiting area. Carl Manderson spotted him and jumped up from his chair.

"It's about time," Carl Manderson said. He was short and stocky, with thinning brown hair and dark brown eyes. Unlike his counterparts on the other side of town, he was wearing gray slacks and a white shirt instead of the usual shorts and jersey, the required casual dress along the water in the summer. "Do you know how long I've been waiting here?"

"Have you had a chance to talk to Sergeant Dupoulis?"

"I didn't come here to talk to a sergeant." Manderson was on his feet and barely able to keep from charging Joe on the other side of the small room. "I want to know what you're going to do about this Harris guy."

Joe offered a few words meant to mollify the man long enough to get him into his office. He made a point of thanking Ken for taking over in his absence even though he was pretty sure the exchange was lost on Mr. Manderson. The irate man didn't seem the least satisfied now that he had jerked the chief from his other duties. He marched into the chief's office on stiff legs with rigid arms.

"This may not be a problem for us to solve," Joe said after he'd listened to a series of garbled accusations against Leo Harris.

"He's cheating us, all of us, anyone who invests with him," the man said. "My wife told me it sounded fishy. I should have listened to my wife."

"If you think Mr. Harris has misled you on an investment, you should talk to the appropriate authorities." Joe reached for a notebook but before he could give Mr. Manderson a referral, the aggrieved man went on.

"That won't do any good," Carl said. "I already tried that."

"Who did you talk to?"

Carl listed the name of an office in Boston.

"And this was when?"

"Late spring, in May, I think," Carl said, nodding to confirm the timing. "Look, let's not get technical. You need to act."

"I need accurate information," Joe said. "If you could tell me when you filed your complaint."

"I didn't file a complaint," Carl said with anger unabated. "I called a couple of people and told them things were fishy."

"And what came about from that?" Joe had the startling image of Carl Manderson calling a contract killer to come out and take care of Leo Harris.

"Nothing, absolutely nothing."

"And when was this exactly?"

"What does that matter? Jeez, about two months maybe before, well, before that poor woman drowned. I know things are bad now, everyone so sad, but life doesn't stop. I felt so sorry for Cecily. I told her it wasn't anything personal."

"Told who?" Joe asked.

"Mrs. Harris."

"When did you tell her this?"

"When? Which time? I told her after that man's funeral. But I told her before that it wasn't personal, my complaint against her husband."

Joe tried a few more questions, to calm down Mr. Manderson. If nothing else, he was a vivid example of how emotional behavior could interfere with clear thinking.

"I felt bad for her from the beginning. I saw her at North Station, waiting for her train, same as me. Anyway, the people I called didn't do anything, so I called someone else. I'd just been to a lawyer and I felt like things might happen, so I told her I didn't mean her any harm, nothing personal, but I wanted out of that investment plan."

"And what did she say?"

"I don't remember. I told her I just wanted to be protected, that's all. Anyway, I haven't gotten anywhere."

"What else have you done?

"I told Leo I wanted my money back. I wanted to disinvest."

This seemed to be the refrain of the day, Joe thought. "So, you've given Mr. Harris a written request to return your funds? Did you do this through a broker?" This wasn't his business, and way outside his field of expertise, but Joe knew that sometimes just giving the aggrieved a chance to talk helped them over a hump of what to do next, how to cope and what steps to take. Joe sensed that Carl needed to talk, and Joe was willing to listen and do whatever was necessary to calm him down. In a small town, a resident shouldn't leave the police station feeling worse than when he went in.

Carl shook his head, looking disgusted, and began rubbing his thigh, as though the fabric chafed his skin. "I tried to talk to a few of Leo's friends, but they wouldn't talk to me." He picked at an imperfection in the weave, tugging at it as though it were a speck of dust that could be removed. "That Randall—I know I shouldn't say anything after what just happened. I don't mean anything negative about him. He was a good man." He tried to rub the imperfection away, perhaps pressing it back into the weave.

"Did he offer any suggestions?"

"He said he didn't have anything to do with it so he couldn't help me."

"That must have been frustrating." Joe hoped Carl was winding down now that he'd said what he had to say.

"I should have known. They're all friends over there."

"Did he say anything helpful?"

"I just said." Carl glared at the chief. "He insisted he wasn't part of that, hadn't invested anything with Leo." Carl jutted his head toward Joe. "That should make you think."

"I may not understand exactly what you're saying, Mr. Manderson." Joe tried to pull these threads together for one clear image. "You invested money with Leo Harris, and when you became dissatisfied with the results—"

"No results!"

"If I may," Joe said, trying to reclaim the conversation, "when you were dissatisfied, you spoke with Randall Connolly. Why Mr. Connolly?"

"Him and Leo are friends. I figured he'd be one of the investors. That's what Leo said at the beginning. 'It's not for just anyone, Carl. I don't want just anyone in this.' So when things went South I figured a few of us could rally all the investors and bring Leo back on track and at least get our money back."

"So you talked to Randall."

"I did."

"And Randall said he wasn't part of the investment," Joe said.

"That's right. Exactly that."

"Did you talk to anyone else?"

"The Eatons. Old Mrs. Eaton has left everything in her daughter-in-law's hands, but they didn't invest either. And there were a few folks at the end of the point, the Priestlys."

"You spoke to Mr. Priestly?" Joe managed not to smile, knowing Carl Manderson would probably misconstrue it, and Joe didn't know how he'd explain his admiration for the one man on the peninsula who didn't seem the least bit intimidated by the Priestlys. Most of the peninsula residents showed nothing but deference for them, which did not extend to the rest of the town. The farther away from that neighborhood anyone went, the less regard one encountered for the family at the end of it.

"So you didn't find any other investors in your neighborhood?"

Carl Manderson shook his head, his shoulders rocking slightly as though he was comforting himself. He slid back in the chair, as though finally willing to be comfortable. "No one. But I know he has other investors."

"I'm going to give you a few names to call, Mr. Manderson. One is with the SEC and another is with the attorney general, just to get you started on a way to learn more. If the lawyer wasn't helpful, perhaps these offices will be."

"I didn't say he wasn't helpful," the man said with a look of resolve that made Joe wonder what he might have had in mind if he hadn't been a law-abiding citizen, which Joe now hoped he was.

"This won't ruin me but it'll hurt," the man said, his hands clasped in his lap.

Probably his pride more than his pocketbook, Joe thought as he rummaged on his desk for a pad of notepaper.

"Leo won't take my calls now. I'm shut out of everything. He gets even with dissatisfied investors by shunning us," Carl said. "And the rest of the place won't even talk to us now. People like the Harrises are untouchable."

"This is the list," Joe said, handing the other man a small sheet of paper. Carl took it but barely seemed to notice he had something in his hand now.

"Well, I know how that works," he said, more to himself than Joe.

"Mr. Manderson, I would caution you to deal with this in a careful, legal manner, getting help where it's offered. This may require patience," Joe added, wondering if he should be more worried about the man sitting in his office.

"Patience." He swore softly. "You can't imagine what it's doing to my wife." Joe looked at him, surprised to see what appeared to be genuine anguish. Whatever was happening to his wife, it was tearing Carl Manderson apart. "I want you to look into this and tell him he can be arrested."

Joe only shook his head.

"I thought Randall would help," Carl said, his breathing heavy. "I didn't know them well, Deb and Randall, that is, but just in passing. They seemed nice. Deb was nice to my wife, Edie. I thought he would help." He looked down at the notepaper in his hand.

"And the Eatons," Carl continued. "Babs and her mother-in-law are nice. We used to use their little dinghy to sail around the harbor." He glanced out the window. "I'm not a sailor and neither is Edie, but it was fun. It was okay. I don't get the sailing obsession, but that's okay." He looked at Joe as though finally realizing where he was and what he was doing. "I've gone too far, haven't I?" He looked around the room, perhaps reassessing and rethinking. "This isn't the place for us. I came out of Worcester County. I made every penny we have. I started with one truck, and now I have fleets all across the country. I like hard work, the real stuff, with your hands. I don't belong here. No one makes anything. They just move money around."

Carl stood abruptly and thanked him. "Maybe that's the answer. It's like a business. Everybody jockeying for position. Take your lumps and move on. It's not that much money. Well, yes, it is. But I've still got plenty. But Edie's feelings were hurt. She was made to feel, well, less. We raised two good kids. They were always respectful to their mother. But here, it's all looking down your nose at others. This place isn't for us." He looked down at the slip of paper in his hand. "Think I'll get my money back?" He gave Joe a meager smile. "I don't."

CHAPTER FIFTEEN

On Friday morning, Annie lay in bed and gazed up at the ceiling, trying to gauge the wind from the way the shadows flickered. She wondered if her sister had ever done the same. They weren't alike though they had been close growing up, a pair of opposites who leaned on each other in order to keep their footing in different worlds.

The bedroom occupied the second floor. Annie impishly liked to tell people that the bedroom occupied the entire second floor. When she did so, their eyes widened as they imagined the sheer size of such a space. That's when she quickly jumped in to explain the bedroom was a normal-sized room. It was the house that was small.

When Deb and Randall first told Annie they were building a house in Mellingham so they could be near the water, instead of buying something larger in one of the tonier suburbs west of Boston, Annie understood perfectly. But when they told her about the restrictions on the property—the house would replace a small garage and the new structure had to conform to the original footprint—she was sure they would regret their decision.

When she at last saw the house, she had to laugh and congratulate them on their ingenuity. The cottage, as it was erroneously called, was three stories, three rooms stacked one on top of the other, with the top floor overlooking the marsh and inner harbor but also with a view almost all the way to the outer islands. Deb and Randall could see their boat, the water, and the ocean. People, strangers and friends alike, told them the house would never sell, at least not for anything near what it was worth, because few people had enough imagination to appreciate it. But Deb and Randall didn't care. They loved it, and Annie loved visiting them there. And now it looked like she might actually live here.

The night before, she had given up sleeping on the sofa in the living room and moved into the one and only bedroom and unpacked her bag. Over the years Deb and Randall had become good friends with the owner of the Agawam Inn, across the street. They could always count on a certain suite when they wanted to host guests for the weekend or longer. Whenever Annie visited, she slept on the top floor, in Deb and Randall's shared office space and workroom.

Annie was used to living modestly as an adult despite growing up with the many advantages and privileges of life in Mellingham, and she wasn't impressed by luxury. She enjoyed camping out on the third floor but she had also disliked the idea of keeping her sister and brother-in-law from their desks. But last night, as she climbed the stairs from the first to the second floor, she knew she had to accept what had happened and move on. She either lived in the house or she sold it. No more could she pretend she was visiting and spread out a sleeping bag on an air mattress.

A warm morning breeze drifted in through the wide-open windows as Annie went about putting away her things in the second floor bedroom. She heard herself saying, Deb won't mind if I put my things in here. Deb won't mind if I move this. Deb won't mind if I sell this. Annie had gone through a brief period when she had resented Randall for surviving his wife, wishing he'd been on that sailboat too so he could rescue her. But she got over it quickly. Now she felt guilty for not realizing how depressed he was over Deb's death. As deeply as she missed her sister, she couldn't imagine feeling such despair that she'd want to kill herself. Her heart ached for him.

Annie picked up a crystal paperweight with bits of colored glass suspended in the center and wondered why they had it. She didn't like the color of the sheets, the coffee mugs were too light to use on a boat, and the plates seemed too delicate, too feminine for the sister she had grown up with. She wondered why she hadn't noticed these things before. And then she came across a painted metal tray that had been their mother's and began weeping. She couldn't understand what was happening to her. Perhaps this volatility was part of grieving.

When the police had arrived at Annie's apartment in Watertown late that Sunday afternoon, she had understood at once something had happened. She had sat with her lost sister's husband into Friday night, but when he clearly needed to be alone, she had left Mellingham and driven back to her own apartment. Saturday had been a nightmare she couldn't quite push through, talking to Randall by phone off and on through the day. She thought they were both doing better, lying to themselves and each other.

And then she heard the knock on the door, the knock that didn't sound like any of her friends, and she knew in her bones she should have stayed in Mellingham, holding onto Randall and letting him hold onto her. She wouldn't have guessed Randall would use a gun, but once she knew Randall was dead, the words flashed through her head before the officer could even say them—"by his own hand."

These thoughts came to her while she was thinking about other things, and she feared she would hear them for the rest of her life and never feel normal again. She was afraid she'd take up a conversation with a casual acquaintance in the grocery store and suddenly break off and start talking about her interview with the HazMat contractor, or the confusing conversation she'd had with the funeral home.

She took as a good sign the realization that she was hungry and begun rummaging through the kitchen for something substantial to eat. She'd had nothing but cereal and toast since she'd arrived and began to feel the need of real food. She was reading the sell-by date on a carton of eggs when she heard a knocking on the glass sliders opening onto the deck.

"Oh, I'm so glad you're here!" A woman in her fifties stepped back from the glass as Annie approached. "I'm Babs Eaton. I live just down the road." She held cuttings from a rose of sharon in both hands, her gnarled fingers twining among the smaller twigs.

Annie was about to invite her in when Babs continued.

"I'm sure you have much to do, what with the house and
. . . " Her face paled and she grew apologetic. "Really, I'm very
sorry about your sister and her husband." Annie thanked her for
her sympathies.

"We live just over there," Babs nodded in the southerly
direction. "We've invited a few friends over for afternoon tea. I
was hoping you'd join us. My mother-in-law knew your family
rather well before she, well, she's in the early stages of
Alzheimer's and it shows in odd ways. Anyway, she knew your
parents and she remembers your sister, that's one thing that's
still clear to her, and I know she'd love to see you. She may
remember you from when you were a child."

To her own surprise, Annie said yes. The minute she
mentioned that Coralee Eaton knew Deb, Annie felt a tug she
couldn't and wouldn't ignore. As a result, six hours later she
found herself walking down the driveway of an early twentieth-
century imitation of a French chateau, with a mansard roof atop a
house of dusky pink bricks. A series of topiaries surrounded a
small fountain circled by the driveway. The door was open and
Annie peered through the screen down a hallway to the back of
the house, where another screen door framed the inner harbor
and the sun gleaming on little sailboats riding at anchor.

"Oh, your timing is perfect." Babs Eaton came in
through the terrace door and hurried down the hall, drawing in
Annie with a flourish. "I'm so glad you've come. My mother-in-
law, Coralee, was delighted to hear you'd accepted our invitation
and has been asking me about it repeatedly since I told her."
Babs led Annie down the hall but stopped before they reached
the door to the terrace. "I don't know if you know anything
about dementia but those succumbing to it tend to develop some
annoying habits like repeating themselves, asking the same
question again and again, forgetting whatever you've told them.
It can be very frustrating until you accept it, and then it's just a
different way of relating to someone."

"That's not the kind of thing that bothers me at all,"
Annie said. And truthfully, as she stood on the doorsill looking
out at the calm waters and crystal blue sky, at the flowers lining
the bottom of the garden buffeted from the shore by crushes of

flowering hydrangeas, she thought no one could ever be bothered by anything if they lived here. She had become so used to living in tight urban quarters, marveling at the sight of the occasional daffodil or rose bush, that she felt in danger of being overwhelmed by nature's beauty. "I'm looking forward to meeting your mother-in-law again. I vaguely remember her from my childhood, and I'm so glad she remembers my sister and our family. I'd like to remember good things about my sister."

Annie thought she saw something more than gratitude in Babs's expression, but it disappeared so quickly that she put it down to her imagination. She followed her hostess out to the flagstone terrace where three couples and Mrs. Coralee Eaton were settled around a glass table. Babs made the introductions.

Annie did her best to follow the conversation, silently repeating names and physical details as she listened to stories about the current banking crisis (that was Dave Winslow, and his wife was Betty, who had pure white-blond hair in a short ponytail and listened with alert eyes), reports from town hall on a predictable increase in property taxes (that was Louise Colter and her husband, a man with very large ears), and suggestions for interesting places to retire to (that came from Andy and Liz Peters, who seemed to finish each other's sentences as well as their plates).

"I would never want to live anywhere else," Coralee said, leaning towards Annie. "I've always lived here. At least until I came here. Didn't I, Babs?"

After a few of these offerings Annie didn't work as hard to follow Coralee's conversation. She listened to reminiscences and waited for the odd comment about her sister.

"Good sailor," Louise said after the obligatory condolences. "She offered to help with our high school sailing class. As expensive as this town is," she went on, "we don't raise enough in property taxes to pay for everything the school needs." Annie heard someone groan and whisper, Here it comes.

"Interesting how people on this end of town always make the most noise about taxes," Betty said almost to herself. There was a lull in the conversation, as though one guest had insulted another, but the voices burst forth again, the chatter rushing in to fill the silence and cover a general awkwardness.

Annie studied Betty out of the corner of her eye. She hardly looked like someone who would rock the boat or take the side of the workers. Her husband looked annoyed but the conversation moved in another direction, and Annie heard someone whispering in her ear.

"It's always that way," Coralee said, leaning closer to Annie. "This side of town and that side of town—divisions, divisions. It's been going on for centuries. They say a sailor came into the harbor over two hundred years ago to steal away his lady love after her father forbade the marriage. The young man was very unsuitable, and the father sent him away. But he came back. He dropped anchor one night right out there." She waved her fingers at a nearby inlet where nothing that drew more than two feet on a centerboard would be able to navigate even at high tide. "But it did not end well."

"It's one of those local legends," Babs said, giving her mother-in-law a smile.

"More than a legend, a great tragedy," the old woman said. "The young lady climbed out of her window disguised as a man and ran down to the water's edge to meet her lover. Her father saw a strange man in the garden and he got his pistol and shot her, only feet from her lover. Her lover heard the gunfire, and he fled, not knowing his lady love lay dead near by."

"It's a legend from the time of the Revolution," Babs said.

"Some say it was a member of Lafayette's army," Coralee continued.

Babs reached for a plate of cake and held it out to Annie, who shook her head.

"It's certainly a very romantic story," Annie said.

"It is said the sailor never reconciled himself to the loss of his beloved, and to this day he walks the shore looking for her, hoping he will come upon her and they will flee together." Coralee Eaton pulled her plate towards her and began to poke at the food with her fingers. Louise tried to conceal a frown, and one of the husbands looked away and began to make noises about how late it was getting.

"I have seen him myself," Coralee said, pushing a fragment of cucumber into her mouth. "He comes late at night.

He walks along the shore looking and looking and looking. A tragic figure. The light of love shines from him—gold and shimmering."

Babs leaned towards Annie and whispered, "The story morphs into something new every now and then. Once there was a skiff of sailors who rowed the man to shore to help him search."

"I told the story to your sister." Coralee nodded to herself as she recalled the incident. "She too lived close to the water. I thought she should know in case she encountered him sometime late at night. I wouldn't want her to be frightened."

"That was thoughtful of you, to tell her," Annie said.

"He is always armed, you know." The old woman nodded, knowingly.

"I'm sure she appreciated the warning." The conversation morphed again into more local topics—zoning and development issues—and Coralee fell into a light slumber.

Annie rose and said her goodbyes and thanked Babs for including her. Before she could leave the table, however, Coralee awoke, grabbed Annie's wrist and pulled her close.

"I told her just as I am telling you because he wanders along the shore looking for her. He is tragic in his sorrow but dogged in his devotion." The spittle had begun to form at the corners of Coralee's mouth and the expression in her eyes became confused. She gazed up into Annie's face as though perplexed. "You mustn't discount him, you know."

"I won't. Thank you for warning me, Coralee." Annie offered another smile of reassurance, and as the old woman relaxed her grip, Annie slipped away.

"I'm so sorry," Babs said as she caught up with Annie, to walk her to the door. "But thank you for being so kind with her. She does enjoy seeing people."

"Will you come again?" Unexpectedly, Coralee materialized behind Babs and Annie. She might be losing her mental faculties but she kept her physical agility. The old woman smiled with a look of mild confusion and anticipation, turning from one woman to the other. She said to Babs, "You know, he really loved her." She turned to Annie. "Really, he did. It was so obvious."

"I'm sure he did," Annie said. "It's a lovely bit of history."

"It didn't happen so long ago," Coralee said. "They were still young—such a pity." She began to shake her head, as if to scatter the sad memories, and reached out for a table to steady herself, as though she'd made herself dizzy. She turned and headed back down the hallway, to the terrace.

"I'm sorry," Babs said, her voice barely above a whisper. "It's hard to know when she's going to make sense and when she's, well, not."

Annie thanked Babs, who hurried after her mother-in-law, and turned to the front door. She rested her hand on the screen as she glanced into the room on her left, which seemed to her a man's room with leather furniture and walls painted red and a large teak cabinet holding a number of weapons. Annie stared at the piece of furniture and its contents, a gun cabinet standing in full view of anyone who came through the door. Babs hadn't said anything about another member of the family—husband or father or son or anyone else, but then there was no reason why she should. She wondered if the man in question was the kind who flinched at the mere thought of a social event, and stayed only long enough to greet the guests, before making his excuses and fleeing to another part of town. Annie forced herself to pull away and step onto the front stoop, letting the screen door slam shut behind her.

CHAPTER SIXTEEN

Joe caught sight of Annie Beckwith strolling down the hill towards her house, and pulled over to the side of the road, waiting to see where she went. When she turned into her driveway, he decided now was as good a time as any to bring her up to date on what he had learned. He was curious to hear her reaction to the news about the vang.

The shingled house was set at the end of a short gravel drive, not far from the marsh, and surrounded by lawn. The cottage, as it was called, was obscured from the street on one side and well hidden from houses on the other by tall poplars and pines. Since this had been the site of a garage at one time, nothing anyone wanted to look at, for the house above, on the hill, landscapers had done their best to hide it. That was when no one thought the marsh was worth looking at.

As picturesque as the marsh was, Joe knew what that was like to walk on—squishy, unstable much of the year, but dry and hard at other times. It absorbed the storm surges typical for New England, hosted most coastal wildlife during at least part of the life cycle, and filtered storm water flowing into the ocean. In some areas farther north along the coast farmers still grew and harvested salt marsh hay annually. The marsh in Mellingham had been filled in along the edges over the years, though that had stopped a few decades ago as neighbors and town officials grew ever more environmentally conscious and observant.

The driveway entrance to the cottage broke through a stonewall that ran from the edge of the marsh up to the top of the slope and beginning of Brewster Street. Joe turned in and parked near the house. The front door stood open and Joe knocked on the screen. He prepared himself for an awkward interview.

Annie Beckwith greeted Joe and led him into the main room on the first floor. He knew the small house had raised a few eyebrows when the design was first proposed for a building permit, but he tacitly congratulated the architect, whoever he was, for his imaginative response to the problem. Joe accepted a glass of iced tea and sat down on a chair facing the deck.

He could see the harbor, with the lobster boats lying still on the incoming tide, a few small sailboats roughing each other on their painters along the town dock, motor and sail boats tugging at their moorings in the inner harbor. On the opposite shore he could see parts of the Mellingham Marina.

Joe noted the absence of curtains or shades on this side of the house, since there were no near neighbors, but he wondered what someone on the other shore might see. What did people on the other side look out on late at night, when they were prowling around unable to sleep at two in the morning? He recalled the apartment he had rented when he'd first arrived in Mellingham, the first floor of an old house occupied by an elderly woman, who lived on the second floor. Mrs. Alesander now lived with her daughter, her own apartment rented to strangers, but she and Joe's mother still chatted on the phone every week. The house sat safely away from the coast, but he could see parts of the harbor through the trees.

"This can't be a social call," Annie said, sitting down on the sofa. Deb had decorated the first floor with rattan furniture usually found in a summerhouse, and the sofa creaked like a frozen pond as a curious animal tested it for safety.

Joe placed the sweating glass on a coaster and sat forward. "We've come across something on the Lady Mistral that has confused us, so I thought I'd bring it to you."

"That sounds odd," Annie said. "What is it?"

"It seems the vang gave way because of a poor repair." Joe waited for Annie's reaction. She began to nod as if to encourage him to continue. She was attentive and patient. "We don't know if this had anything to do with your sister's death of if it's only a coincidence." He paused, waited. "The bolts in the boom to hold the vang were secured with plastic wood."

"What?" Annie's face went blank, and Joe watched as her expressions changed. First, not understanding, then grasping the technical point, then shock, and finally dismay. Behind that he could see the anger building. "What did you say?" She moved to the edge of the sofa, the heels of her palms pressed hard on her knees.

"It looks like someone resized the bolt holes and used plastic wood to fit the bolts and secure them into the new holes." Joe understood the reaction he was seeing. Unless Annie Beckwith was an award-winning actress, this discovery was news to her.

"My family has been taking our boats to the Mellingham Marina for years," she said. "They couldn't make that kind of mistake. They wouldn't." She struggled on, trying to convince herself that this could have happened. Surely, no one who worked with boats could have done this. Joe listened, then decided it was time to end her floundering. She hadn't known, he concluded, and it was time to take the next step.

"I've spoken with Hugh Trask. He has the Lady Mistral in dry dock and is going to keep her there," Joe said. "Meanwhile, I want to make sure I understand what happened."

"Hugh knows about this?" Annie said.

"I asked him to keep it to himself until I'm through looking into it."

Annie nodded but she was obviously confused, as though she didn't really understand and wasn't sure if she should be angry or not. She was growing numb, sliding into a state of incomprehension.

As if to better grasp what he had told her, she stood and walked to the sliding glass doors, where she pushed open the screen, standing on the sill leading to the deck. She stared at the harbor and the marina in the distance, as though an explanation could be visible from this side of the water. She swung around to face him. "But why? Why would someone do that?"

"That's what I have to find out, Ms Beckwith," Joe said. "Hugh Trask is confident the changes with plastic wood didn't happen in his marina. If the boat was tampered with, only a few people could have done it, and only a few people would have known how dangerous an unstable vang system could be."

"There aren't many people who could have done it," Annie said. "But who would want to? Why? Why hurt Deb?" She turned a face contorted with pain, and Joe remembered she was the older sister who fell off her bike in the center of town, skidding around corners, while her younger sister, Deb, watched from the sidewalk, arms akimbo and a moue of affectionate disapproval on her lips.

"Do you know of anyone who disliked your sister?"

"So, you think it was Deb they were after?" Annie walked back into the living room and faced Joe, her hands hanging by her side, a look of helplessness on her face.

"They could have been after Cecily Harris. Or you. We don't know."

Annie sat down again, and the rattan sofa slid a few inches on the bare flooring. "Well, realistically, there aren't many people who could get at the boat. The first person who comes to mind is someone at the yacht club. Lincoln Walsh is the club captain. He's there all the time, even at night sometimes." Annie paused. "When I say something like that it seems a totally bizarre idea. I was thinking he's someone who would have seen anyone going out because he's there, on the spot, late at night sometimes."

"How do you know this? I thought the launch closed at five or six, and the club soon after."

"Yes, that's right, but sometimes I can see a light on late at night, and I mentioned it to him once and he said he had a late call about a damaged boat and stayed to finish up the loose ends."

"Does that seem unusual to you?"

"Not really," Annie said as she paused to think this over. "Okay, Lincoln but for no reason except that he had access to the Lady Mistral, knows how to rig a vang, and is good at working on boats."

"And after Lincoln?" Joe asked. "I know this is hard, but was there any trouble between your sister and her husband?"

"Randall?" The color drained from Annie's face. She shook her head. "Randall could have been out on the boat, but

Lincoln told me he never boarded the boat without Deb. If he wanted out of the marriage, he could have just asked."

"Any problem with neighbors?" Joe waited. "Tell me about Cecily Harris. She and Deb were friends, but that's all I know."

Annie laughed, but without humor. "It's hard if not impossible to see Cecily in the role of villain—a sailor who knew how to sabotage a boat and create maximum danger for the skipper." Annie shook her head. "It isn't plausible. To me, Cecily is just the timid third wife of the scion of one of the town's oldest families, the unexpected trophy wife of one of Randall's friends. Cecily is so blonde and curvy, she's almost a caricature." She stopped. "God, that sounds so catty. I'm sorry. She's perfectly nice and I can't stand the way I'm talking. Does this kind of thing, sudden death, I mean, always turn people into monsters?"

"It's understandable, Miss Beckwith. You'd rather have your sister alive than her friend."

Annie's gratitude spread over her face. She relaxed and her eyes grew moist. "Deb seemed to like her and they certainly got along."

"Were they close?"

"I'm not sure I know how to answer that," Annie said, leaning back and pursing her lips. "Deb and Cecily bought tables together at local fundraisers, rounding up friends to make a table of eight or ten, at $100 or $1,000 a plate. They organized dances at the yacht club, book clubs and treks into Boston. They made an odd pair, but Deb never talked about her affectionately, like a dear friend from school or something, and I rarely saw them together. I heard about Cecily more than I saw her, so I didn't get to see what the friendship was like between them." She paused. "I guess they were friends. They did things together."

"I understand Deb was teaching Cecily to swim," Joe said. "And the sailing lessons might have been an extension of that. Is there any reason why her husband, Leo Harris, wasn't teaching her? Was there any trouble between your family and the Harrises?"

"Not that I ever heard." Annie turned to gaze out the open glass doors onto the deck. "But now that you say it, I haven't seen Leo's boat in the water. He's the only other owner of a 210 left from our once very respectable fleet." She smiled, recalling earlier times. "But putting Leo on the list is as absurd as including Lincoln or Cecily or Randall. Leo raced with a vengeance, but he's a sportsman. After a race he always made a point to give a slap on the back and offer a handshake and a few words of encouragement or congratulations to the other racers, no matter who won. Leo's grandfather had been one of the founders of the yacht club. I can't imagine Leo damaging a boat for any reason. And why would he want to kill Deb or Cecily? I mean if he wanted to kill his wife, there have to be easier ways." Annie's consternation collapsed into a deep blush. "God, that sounds awful." She clapped a hand over her eyes.

Yes, thought Joe as he listened to the gravel crunch under his feet. Annie Beckwith hit on a crucial point. There had to be easier ways to ensure someone's death than rigging an accident on a racing boat. And yet, that was the weapon of choice. Unless murder was not the intent, and sabotage was the goal.

CHAPTER SEVENTEEN

Since marrying Gwen McDuffy and formalizing their relationship, as his stepchildren liked to describe it, Joe had found himself increasingly conscious of how he spent his weekends. It seemed he wanted to take his new family to all the places he cared about and new ones he wondered about. Jennie smiled patronizingly and rolled her eyes, leading Joe to believe she would be a formidable figure one day, and Philip lowered his chin and studied him as though he were an ant under a microscope. But they got in the car when told and bickered happily in the back seat. Joe thought they were too old for this but Gwen said they were just catching up on parts of their childhood they had missed. She sat contentedly in the front seat gazing out the window.

The only fly in the ointment anointing his happiness at the moment was a question that had come to him at the most inopportune time, when he was loading up the car for their Saturday morning trip to New Hampshire. He'd figured out how to resolve the question, and hoped his family wouldn't catch on until it was too late.

Joe cruised north along Route 95 into New Hampshire. Every few minutes Gwen glanced over at him to see if he was listening to Philip in the back seat explaining the virtues of different kinds of rigging and sails. In the space of barely a week her son had been transformed into a stranger, albeit a charming and interesting one. Joe suppressed a smile and resettled in his seat. He hit the directional signal and began to turn.

"This isn't the way, Pae." Philip leaned forward, his hand gripping the leather head rest of Joe's seat.

"We're taking a slight detour," Joe said. Gwen frowned.

In the rear view mirror Joe could see Jennie rolling her eyes. "Boats!" she whispered so everyone could hear.

Joe guessed the only reason Jennie wasn't interested in sailing was because Philip was. She'd get over it and then, Joe realized, he'd probably have to buy something for her too.

Joe drove along a river wending its way through the marsh until he came to a dirt road. A wooden sign dangling from a single hook on a crosspiece announced the Greenview Marina. He drove into a dirt lot and pulled up to a bank of trees and brush to park. In front of them was a wide river bordered by green marsh. It was a visual landscape different from what he was used to, but just as beautiful. No ocean view here but this too was New England on the water. The four climbed out and walked toward the river and its row of docks. Most of the boats tied up were motorboats, but a few small sailboats bobbed alongside them. A large German shepherd trotted out from the side of a warehouse and Jennie immediately approached it. Well trained, he thought, to not bark at visitors during regular hours.

"Why don't we have a dog?" Jennie said, to the dog.

"Because we have a cat," Philip said.

Gwen smiled and strolled toward the water. She and Philip walked out onto the docks and she listened as he repeated his latest conversation with Hinkie Trask.

The warehouse was open along the front, and Joe could see three or four boats on cradles deep inside. He turned to a dilapidated door cut into one corner of the warehouse, and entered a small room, like a closet jutting into a living room. The office was little more than a shed, and the desk was cluttered with papers, odd bits of equipment, and a crushed paper bag on which sat the remnants of a sandwich.

"Yo! Can I help you, sir?" The question came from a man who looked to be in his sixties; he appeared in the opposite doorway and peered at Joe with the squinting, peering expression of the myopic. His khaki pants were stained with oil and his heavy khaki shirt had probably been washed and ironed as recently as this morning but was already showing signs of a busy day. The smell of motor oil leaked from the man's clothing.

"I hope so," Joe said. "I'm trying to track down a sail boat."

"Anything particular?" He reached for a rag hanging on a peg near the door and wiped his hands, then reached for a jar of damp wipes to finish the job. "Harry." He extended his hand and Joe took it.

"Yes, in fact." Joe reached into a shirt pocket and pulled out a photograph printed from the web. "I saw this and I wanted to get a better look at it." He held it out to him.

"Hmm."

"It doesn't say where it's berthed but I think it's here." Joe waited for him to agree or disagree. Joe had asked Mindy Dodge to find out what she could about the Harrises, and she had come up with a few surprises. Joe wasn't sure how relevant they were, but they made him curious. One of the surprises had been the information about Leo Harris's boat. Joe already knew it wasn't in the water this summer and might be for sale. But Mindy gave him a list of six marinas in the coastal New Hampshire area, with a gut feeling on which one was the most likely. Harry stared at the photograph, trying to recall the boat.

"I'm pretty good at placing these, but I need to check this one." He handed the paper back and headed for a file cabinet. "We get boats in here sometimes for just a single season. The regulars I know right away, but some of the short termers I'm not so sure about." He pulled open a drawer and began to finger the files.

"It's a 210 put up for sale this summer or last summer. Not sure," Joe said.

Joe went to stand in the doorway, watching Gwen and Philip on the dock and Jennie playing with the dog. A pair of teenagers marched across the parking lot to the ramp and headed down it, walking along till they turned onto another float and dropped their bags onto the boat in the first slip. They jumped in and Philip wandered closer, leaning down to ask a question.

"Did you say a 210?" Harry pulled out a folder, opened it, and laid it on the file drawer, reading. "Yup. Came in last fall for some work. Stored over winter. Put out in the spring. I remember the guy taking photographs. Never had it picked up. Said he thought he'd be more likely to sell it if people could sail it right away. It's out here." He turned around from the cabinet and handed him a glossy photograph.

"Is the owner from around here?"

Harry shook his head. "No, he's from Massachusetts. Mellingham, it says here."

Joe nodded, waiting while the other man continued reading.

"I saw the photos he took—they weren't very good—so I offered to take one for him," Harry continued. "He said no, that was all right, but they really were pretty bad and I knew he'd see that as soon as he posted them on the Internet. So I took some anyway, just in case he wanted them. I emailed him but he never got back to me." He paused while Joe pretended to study the photograph. "Nice boat. You interested?"

"Maybe." Joe was very interested in the photograph.

"Make an offer," Harry said. "I'm sure he'd take anything reasonable."

Joe glanced up at him and wondered if this was a hint that Leo Harris hadn't paid his bill yet. "You think so?"

"Yeah," Harry said. "He didn't seem too happy about selling—sort of got the feeling he had his back to the wall. He didn't say anything, but you can tell. I've been watching boats come and go so long, I can tell what kind of sale it is. Some people sell so's they can move up. They price things all over the place but they know deep down what they want, and that's the price they'll take—the amount they need to get over the hump to the new boat. Some sell cuz they have to, they need the money, you know, but they're fighting it every step of the way. You could offer them top dollar and they'd still hold back, dragging their oars. You just know how much they hate the idea of letting the old thing go. And some sell cuz the wife, sometimes the husband, or the dad, or someone in the family, says, get rid of that thing. It's costing us too much." He scratched under his chin. "I can always tell."

Joe and Harry stared another moment at the papers in Joe's hand.

"He'll take a decent offer, maybe a little lower," Harry said into the quiet.

Harry went on talking, about other sailboats for sale, some here in storage that he could look at, some on slips right now, ready to go if Joe was interested. He knew people who kept their boats nearby if not in use and he could call them up while he and his family looked around. He was ready to help in any way he could. "You're not really interested in that boat, are you?"

Joe shook his head. "I'm glad to have the information, though."

"I could tell he was in trouble. I can always tell." He shook his head and followed Joe to the door. "You folks sail?"

"I just started my boy on a Penguin," Joe said. The other man smiled, and Joe felt he'd redeemed himself.

Harry and Joe strolled towards the ramp. Harry talked about sailing on the river, the skills sailers acquired as they learned to navigate the shallow water and shifting bottom to the open sea. And through it all the picture of the green 210 flashed in Joe's memory.

Leo Harris was selling his boat. He had brought it up to Newington, New Hampshire, for repairs and storage, and then put it up for sale. This was as unexpected as snow in July, as snail mail on Sunday, as ten years without a war. But the boat was on the market. And Joe had the feeling that no one in Mellingham knew anything about it, and that was the intent.

CHAPTER EIGHTEEN

On Monday morning, Joe went into the office early, to take advantage of the quiet time to sort through what he had learned about Leo Harris over the last few days, reviewing Mindy's research and what he'd learned at the marina in New Hampshire. A flash of light on his office window broke Joe's concentration and he looked up. Through the window he watched a covered black pickup pull into a department parking space. He'd forgotten that Ken Dupoulis was on duty this morning even though he worked through the weekend. Ken's great love was hunting, anything he could dress for his home freezer. If working extra hours in the summer, when everyone else wanted time off, meant he could have more time for hunting in the fall and winter, then he was available. The truck door slammed, and a moment later Ken greeted him in his office doorway.

"How was your day off in New Hampshire," Ken said. "Did you get those sails for Philip?"

"A new set of nylon sails for the recently christened Explorer," Joe said, swiveling in his chair toward the doorway.

"He's gonna make a pretty good sailor." Despite growing up so close to the water that he could smell the tide change, Ken had no interest in going out on the ocean. He could sail and swim but he loved inland waterways, rivers with fish and trails that led to rabbit or something else.

"He has the enthusiasm for it, and a pretty good teacher, Hinkie Trask." Joe reached behind him for a file. "I made a stop along the way, at a marina on the Piscatagua." He handed a sheet of paper to Ken. "Leo Harris has his boat for sale up there. It's on the Internet too, but it seems no one down here knows about it."

"And Carl Manderson thinks Leo is cheating him," Ken said, leaning against the door jamb as he studied the paper advertising Leo Harris's 210. "And that plastic wood. Nothing is what it seems, is it?"

"I don't know there's any connection," Joe said. He knew Ken was waiting for him to add something, because the implications were obvious.

"An investor complains and the man named in the complaint shows signs of financial distress, which he then attempts to conceal." Ken frowned over the paper.

Joe leaned back and rested his arms on the chair arms. "Things are starting to look different, aren't they?"

"You know what I always wondered?" Ken said, stepping into the office and lowering his voice. "I never heard anything about the Connollys being interested in guns, and I usually hear that sort of thing. And the sister, Annie Beckwith, never asked about where the gun came from. All she said was 'He used a gun?' "

"Yes," Joe said, thinking back. "She seemed too surprised to take it in."

"And she didn't ask for it back after we cleared the house and she didn't ask about it during the interview when she identified the body. The only other thing she ever said was that she never thought Randall was someone who would commit suicide. It's as though the gun didn't even exist."

Joe agreed as he handed Ken another sheet.

"What is it?" Ken said as he started reading. "Oh, the report on the gun Randall used." He continued reading, then glanced up. "Really? Is this correct?"

"Mindy wouldn't get something like that wrong," Joe said. "You can see there what she got." He nodded to the report in Ken's hands.

"That's a bad one," Ken said.

"I put Mindy on it right after the death was declared a suicide, before I knew about the plastic wood." Joe hunched his shoulders for a moment before releasing them. "I never liked the idea of two deaths at once without something explaining them, other than coincidence. I know coincidences happen, but this one didn't make sense, and then when she couldn't track the weapon, I sent her back to keep looking."

"Lucky we still had the photographs," Ken said.

"I half-expected Mrs. Eaton to ask for it back but she never did."

"Who had the weapons license in that house?"

"The older Mrs. Eaton, Coralee Eaton," Joe said. The two men lapsed into silence.

"I can see why I never heard about the Eatons being collectors," Ken said. "Collectors usually talk about their collections, like their pets or their children. But you never heard anything like that about the Eatons. So what's next?" Ken said, handing back the sheet.

"I want to know how Randall Connolly got hold of the weapon he used. Annie Beckwith is the obvious person to ask, even though she was oblivious to it when she was told about her brother-in-law."

"Is she the only heir?"

Joe nodded.

"Was there ever any suggestion that she was worth looking into?"

"I get your point," Joe said. "When the police arrived at her apartment, there were several other people there—and they'd been there since Friday evening, staying with Annie Beckwith throughout the night. Someone was with her from the time she called a friend Friday night to when police arrived on Sunday afternoon. She has half a dozen women for alibis."

"Lucky woman, friends when you really need them." Ken jerked upright. "I didn't mean that to sound snarky."

"I understand." Joe lifted a hand to reassure him.

"So, how much will she get? Any idea yet? That house is tiny but it has to be worth something, right on the marsh with that view of the harbor," Ken said.

"I talked to Max Hasden, the family attorney who's handling the estate. Apparently he and Randall went to school together and he's been handling the family's business affairs for years," Joe said, recalling his conversation with Max Hasden. "She stands to inherit several million dollars."

Ken whistled and gazed out the window. "Wow! You could do a lot with that kind of money."

Joe almost laughed out loud. "You have ideas for that kind of money, do you?"

Ken blushed. He had given up on his diet of a few years ago and returned to his quiet pudgy self. No longer cranky in response to the slightest comment, he tried to stop the blush rushing up his neck and over his cheeks. He appeared uncomfortably warm and tried to hide his embarrassment by looking down; his thick sandy hair flopped over his forehead, but he only grew redder. "I was thinking of a new rifle."

At that Joe did laugh out loud. "You could buy an entire arsenal. You could buy a manufacturer."

Ken's face paled. "Jeez, no, chief. That kind of money can change your life. It would ruin everything for me. I wouldn't want to live with that much money. It would own you."

He was right, of course, but few people could free themselves of greed enough to recognize that. Too much money, however much that was, ruined lives.

"One good rifle for hunting. That's all I need. Well, maybe one more would be okay." Ken frowned as he repeated this in a soft voice. He took a deep breath. "Okay. I'll follow up on the information Carl Manderson left and coordinate with Mindy and go from there."

"And I think I'll have another chat with Annie Beckwith," Joe said.

CHAPTER NINETEEN

Joe hung up the phone, slipped the glossy photos into an envelope, and five minutes later drove into Annie Beckwith's driveway. The gravel crunched under his tires in the heavy summer quiet.

Since first broaching the subject of the plastic wood on the boom, and what that could mean, Joe had noticed a gradual withdrawal in Annie Beckwith, a slowly dropping temperature, until now he felt the formality of her greeting and initial responses. It could be grief, he considered, or shock or something more serious. He placed the glossy photos on the coffee table. The house was designed to give an open, airy feel, and Joe idly wondered if winter felt colder here than in another, more traditionally designed and furnished house. He moved the photos closer to Annie and lined them up in front of her.

Annie leaned forward and looked at each one, then went back and studied each photo separately, pulling it toward her with her fingernail on the white border. "This is the—" She closed her eyes for a moment. "This is the one Randall used?"

Joe explained that he had held it in the evidence room, but after it had been examined and photographed and Randall's death ruled a suicide, one of Joe's men had cleaned it up and taken additional photographs of it. Those were the ones she was looking at now. "Do you recognize it?"

Annie stared at the photos as though something might emerge, and then she looked at them as though they were curiosities. She pushed herself back against the sofa cushions and shook her head. "No, I never even knew they had guns here. Deb never mentioned it. I had no idea they were into guns." She turned to look directly at Joe, as though awaiting an explanation. "No one in our family ever did any hunting or anything like that. It just wasn't our thing."

"Is there any chance he was starting a collection?" Joe knew where the gun came from, but he wanted a sense of whether or not she knew. He wanted to explore possibilities, looking for reactions, deceptions, or anything else that would tell him which direction to take.

Annie gave a rough laugh and waved her hand. "Have you noticed this place?" Her smile warmed. "My sister and Randall barely collected enough furniture for guests." She patted the raw silk pillow next to her and ran her hand along the tasseled edge. "I gave her this, sort of a housewarming gift. She said it would stand out as the nicest thing she had because she had given herself one month to do everything to get the house ready to occupy and that meant she had no time for frills."

Joe offered a compliment.

"Thanks. But if Deb and Randall had suddenly decided to start collecting useless objects, including little antiques, I would have noticed. That would have been a sea change in them." She stared sadly at the photograph of the gun, but her expression turned into a frown. She was catching on. She sat up and stared at him. "Does this mean—Are you saying—"

"We want to make sure there are no unanswered questions," Joe said. "I brought you these photos to examine because I really want to know where the gun came from and when he got it."

"But if it wasn't his?" She moved to the edge of the sofa. "Chief?"

Joe judged the time right to delve into the real reason for his visit. "Do you remember the last time you talked to your sister?"

"Of course. It was the week before, the Friday before, exactly a week. She called me to ask when I was coming out next and we arranged for me to come out in a week." Her expression softening as she turned her head to collect the memory. "She said she had something to talk to me about, something to go over with me. She wanted my advice." She looked through the glass doors. "Well, maybe not advice. I think she liked to bounce things off me, get my feedback, before she made a decision. She liked to know as much as she could before she went forward. So I guess she wanted to try out something on me. See what I thought of a new idea."

"Do you know what that was?" The danger of questioning her now, after she had seen the gun and knew about the plastic wood, was the editing of memories, the introduction of suspicion where there had been none. But it was too late to catch her first impressions, too much time had passed for that. "Did she say anything specific?"

"Deb's last phone call wasn't mysterious so much as confusing." Annie paused to collect her thoughts. "She said she had something she wanted to talk about and I asked if this was about Randall. I don't know why I asked that, because I never thought of them having problems. She sounded worried, so I was thinking maybe Randall was sick or in trouble or something. It was just a gut reaction. The minute I said it I felt I'd overstepped a line. But instead of laughing it off, Deb just said no, this is quite different. She was serious the whole phone call." Annie shook her head. "I took her at her word and left it. I figured it couldn't be too important. Not something drastic at least."

Joe could feel the change in Annie, the regret and remorse at not having sensed that her sister could be in trouble or in danger. "Was there anything else you talked about?"

"I asked what her plans were and was she going anywhere, thinking that might be one thing she wanted to tell me. I got the idea—absurd when you think about it—that she and Randall were going to take a long trip and she wanted me to house sit or something like that." She rubbed her hand over her face and looked across at Joe sheepishly. "I'm a lazy thinker. I know it. But when she said it could wait, I let it go. I was glad not to have anything else on my plate. I was feeling kind of overwhelmed, with work not going well and all." She shifted again on the sofa. "Then she said she couldn't talk and changed the subject, got all cheery and businesslike. I figured someone came along and she didn't want them to hear what she was saying or that she was worried about anything."

"Had anything happened recently in her life?"

Annie shook her head slowly, side to side, her eyes fixed on Joe. "I know she'd been sailing a few days before, her and Randall. She sent me a photo she took of the broken marker on Hidden Rock. She and Randall were going to get up a petition to have it fixed sooner rather than later."

"Where did they usually sail when they went out?"

"Just out. They might go down the coast to see the skyline or up to Cape Ann. Randall liked seeing the Boston skyline from the water—he said it put everything in perspective." She frowned. "They weren't having trouble. I can't believe . . ."

"Did your sister ever suggest they weren't getting along?"

"Never. They were always happy when I saw them. And it wasn't an act. They really were happy together," Annie said, leaning forward in her desperation to convince Joe—or herself.

"You're not thinking Randall . . . and then . . ." She glanced at the gun and then shut her eyes. "I can't believe that. I won't. Nothing will ever convince me."

"We are only trying to make sure we have everything sorted out, Miss Beckwith. I just want to make sure I understand what happened. We have new information and I want to make sure I'm not missing anything."

"Okay." Annie exhaled and made a poor effort to smile.

Joe stood up. "We'll keep you informed of everything we learn, Miss Beckwith." She was gracious and polite as she walked the chief to the door but underneath he could sense the shift from grief to uncertainty and growing confusion. The confrontation with the weapon that had killed her brother-in-law had split her open.

CHAPTER TWENTY

The Eaton house was barely a quarter mile from Annie Beckwith's, and Joe knew that many neighbors walked short distances to each other's homes or private beaches or tennis courts or swimming pools. Brewster Street saw very little vehicular traffic. He pulled into the Eaton driveway, parked, looked through the screen door to the terrace beyond. He caught a glimpse of Babs and Mrs. Eaton. He pulled the old doorbell and heard a distant ringing.

Designed as a French chateau, the house centered on a long hallway, running from the front door to the back and opening onto the terrace and lawn. The hallway ran past four rooms, two on each side. The living and dining rooms at the back of the house, looking out onto the harbor, were open to the hallway, their pocket doors tucked away out of sight, turning the back of the house into one large room. This area had the feeling of shabby gentility, the result of redecorating undertaken probably thirty or forty years ago and nothing since then. The interest in fashion had waned, and the rooms remained welcoming and, because of their neglect, unintimidating. The two front rooms were smaller, with doors that stood ajar.

Babs listened to Joe's explanation for his visit and nodded as she turned from the living room. "We can go right in," she said, motioning to the hallway and a small room near the front door. "My mother-in-law is on the terrace and she's sure to become unsettled if she sees a policeman in the house."

100

"Of course," Joe said. "I understand." He followed Babs into the small room that felt like a man's study, with leather chairs, an old wooden desk, and floor-to-ceiling bookshelves filled with leather-bound books, small plaques and trophies, and bronze statues. On one wall stood a tall glass case sitting atop a low bureau with three shallow drawers. This was the gun cabinet.

Babs motioned him to a chair, but Joe declined.

"This won't take long," he said, pulling the photos out of the envelope and handing them to her. Babs studied the top one, the group of three resting in her right palm. She examined the first one, then glanced at the second and third.

She looked up. "Yes, I recognize it."

He knew she would.

She nodded to the glass case and after a moment moved toward it. The gun cabinet stood at least seven feet, with three drawers in the lower section and two glass doors above. Inside the upper half were four small ammunition drawers on either side at eye level. The teak Victorian case held at least a dozen small weapons fixed on brackets attached to the back wall. The space between the small ammunition drawers was empty.

"It would have been here," Babs said. "They were a pair, you know. I was always reminded if I looked into the room because the arrangement had been upset. It's all uneven now."

"Do you know when you last saw this one?" Joe held out the photographs again.

"This one?" He held up the photographs.

Babs shook her head. "I'm afraid I can't tell you when it disappeared. I never come in here unless I have to. Em cleans the room only once a month, but otherwise no one comes in here." she asked.

Joe understood her reluctance to enter the room. "The cabinet door has a key in it. Is that always the case?"

"Yes." She stared at the key sitting in the lock on the right-hand door, a gold tassel hanging still against the wood. She took a step back, perhaps to break the spell of the case and its contents, and turned to Joe. "When I heard about Randall, I had the most awful feeling. He came by the day after his wife, after Deb, was lost, and he looked horrible. The dark circles under his eyes, his hand not shaking but not right either, awkward, jerky. I left him in the hallway for just a moment when Coralee cried out. It was only a moment."

"And the door to this room was open?"

"It was." She sighed as though finally giving up a burden. "It was, god help me, it was."

"Why did he come by? Did he give you a reason, or was that the kind of thing he normally did, just dropping by?" Joe asked.

"No, no, never. We were friends and neighbors but we didn't drop in on each other quite so casually," Babs said. She glanced at the cabinet before continuing. "I guess we're rather private people, you could say."

"So, he had some reason for coming by?" Joe felt the tug of her wanting to avoid the conversation and nudged her gently back onto the topic.

"Yes, yes, he did." Her voice fell to a whisper.

"And what was that?"

She lifted her head and stared at him, as though just coming to be aware of him. "What was it? It was a surprise, to me, at least. He wanted to have a very quiet service, something very private and personal, but he feared that their house, being so close to the road, would bring gawkers." She clasped her hands and pressed them to her chest. "I understood what he wanted and offered our lawn, down to the water. It seemed to help him. He calmed down and was more relaxed after that. He talked about the service, something very small. He was going to have a bouquet to set afloat. A pastor. A few words. A few friends."

Joe could imagine the crush Randall felt to do anything to avoid facing the finality of Deb's death.

"I could see how awful it was for him," she said. "I was very fond of Deb. We felt fortunate to live next door to them both."

Joe slipped the photos back into the envelope and followed Babs to the hallway. "When was the last time Em would have come in to clean?"

Babs walked into the hall and stood, staring at the opposite wall, as though she needed the time to gather strength, then she turned to face him. "Em? I'm not sure. I know she has a system, for getting through the whole house, making sure some rooms are done regularly, since we're in them more often. This room and a couple of the guest bedrooms are done once a month, at the beginning. So, about three weeks ago." She closed her eyes, the sorrow falling upon her again, as though she could have stopped Randall if she'd just known.

"When was the last time you were in here?" Joe asked.

"When I pushed the door wide open for Em, to make sure she knew I meant for her to clean it," she said. "I don't know if that's the same as coming into the room, but before that I don't know." She gave her head a sharp shake, like a twitch. "I don't mean to be so awkward about all this."

"I understand," Joe said. "You're actually being a big help. I appreciate it."

"I don't come in here unless I have a specific reason to. I only keep it this way because Coralee looks in sometimes and I think it would throw her off if she found it changed. But when I can, as soon as I can, it's all going. All of it."

He wasn't surprised. But he wondered when Em or someone else would have noticed the missing weapon and reported it to the police as stolen, or merely assumed it had been mislaid somewhere else in the house. The cabinet held a collection of objects regarded in much the same way as a collection of jade bowls or china figurines. The first thought of the owners would not be that a weapon had disappeared but that a valuable object had been mishandled somewhere in the house. If Joe had not been able to identify it, it might have remained just an unusual weapon used in Randall's suicide.

Joe had last seen the weapon over eight years ago, when he investigated the death of John Eaton. Mrs. Eaton had identified the weapon's twin after the death of her son, John. The weapon used in John's death, the commission of a crime, had been held and then transferred for storage, where it still sat, earning storage fees that Mrs. Eaton paid. She had never asked for the return of the weapon, and Joe had never offered to arrange it.

CHAPTER TWENTY-ONE

Later that afternoon Joe crossed the deck at the Mellingham Yacht Club. The spacing of the thick oiled planks allowed a view of the quiet waves beneath, and contrasted with the bright white of the tall railings. Joe took a short detour to the foot of the ramp to take in the full view of the harbor. No races were scheduled for the day, and the junior sailors sat or sprawled on a float while the instructor took them over some of the finer points of racing. The boys and girls might never grow up to own boats and race in these waters, but they were enjoying a rarefied experience. Joe guessed that Philip was soaking up the same information from his private tutor, Hinkie Trask.

"Quite the view, isn't it?"

Joe returned Lincoln's greeting and the two men watched the juniors launch their small sailboats. "My son has taken up sailing on a Penguin. He took to it far better than I thought he would." Indeed, Joe was privately thrilled at the enthusiasm and native skill Philip demonstrated.

"Hinkie's a good teacher," Lincoln said.

Joe straightened up. "So you've seen them going out?"

"Once or twice," Lincoln said. "They were tacking over toward the beach there, then around the little islands. For those boats those rock piles are islands. For the rest, they're hazards."

Joe smiled; he had to agree with that. "I've tried to warn him about sailing too close to anything. I don't want to hear about him scraping bottom and having to swim back in, pulling that little boat behind him."

"At that age they treat their boats like a new car—fussing over it, checking for scratches or dings." Lincoln glanced behind him at a couple arriving on the deck; they waved and continued on into the open storage area where the walls were lined with lockers.

"I suppose things will get pretty busy soon," Joe said. "Got a minute?" He followed Lincoln into the small office.

When the previous captain had retired unexpectedly after a car accident, the club members worried they'd never find a good replacement. But Lincoln came with strong references from a sister yacht club in Florida, and was immediately taken on. He knew how to work with the diverse personalities of club members, and in only his second year had earned a loyal following. Joe closed the door to the office and took a moment to study the bulletin board, with its notices. He glanced through the doorway into the small back room. "I hope they don't expect you to sleep here too?" Joe said when he noticed the cot.

Lincoln laughed. "I'm dedicated but not that dedicated."

Joe took a step into the room. "That cot doesn't look very comfortable." Joe appreciated Lincoln's professionalism as he turned to the long counter that served as a desk in front of the large window. He cleared a spot and leaned against it. Joe returned to the main room.

"Whatever you need, Chief."

"I'm here for some basic information. I want to know who could have gone out to the Lady Mistral in the days before Deb and Cecily went out."

If Lincoln was disturbed at the question, he didn't show it. Joe saw a slight flicker of surprise but nothing more. The other man reached for a white-plastic three-ring binder and flipped it open.

"If we had to keep track of who goes out," Lincoln said, "it would be impossible. But if there's anything unusual about the day I note it here, in the log." He stood up and flipped over the pages to the first date, three days before Deb was lost at sea, and swiveled the binder so Joe could read it. Joe ran his finger down the page and turned to the next one.

"What about this boat?" Joe tapped his finger on a name and date.

"They're up from Cohasset, on their way to Maine."
Lincoln said. He reached for another binder and opened that also.
"We have reciprocal agreements with a few other yacht clubs, so
when a mooring is available here, while the owners are sailing
elsewhere, we let visitors use them. We usually have three or
four skippers who sail for a period of weeks during the summer
and leave their moorings available through us."

"How many were available on the nights in question,
and how many were in use?"

"About three were available, and two were in use,"
Lincoln said. "Two are in use right now. One is a long-term
guest, in a day sailor. The owners are Bunny and Steve Farrell.
The other is a boat that has been here since late June. The
Golden Wings." He pointed through the window at a sloop
deeper into the harbor. "It's for sale and the owner is hoping if
he leaves it here for part of the summer he'll get a buyer."

"Any interest so far?"

Lincoln shook his head.

"What about the other mooring, the third one?"

"That was a small one, a Lightning up from Sandwich. It
went on to Oqunquit." He pulled out a sheet and held it out to
Joe, who read the travel plan, and made a note of name and
contact information before handing it back.

"That's helpful."

"They have to have reservations, and we usually get the
call from the other yacht club," Lincoln said. "It's not possible
for anyone to just show up and ask for a berth."

Joe's head reared back. "No one just shows up asking to
lie over?"

"I don't mean that," Lincoln said, backtracking. "That
definitely happens. And it used to be the norm, but no longer.
Too many people out sailing these days. If a skipper has trouble
and wants to make a stop, to set things right, well, of course,
we'll accommodate. But that means they'll tie up here, on one of
the floats."

"Anyone here on a float during the week before the
accident?" Joe asked, but he knew the answer. Lincoln shook his
head and Joe picked up a heavy sheet of glossy poster board

listing names and telephone numbers. "This the membership list for the season?"

Lincoln looked uneasy and Joe guessed he was weighing the prospect of taking something out of the hand of the chief of police or allowing him to read confidential information. "It makes it easier for the members to reach each other. It comes out every May and then we update it each month in case someone joins later in the season. That doesn't happen often, but once in a while."

"Good service," Joe said, slipping the white and blue sheet onto a pile of them on the counter. He'd seen what he wanted to see.

He thanked Lincoln and crossed the deck to the railing once again, admiring the junior sailors now tacking their way out of the harbor, the sailboats looking crowded but well spaced by tide and wind. A few struggled to stay the course set out for them, and Joe felt a twinge of envy for their youth and freedom. They were fortunate youngsters to have such opportunities handed to them.

On a day like this, Mellingham shared only its beauty, but there was more to the scene. The rocky shore opposite could easily destroy anything tossed against it in a hurricane, and just as easily launch a small dinghy. Joe caught a glimpse of the Harris house through the trees, and wondered that Lincoln didn't mention Leo's mooring also lying unused this season and his membership dues unpaid. For probably the first time in his adult life, Joe calculated, Leo Harris had not paid his dues to the Mellingham Yacht Club, and everyone could see the evidence for themselves in the names missing from the membership list. The gap left by the two missing 210s, one for sale in New Hampshire and the other dry-docked in a marina, seemed full of import.

CHAPTER TWENTY-TWO

The more Annie Beckwith thought about her conversation with Chief Silva that morning, the more disturbed she felt. She had struggled to accept Deb's death and not hold it against Cecily. The woman had obviously been traumatized by the experience and felt miserable. Once in a while Annie spotted her getting in or out of her car in Mellingham, and the expression on her face made Annie squirm, but there was nothing she could do. Cecily wasn't responsible just because she was a poor sailor. And then Randall's death had shocked Annie almost into a stupor.

But now Chief Silva kept showing up with odd bits of information, seemingly little things that might have been nothing each by itself, but together . . . Well, Annie began to shiver whenever she thought about it. That's when she shook herself and said enough. If there is more to know, she has to look hard at the facts and understand them.

It was the tampering with the vang that most concerned her. How did they do it? How did they get out to the Lady Mistral, remove the fittings and replace them? And when? When did they do this? The plastic wood had to be dry enough to hold the vang at least long enough for Deb not to notice, for her to clip on the vang and move back to the tiller. How would someone do this if the boat weren't in a marina? Deb had called the week before, on Friday afternoon, and she was gone the next Friday. Lincoln said no one went out to the Lady Mistral except Deb and Randall between the time the married couple had gone for a sail and the fateful afternoon, when Deb and Cecily went out together. So, if the tamperer didn't get to the Lady Mistral from the yacht club, or from the shore during daylight, then it must have been at night, and perhaps from this side of the harbor. And it was easy to launch a dinghy from this side because Annie and Deb had done it dozens of times as teenagers.

Annie had no trouble finding the path that ran along the shore out to the end of the peninsula. After so many years she feared she'd get lost and find herself walking into a neighbor's garden but the path was right where she expected it to be. She found the opening in the trees and picked up the path at the foot of the Eaton property. She glanced up at the house and the now empty terrace, thinking how easy it would be for someone to sneak down the lawn, hidden by gardens, across the path and lawn to Deb and Randall's cottage. Anyone in one of these houses could to it. She tried to imagine Babs or even Coralee taking a gun from that cabinet she'd seen, leaving the house late at night, and making her way to the cottage. It was so simple that she was stunned she hadn't thought about it before. But the idea was absurd.

Annie gave herself a mental shake and turned her attention to the path. She followed it along the water, sometimes jumping among the rocks, in other areas walking along the foot of a garden or lawn. The path swerved out toward the water and then ran between yew trees and firs, moving from light to shade, from dry heat to cool damp. During their childhood, finding places to explore near the water was an afternoon desideratum.

The path was easy to follow for the most part—no roots sticking up ready to trip the unwary, no piles of leaves or other debris ready to trap the unobservant, and no concealed holes ready to break an ankle. No branches hung over the path ready to slap a face or knock off a hat. No section had fallen into the water, requiring a leap to the next dry spot, or a clambering to higher ground. The path was, in short, still used and maintained.

Annie slowed her step and considered this. During her childhood only a few neighborhood kids bothered to run up and down along the shore, and the pathways down to the shore path were more traveled than the path itself, which was crossed to get to the water and the dinghy occasionally tied up there.

It struck Annie as odd that something that was a nineteenth-century practice—maintaining shore paths—had been revived in the twenty-first century. Annie recalled her grandmother's stories of shore walks in the evening. After a summer supper, when it was still light, the family meandered down to the cliff edge on the other side of the peninsula, took a path running in either direction, and strolled along the cliffs looking down on the rocks or a beach, watching the late sailing boats making their way home. Her father had tagged along as a young boy, and grandparents and parents always followed or led a courting couple. How quaint, Annie thought, as she had listened to her grandmother reminisce. And yet, here was the same kind of path, a little rougher, and this time on the inner harbor.

Her meandering thoughts occupied her till she came to a wall of azaleas and saw the path had ended. She pushed her way through and found herself looking up at a large white clapboard house. She recognized it. She was in Leo Harris's yard. The continuation of the path on the other side of the yard wasn't immediately visible, and Annie wondered if they'd closed it off, tired of people traipsing across the lawn at all hours. When she saw someone on the terrace on the other side of the house walking toward her, she immediately raised her hand and waved. She hadn't expected to meet anyone, and cast around in her imagination for an explanation.

"You're not quite Venus rising from the ocean, but just as good." Leo came toward her with a broad smile and wave of his arm. "Come on over. Good girl for coming to us. Good girl."

Really, thought Annie, as they gave each other a quick kiss, I'm not a dog.

"You found the old path, did you?" He turned as he spoke, swallowing the last words of his question.

"Right where I left it last time," Annie said, following Leo to the patio.

"Have a drink."

Before Annie could demure he tapped out an order to the housekeeper on a cell phone set up on the table as a call system. She knew he liked his comforts but this one seemed to be going a bit far.

"And something to eat. You must, I insist." He tapped in the order for another plate along with the drink, and directed her to a chair. "I just started and I'm delighted to have company."

"I had no intention of interrupting your lunch. Really." Annie looked around for Cecily but she was nowhere in sight.

"My wife's gone off with some of her friends," Leo said as he waved his hand in the direction of the approaching housekeeper, a woman in her forties whom Annie knew as Cathy. She smiled at Annie, placed a luncheon plate and cutlery in front of her, and rearranged the serving bowls so they were within reach. Leo pulled out a chilled bottle and poured Annie a glass of white wine. He turned aside to cough, a heavy sound that made Annie wonder if he was getting over a summer cold.

"You could never interrupt. You're family." Leo sat down again and began to serve himself. Annie appreciated that he was doing it to keep her company, and succumbed to the cordiality of her host. Besides, she knew what a good cook Cathy was.

"It looks like someone takes care of the path," Annie said after sampling Cathy's curried chicken salad with raisins and slivered almonds.

"That's very observant of you, Annie." Leo poked his fork in the air for emphasis. He lowered his voice and leaned toward her, whispering. "I'm surprised you made it this far. We have some unfriendly new neighbors." He winked at her.

"Carl Manderson? I think Randall mentioned him." Annie tried to remember if her brother-in-law had told her anything memorable about the man.

"He's a bit high strung." Leo plunged back into his lunch again.

"He doesn't own any part of that path, does he?"

"He's not right on the shore, no." Leo shook his head and shoved his plate away. "But he's gone kind of crazy for Babs and her mother-in-law. He thinks anyone walking along the shore is out to do them no good." He spoke roughly, his voice scratchy and breathy.

Annie stopped eating and lowered her fork. "That does sound crazy. I thought he was married. I've met his wife. Are they divorced now? Is Babs aware of this obsession? I'm surprised she hasn't called the police."

Leo laughed, a bark that startled the birds blanketing the lower lawn so they lifted into the air like dust from an old oriental carpet being shaken out a window. His laugh turned into a cough. "She's the last one to call the police, Annie dear."

"I met her. She seemed rather nice." Annie thought back to her pleasant tea with Coralee and Babs and their guests. "I found mother and daughter very pleasant."

"Daughter-in-law." Leo corrected her.

"Oh, yes, of course. Babs was quite clear about the relationship." Annie frowned. "But Coralee referred to her as her daughter."

"She may well have, my dear. Old Mrs. Eaton is very dotty these days." Leo sat up and poured himself another glass of wine. Annie noticed that he handled it as though it were water, there to quench his thirst with no taste of any significance.

"Babs warned me about her mother-in-law, and she did seem a bit off, but I thought she was all right most of the time. I don't mind people with dementia." Annie had liked Coralee, and hated hearing her spoken of disparagingly.

"She imagines things that aren't there and doesn't see what is." Leo sat back in his chair and offered this description of the old woman as though it were the greatest wisdom.

"That sounds like a lot of people," Annie said. "She told me about the sailor who came for his lady love so they could elope, and how the girl's father shot her by mistake as she was running down to meet her lover." Annie smiled and shook her head.

"Fanciful tale. She probably made it up."

"She thinks it's part of Mellingham's lore. Insists she sees the lover walking the lane looking for his bride." To Annie's surprise, Leo's eyes narrowed and for a moment she thought she saw something flash in them—anger, surprise, hostility? But then it was gone, and the light flickered across the china.

"Hmm. She's going gaga. They'll put her away soon." Leo seemed to grow surly.

"Babs is quite good with her." Annie shifted in her seat. She liked Babs, especially the way she was playful and loving toward the older woman. Annie suddenly had the wild thought that Leo had a reason for disliking the Eatons, as if they had injured him in some way. Her glance went to the wall of flowering shrubbery. A path along the shore would have made advances to Babs by someone like Leo easier than otherwise. If not welcome, his arrival would have been awkward at best. Leo was on his third marriage, and he had never had a reputation for fidelity.

"Knows which side her bread is buttered on," Leo said. He turned his chair so he could face the water, and Annie took the hint.

"I recall a son, a good bit older than I am, so not someone I would have known growing up. Is he still around?"

Leo tipped his head to the side and gave her a curious smile. "You have been out of touch with Mellingham, haven't you?" His voice dropped to an unsuspected softness, as though protecting secret information.

"Hmm. I guess I'm supposed to know what happened to Coralee's son." Annie waited. She hated sparring with people like Leo, but she wanted to know what he knew.

"There was only one child in the Eaton family. Babs Eaton is John Eaton's widow."

"I should have remembered that."

"She shot him."

"What?"

"Spent a year in prison for involuntary manslaughter." Leo yawned. "Some people think she got off easy and some people think she shouldn't have gone to prison at all."

"What happened?"

"She claimed her husband was abusive and she was in fear of her life. So she shot him. Dead. One shot to the heart." Leo looked over at her, watching for her reaction. Her first reaction, which she had managed to swallow because of its naivete was, Here in Mellingham? Instead, she willed herself to remain calm.

"When did this happen?"

Leo frowned. "Seven or eight years ago she was released. Coralee insisted she come here to live. She did. And that was that." Annie quickly counted back. The incident would have happened just before Deb and Randall moved here, during the dead space when no Beckwiths lived in Mellingham.

"Do you think Coralee really understands what happened?" Annie asked.

"Understands?" Leo paused. "If you mean did she have all her marbles back then, yes, she did. She wanted Babs near her. John and Babs had no children, and Coralee always liked Babs."

"And the town accepted her?"

"Of course." Leo gave Annie a disdainful glance. "Mrs. Eaton is, after all, Mrs. Eaton."

Annie tried to change the subject again, hoping she wasn't putting her foot into anything else. She didn't seem to be blessed with tact these days. "You have the perfect view, Leo." The silence between them became comfortable again, and Annie attributed that to the jewel like surface in front of them—the beginning of the harbor and the array of boats creaking on the wake of a passing motor boat. They faced not only the yacht club on the other shore but the two empty moorings, one for Lady Mistral and the other for Leo's boat.

Leo turned around to study her. She smiled, an awkward smile.

"I'd live on a boat if I could. Never set foot on land unless I had to," Annie said.

"Even after all . . ."

"Yes, even after all . . . that." She closed her eyes and let the sun warm her, feeling it reach along her ear lobes, find the part in her dark brown hair, heat the ring on her finger. "It could have been a car that killed her." But it wasn't.

"Hmm. That sounds very fatalistic." Leo turned back to the view of the harbor.

"Lincoln said you haven't been out recently." Annie knew it was a risk, but she wasn't here to get a free lunch. "Is your boat okay?"

"She's fine." He hunched down in his chair. Perhaps realizing he sounded surly, he sat up and turned to her again.

"Too much going on right now. I haven't had a chance to even think about taking her out."

"Too bad." Annie nodded. "I know what you mean, though. I wasn't thinking of sailing again for a while—too much to do to straighten out Deb and Randall's estate—but not sailing at a time like this." She lifted her hand to indicate the clear sky and deep blue water. Storm clouds hung at the mouth of the bay, as though loathe to mar the beauty of the day in Mellingham.

"Plus you haven't got a boat," Leo said.

"True," Annie said, a bit miffed at Leo's comeback. "Anyway, thanks for the lunch. That was delicious," she said as she stood up.

"If you need any help with the estate, let me know. Randall was pretty open with me on his finances. He was going to come in on a deal I have going." He stood, his thick arms still muscular. "You might want to consider it. I can get some information over to you if you're interested."

"Probably not," she said. "That's not my forte. I'll stick to sailing. I put my name in at the club in case anyone's looking for a crew."

"Good idea." Leo nodded. "Not as many sailors as there used to be. Can't really understand it. The younger ones certainly have the money for it."

He repeated his offer to let her in on his investment and they parted. She felt him watching her as she crossed the lawn, but when she turned to wave, he was gone.

CHAPTER TWENTY-THREE

Annie's brief conversation with Leo unsettled her but not in the way she would have expected. She had always been drawn to the water, and happily set out to sail whenever she could. But now, with the Lady Mistral in dry dock and no other boat available to her, she felt doubly bereft, like an exile—unable to claim a homeland that she could see and smell and touch. The degree of pain from the loss of being able to sail surprised her with its intensity. She knew she'd sail again but that seemed only an abstract idea.

The soft ground beneath her feet began to give way, and she was surprised to find she'd been standing and staring at the water so long that the bank had begun to collapse. Out on the water a small blue and white day sailor bobbed as a man and woman clambered into a yellow rubber dinghy and rowed deeper into the harbor. Annie didn't recognize the day sailor but she did recognize the mooring. It was one of the few available for rent during the summer months, when the owners were out cruising somewhere along the coast, or simply not able to put their own boat in the water for the season. Leo had not put his boat in the water yet, but he hadn't apparently thought about renting his mooring.

Annie waved to the rowers when they looked in her direction, and they waved back. She guessed they were heading toward the town dock, where they could tie up and buy provisions and perhaps have a late lunch. An hour later, as she walked through the small town park on her way to the public library, she spotted them crossing the street in front of the small grocery store, each one carrying two canvas bags. They walked to the town dock, and the woman stopped and waited for her at the top of the ramp while her husband walked down to the dinghy.

"Hello!" she called out.

Annie nodded and greeted her as she drew closer. "I saw you on the water earlier."

The woman introduced herself as Bunny Farrell, "and that's my husband, Steve." Steve waved from the dock, where he was positioning the dinghy for the return trip to their boat.

"Are you spending part of the summer here?" Annie asked. On her walk down she had recalled seeing the day sailor on the mooring a few times earlier in the summer, and noted that it was the same one from week to week.

"We thought we'd give it a try," Bunny said. "We're usually down in Florida, so this is a different treat for us." She glanced down at Steve, who was now loading small bags into the dinghy, positioning them for an even distribution of weight. "It was my husband's idea. And the yacht club has been a big help, very welcoming."

"The mooring is convenient," Annie said. "Close enough so you can row into town." She nodded to the bags. "Where do you go from here?"

"Not sure. Maybe Maine." She handed off the canvas bags to her husband. "Do you live around here?"

Annie pointed to the shingle house on the marsh. "You can just see it from here."

"Oh, yes," Bunny said. "We noticed it the other night when we had supper at the Blue Lobster. So pretty shining through the trees."

Annie's imagination snagged first on the "shining through the trees" because it reminded her of Coralee's story about the sailor coming for his lady love but she quickly moved on to something else. "Were you rowing back at that hour? After it got dark?"

"Oh, sure," Bunny said. "We often do. It's so lovely then. Of course almost no one else is out, just one or two staying on their boat or fixing something. The harbor is so quiet at night. Just lovely."

"Yes," Annie thought, wondering what she could ask without raising suspicions. "So, you've been here a few weeks then?"

"About a month," Bunny said. "Terrible about that sailing accident, isn't it?"

"Yes," Annie said, stiffening. "The woman was my sister, Deb."

Bunny immediately offered her condolences and shifted the conversation in the expected direction. It was too late, Annie realized, to probe Bunny and her husband's experiences rowing around the harbor late at night. But if she couldn't ask the questions, perhaps Chief Joe Silva would.

CHAPTER TWENTY-FOUR

Annie left Bunny and Steve to row back to their boat and went on her way to the library. Leo's gossip about Babs Eaton had unsettled her. She had liked her neighbor, enjoyed her company and admired the way she dealt with her mother-in-law. And then there were the other guests, who seemed to be comfortable with their hostess. And yet, Leo had reported a gruesome tale, and as much as she tried to set the story aside, it nagged at her. She had to know the truth, one way or the other. Was Leo lying because he held a grudge against Babs, or was there some truth to the story?

Annie arrived at the library at just after four-thirty. She pulled open the heavy oak door and entered the cool quiet of the old building. The librarian glanced at her over the terminal, managed a half smile, and returned to her task. Annie turned into the larger reading room and found a file of old newspapers. She thought back to what Leo had told her, and selected five sheets of microfiche.

After scanning them and finding nothing, Annie turned to the local census reports. There, in the year Leo had vaguely referred to, Annie found Babs Eaton listed as a resident of 8 Brewster Street, along with her mother-in-law and a tenant living in the in-law apartment over the garage, a man aged sixty-eight and listed as retired. Annie continued checking census reports until she found one that recorded Coralee as the only resident at that address—no husband, no son, no daughter-in-law—along with the tenant in the apartment over the garage. Working backward, Annie estimated the year of the trial and pulled out another microfiche. It didn't take her long to find the story—it must have written itself.

Society Wife Shoots Husband

Boston. Police were called to the home of a prominent Mellingham resident on Saturday evening on a complaint of domestic violence and found a man dead and his wife holding a gun. Mrs. Barbara Eaton reported that her husband, John Eaton, had threatened to kill her in a rage, and fearing for her life she wrestled with him for his gun and shot him in self-defense. Her mother-in-law witnessed the event, and confirmed her daughter-in-law had acted in self-defense.

The story continued with the mundane details that always seemed to accompany the sad and tragic story of a marriage gone awry—the multiple calls to the police over several months, the threats, the neighbors' complaints about shouting. Annie scanned the news reports and subsequent installments for the highlights of the trial and Babs's conviction and sentencing. Her life was fodder for the op-ed writers for some time, and Annie noticed in subsequent indexes that they infrequently revisited the Eaton story, perhaps when they were at a loss for something more timely to write about. The Eatons had entered the lore of infamous old New England families.

Annie slipped the microfiche into its box.

"Find what you were looking for?" The librarian stood by the carrel, a number of books nestled in her arm.

"Some local history."

She picked up the microfiche box and looked at the date. Her puzzlement gave way to something else, and she stiffened her posture and presented Annie with her most professional bearing.

"I'm being nosy," Annie said. "I live next door to the Eatons, and I like them very much, but I've been hearing stories, so I want to separate fact from fiction." Annie waited for the librarian to comment. "She seems very nice," Annie said, alluding to Babs Eaton.

"She's not a sailor like you but I think you share the shore path." The librarian had accepted Annie's explanation, and extended her own version of the olive branch.

Annie reached for her pocketbook and stood up. "Well, considering what her hand and arm look like, I don't think she'd be able to sail on her own. She'd enjoy being out there but she wouldn't be up to taking the tiller or sheet."

"I used to see her out on the water once in a while," the librarian said. "She never went out very far. And after . . . I never saw her out again."

"Her arm and hand?" Annie began. "From that night?"

"That . . ?" The librarian turned her head enough to see if anyone else was working nearby. "It's a small town. I don't think people wanted to talk to the reporters, so they never got the whole story. Yes, she was taken by ambulance first to the hospital. She had a lot of injuries. But it wasn't the first time." She spoke softly, checking repeatedly to make sure no one else was within hearing. "But that last time, well, she was probably in shock. My neighbor's a nurse and she was on duty that night in the ER. She said they had a terrible time getting the gun out of her hand."

Annie frowned. "How can that be?"

"Her hand was so damaged they had to pry it out of her fist. She couldn't manipulate her fingers in the hospital. I don't know how she managed being in prison, crippled like that."

"Could she sign her name?"

The librarian looked confused, and took a step back. "I shouldn't have said anything."

"Not at all," Annie said. "You've said nothing untoward. I liked Babs before and I like her now." The librarian looked relieved, but she nodded curtly and made an escape, walking briskly among the desks toward the low stacks near the entry.

Annie's neighbor's life was spread across newspaper pages for all to see, and yet Babs seemed nothing like the person described by the reporters. She was the one person Annie felt fully comfortable with in Mellingham. Annie had observed Babs with her mother-in-law and the other guests, and saw only a decent woman conducting herself well, no airs, no pretense, no agenda smoldering below the surface. But the fact remained that

Babs had shot her husband and Annie felt that fact shifting back and forth inside her, refusing to settle.

CHAPTER TWENTY-FIVE

One of the advantages of living in a small town, in Joe's view, was the likelihood of knowing everyone he had to question in order to learn what he needed to know. The downside was that he had to question people he knew and they could easily figure out what he was investigating and start asking their own questions among their friends. He knew he was approaching the moment that would trigger a public awareness of his doubts about Deb and Randall's deaths, but he hoped he could delay it as long as possible.

Joe read the message Annie Beckwith had left at the police station in the late afternoon, suggesting he question the visiting sailors Bunny and Steve Farrell about anything they might have seen on any of their evenings paddling through the harbor. He wondered how she'd come across them, but decided it was inevitable in a town like Mellingham with sailors like Annie Beckwith. He only hoped she wasn't going to start her own investigation and stir things up before he could make real headway.

Emily Hanover, or Em as she was commonly called, occupied one half of a small two-family white-clapboard house. Its two front doors stood side by side in the center, one painted yellow and the other dark blue. The owners had apparently agreed on uniformity in the front garden, and azaleas and hydrangeas concealed the old brick foundation. A thin cement block chimney ran up the outer wall on the left, and the right side, with the dark blue door, had no chimney. Joe raised his hand to lift and drop a small brass seashell knocker on the blue door but the door swung open before he had a chance.

"I saw you drive in," the woman said. Dressed in light blue scrubs with a floral top, Emily Hanover was now in her early fifties. He had always thought her a no-nonsense, thoughtful type who knew her worth and was content with her life. "Come on in, Chief. I'm on my way out but I can give you a few minutes, if that's enough."

Joe stepped into a tiny hall facing a narrow staircase to the second floor. To his right was a large room that ran from front to back, where the kitchen work area sat behind an island. The living and dining area were marked by the arrangement of furniture. The home was tidy, just what Joe expected. He followed her back to the kitchen area.

"Babs told me you'd come by and looked at the gun cupboard," Em said. She poured him a cup of coffee and motioned to the sugar and cream set out on a tray on the counter. "She said you asked about a missing gun."

"The gun we found with Randall belonged to the Eatons, an antique kept in the gun cupboard." Joe fixed his coffee. "A match to the one that killed John Eaton."

"Oh." Em's face tightened. "Does Coralee know this?"

"No." The question intrigued him, and suggested that Em perhaps encountered a pre-disease version of Coralee Eaton.

"I suppose that was sure to happen some day," Em said.

"Can you elaborate on that?"

"The gun cabinet was never locked. All those guns just hanging there, and all that ammunition. I don't think anyone ever thought about it—just more antiquey stuff." She exhaled loudly, blowing softly from pursed lips. "Jeez, I had no idea. You mean, Randall stole a gun from the Eatons for . . ." She swallowed hard and stood up, pressing the coffee mug to her chest. She turned and placed it on the counter. "Sorry, Chief. Sometimes I work in the ER and once in a while we get someone who's been shot. It's an awful thing." Joe waited for her to compose herself. "So you think Randall took a gun from that room?"

"It looks that way," Joe said. "The ammo was there also. I don't want to jump to any conclusions. It seems out of character for Randall to do something like that, but he'd had a shock, with his wife dying as she did."

"Yeah," Em said. "Wow." She turned to look through the windows into the small back yard. She had bordered the yard with a low fence and grew vegetables instead of flowers. A cast-iron table and three chairs sat under a canvas umbrella. The neighborhood was quiet, even during the summer months when students were out of school.

"I'm wondering if you noticed anything, anything at all. Do you remember anything being different, anything changed or different?"

Em turned around and leaned back against the counter with her ankles crossed, her hands braced beside her, frowning as she thought back. "I cleaned that room just before that big neighborhood party the Eatons had. You know, their annual summer do? They have a party for everyone they know out there, usually the neighbors up and down the peninsula. People wait for their invitations," Em said with a smile, "and I guess it's a sign of having arrived." She grew serious again and shook her head. "I didn't notice anything being different."

"Do you recall seeing it then?"

"I think it must have been there," Em began. She stopped to glance at Joe.

"This has nothing to do with either Mrs. Eaton," Joe said. She nodded.

"I'm usually careful about the gun cupboard," Em said almost shyly. "After all that's happened, I take a look at it whenever I'm in the room, you know, like glancing behind a door when you're a kid and afraid of the dark. I'm aware that what I'm doing is a residual fear but I still do it. I think if anything were missing when I went in to clean before the party, I would have noticed. I'd say for sure the gun was there before the party. And the party was that night."

"Was the gun room open for the event?" Joe felt his whole body tense. He didn't want to consider the number of people who could have gone into that room and taken a weapon and ammunition.

"It was." Em tipped her head to the side and gave him a sympathetic look. "Afraid so. Babs opened it because Coralee always insisted. You know she's declining, and I think she no longer understands what that room means. I don't think she even recalls that her son, John, is dead." She shifted slightly, drawing her hands across her stomach. "Or how he died."

"Then, in her case, dementia is a blessing," Joe said.

"I thought she'd start calling that ghost on the shore path Randall," Em said. When Joe looked quizzical, Em explained. "Every now and then she starts telling the story about the Revolutionary-era seaman who wants to marry a local girl, the father objects, and when the girl is trying to elope the father shoots her, thinking it's the seaman. It's always the same, the shimmering golden lover come to claim his bride."

"Does she tell that story when something is going wrong, or is there a real story there?"

"Oh!" Em stood up with her hands on her hips as she thought. "It does tend to come up when something has happened in town. Now that you mention it she started telling me the story again a few weeks ago."

"So, after the party but before Deb's accident on the Lady Mistral?"

"Yes," she said, nodding several times. "That sounds right." She slipped her hands into her pockets. "Of course, Coralee really does have advanced dementia, so I wouldn't try to make too much out of it."

"Have you ever seen anyone on that shore path?"

"Me?" She reared back and gave him a mildly reproving smile. "I have no time for anything like enjoying the view, Chief." She glanced at the clock. "I run on a very tight schedule."

CHAPTER TWENTY-SIX

Joe thought his day was just about over after his interview with Em until his cell beeped. He read the message and headed back to Town Hall, where he spent the next hour sifting through the plan for the senator's security during his annual visit. He appreciated as much as anyone in law enforcement the challenge of walking a thin line between providing security and stifling free activity and making ordinary people feel acutely uncomfortable. When he heard the senator had invited an official from a foreign government, he was relieved to see the US State Department had arranged security. He was glad to see what the Department had set in place, and the notes of approval from the visiting senator's office. Of course, Ellen Priestly had her own views on the senator's visit this year.

"Looks good," the woman standing next to the photocopier said. He started at the sound of the familiar voice. Ann Rose had reached her mid-sixties looking like she was still in her forties. Joe chalked that up to never having children, which required endless sleepless nights, though her programs and kindnesses to the children of Mellingham seemed to take up as much time and attention as mothering her own would have. Her older brother often threatened to name an orphanage in her honor, knowing it would receive more attention and funding than a United Nations Heritage Site in Paris. "At least this year we'll still be able to get to the beach."

Joe turned at the sound of her voice as he slipped the sheets back into the folder. For a moment he'd forgotten how popular the additional photocopier was. He could count on meeting just about everyone here at one time or another. "And we know what would happen if we cut off access to the beach."

"Too right, you do," Ann said. "There is no protest against a beach closing that Ellen Priestly could control or counter or deflect. I have two summer programs going over the weekend, and if the Priestlys and the senator don't like it, they can go elsewhere. I hear there's room in Siberia."

Joe managed, just barely, to suppress a laugh. In previous years the Priestlys had won permits for closing roads and beaches and permits for limited fireworks to entertain the senator and his accompanying guests to the Priestly home. Dozens of residents protested the closing of a beach but few ever mentioned the fireworks because the townspeople could enjoy them from the park or small beaches farther down the coast. But over the years Joe had begun to hear rumblings, in addition to the one very vocal and annual protest he heard every year, from Ann Rose. She had lots of reasons for opposing the fireworks— the noise, the environment, the laws, the danger to children as well as adults. And this year she had those reasons as well as her foster children. And she had enlisted some of her friends to protest with her.

"I suppose you haven't changed your mind about those fireworks," Ann said.

"No, ma'am," Joe said.

"I don't mind those things on the fourth of July, when I can plan for them," Ann said. "But my foster daughter and her husband are coming for the weekend." She paused to turn to him. "And they have a little one." She broke into a broad smile.

"Is this Chandra Stine?"

"But now she's Chandra Oliver, Mrs. Enrique Oliver." Ann looked so happy Joe wouldn't have been surprised if she did a little tap dance.

"You must be very pleased," he said.

"I could bust I'm so excited," she said. "I never thought I'd be a grandmother. After all, we didn't have any children, and now I have a daughter and a granddaughter."

Joe let Ann savor the moment.

"I admit that at first when she told me she was getting married I was upset and worried, very worried. I told her she was too young—nicely, nicely, not meddling, but nicely. After all, she had just turned eighteen, she'd barely finished high school, and now here she was getting married. And now a baby!" Ann took a step back. "She's so young. But I understand."

"She wanted a happy family and now she has one," Joe said, remembering the young teenager who had been Philip's partner in drama programs mounted by the community center. Chandra and his stepson had leaned on each other when they needed a friend who accepted and understood who each one was, and Chandra had been that one for Philip. The young boy had come through some uneasy times, thanks to Chandra and the other people he met there, and Joe became one of the Mellingham Community Center's strongest supporters.

"Her mother's happy for her too," Ann continued. "They stay in touch. I want her to. She has the right to love her mother, and her mother has the right to love her daughter. But it's better if they're not too close. Mrs. Stine still has her struggles."

Joe considered that a major understatement, but all he said was, "I'm happy for all of them," and he meant it.

"So I'm hoping I can persuade you to let us have a peaceful weekend," she said, growing serious. "If there are any fireworks over the Priestly house, that child will be caterwauling all night long, and my husband will be beside himself, not to mention the rest of us."

"I have received a number of letters taking the same position," Joe said, wondering if this was going to be the year when he was caught between the two most vocal and influential factions in Mellingham. This was when retirement began to look appealing.

"They like to show off every summer," Ann went on, nurturing her grievance. "It's obscene."

"I thought your husband and Mr. Priestly were good friends," Joe said.

"Were, Chief, were. They stopped playing golf together a few years ago after Bill Priestly passed along Ellen's view of playing golf with people who weren't going to invest in her husband's company." Ann slapped the papers she'd been copying onto a table and banged them into a somewhat neat pile. "Really. What was she thinking? Or, as my brother would say, What? Was she thinking?"

This was the quality Joe most admired in Ann Rose, the way she could defuse an intense situation, including one of her own creation, with a little humor. It was one of the reasons she was always welcomed on town committees. She turned down most invitations, saying not only was she too busy but she was at the age to retire. And she was going to give it considerable thought. Then she went off and started another program for the youth in Mellingham.

"It will be quieter this year without the big party," Joe said.

"I sure hope so. But it would be even quieter without the fireworks. I would really like to sit on the terrace and admire the view and hold Chandra's little girl on my lap and be a silly old lady," Ann said. "Perhaps I should give Ellen a few pine trees for Christmas. Of course, it might take a few decades before they adequately block the view. Or I could plant some on our property."

"I doubt they'd survive," Joe said.

"True. And if they did, I wouldn't get to see you teaching Philip to sail. When are you going to buy him a bigger boat so you can all go out together?"

"Not for a while. I just bought this one," Joe said, knowing how ridiculous the two of them must have looked. There was barely enough room for his stepson in the boat. "Hinkie has taken over. That little Penguin was a bit cramped for me."

"So I noticed." Ann continued to slap her pages into order. "I saw Hinkie and Philip just the other day again. He's going to be a great sailor. You won't be able to keep up with him."

"I'll rely on you to tell me where he is." Joe gave her a warm smile and put away the file.

"Will do, Chief. Will do."

CHAPTER TWENTY-SEVEN

Philip perched on a stool and leaned over the book spread open before him on the granite counter top. The book was old, a hardcover of less than two hundred pages, but stiff from lack of use. He had pulled a painted metal tray over to hold down one corner and rested his elbow on the lower left hand side, leaving his right hand free to take notes. He scribbled on a sheet of paper until he felt it pulled from under his fingers.

"Hey!"

"You're deaf now too?" Jennie stood with her feet set apart and her hands on her hips. "Mom's been calling you and you can't even hear her."

"What?" He turned a perplexed look to Gwen.

"The tray. I need the tray." Gwen pulled the tray away and offered him a frying pan. Without a moment's hesitation he placed in on the corner and went back to writing.

"What are you reading?" Jennie said, leaning over his shoulder. He waved her away. "What are those drawings?" She leaned in closer. "That book smells."

With that, Philip sat back and glared at his sister. "It's old. I found it this morning on the shelf where they put books for sale at the library."

"Why are they selling their books?" Jennie asked Gwen.

"To raise money to buy more," Gwen said.

"Weird." Jennie rolled her eyes and went to the refrigerator.

"What's the book, Philip. If you're going to read in the kitchen you have to share." Gwen repositioned the tray and placed a square plate with skewers of vegetables on it.

"It's on racing," Philip said. "How to judge the wind and distance and the best way to cross the start line and get ahead."

Joe must have heard him from the other room because he came to the doorway to listen. "You're already into racing?"

"Hinkie's teaching me. We went out again this morning, really early, and we talked about how to set up a simple course for Penguins. He has one, and I have one, and he has two friends who have them, so we have enough for a fleet and we can race." He finished speaking and took a deep breath, glancing cautiously at both Gwen and Joe in case he had miscalculated. Joe and Gwen turned to each other.

"Hinkie Trask," Joe said in case Gwen had forgotten. "When are you planning on going out for this race?"

"Well, we can't do much on the weekend because of the Priestlys," Philip said, growing thoughtful. "So maybe one of the afternoons in the next couple of weeks."

"What about the Priestlys?" Jennie asked.

"They have their usual summer guests and this year they're having fireworks. The town has been asked to limit the area where boats can gather to watch." Joe slipped his hands into the pockets of his khakis. Jennie pulled the book out from under her brother's hands and read the title.

"Thoughts on Small Boat Racing," she read.

"I saw Ellen Priestly in the market yesterday," Gwen said. "She wasn't as excited this year as she usually is. Maybe she's getting tired of hosting the senator."

"Well, I know a few people who are definitely tired of having her hosting him," Joe said. Gwen laughed and handed Joe another platter for the tray. "Whenever you go out, Philip, stay closer to the islands and maybe set up your course between the main island and the beach towards Salem. No one will bother you there. The place will be awash with security very soon."

"Yes sir." Philip bounced off his stool and replied in such a clipped manner that Joe was afraid he'd salute. Instead, the boy grabbed his book and stuffed it into a canvas bag that now held the various small tools a sailor needs but doesn't want to leave on a boat.

CHAPTER TWENTY-EIGHT

Later in the week Joe crossed the town green to the new Town Hall, so spiffy and modern, by Mellingham standards, that getting it approved and built seemed to have exhausted the town fathers (and mothers). For years after it was built not a single building project could make it onto the town warrant for Town Meeting members to discuss. Modernity was not coming to Mellingham, at least not without a pitched battle. And that was one reason Chief Joe Silva was strolling across the town green to the selectmen's offices. Before he reached the stairs, however, Annie Beckwith came through the door and skipped down the steps.

"It's a great day for a sail," Annie said by way of a greeting. "Hard to feel gloomy on a day like this. Have you had a chance to talk to those visitors I mentioned? I left a note at the station."

"I appreciate the information," Joe said, and when it was clear he didn't intend to add anything, she turned to leave. She took a few steps toward the street before turning around. "I see you've got a sailor in the family now."

"You mean Philip?" Mellingham was indeed a small town, and he wondered how many of its residents had discussed his marital state (or lack of it) before he and Gwen finally made it official. Now that he thought about it, he was slightly embarrassed to think he might have damaged Gwen's reputation. But then, that was thinking like his parents, so perhaps he should stop fretting. "Hinkie Trask has taken him under his wing—or sail, I should say—and Philip loves it."

"He'll be good too." Annie nodded enthusiastically, and Joe glimpsed the love, perhaps obsession, that had guided her life. From an early age, he had learned, she only wanted to be on the water, but Deb, not Annie, had been the one to live in Mellingham in sight of their mooring.

"Maybe he'll take you out sometime on his little Penguin," Joe said.

Annie became serious and took a step toward him, her hands drifting away from her sides, as though about to rise to applaud him. "Crewing! That's a great idea. I mean for him." She lifted her hands, palms up, to forestall the objection that would come too late if at all. "I'll have a boat again eventually and I'd love to have a crew."

"I thought you usually went out alone," Joe said, intrigued.

"I do, on the Lady Mistral and anything that size or smaller, but the 210 was meant to have a crew, and it would be a great chance for Philip to learn more." It was obvious that Annie was already calculating on how this could be managed.

"Your boat is still at the marina," Joe said. "And I'll probably have to keep it a while longer." He was surprised she hadn't pressed him to release the boat.

"I understand," she said, taking a step back and slipping her hands into her pockets. He could see the pain of her sister's death was still raw, compounded by the loss of her brother-in-law in such a violent manner. "But, it's okay." She straightened up, lifting her chin, defying sorrow to claim her. "I can go out crewing for others for a while. I should have done this sooner."

"Good idea," Joe said. "Anyone local?"

"I thought about crewing for Leo Harris but he hasn't put his boat in the water yet—and it's pretty late in the season, so probably not for Leo. Too bad. He has a nice boat, another 210," she added with a smile.

"Your family and the Harrises seem to be close," Joe said. He waited while an elderly couple worked their way down the steps and passed by. "Did Randall or your sister ever mention any investment with Leo Harris?"

"With Leo?" Annie pursed her lips and squinted across the town green. "Leo's an independent investment counselor, usually putting together packages or something for investors who like to gamble a bit. I think that's what Randall said." Her expression softened. "In case you haven't guessed, my sister and her husband were not risk takers. Slow and steady, slow and steady." But the smile faded and Joe waited while she composed herself again.

"Did you come across anything in your sister and brother-in-law's papers that could pertain to an investment?"

Annie shook her head slowly, pulling down the corners of her mouth and looking down at the ground.

"Well, if you think of anything that could be relevant, perhaps you can let me know." Joe stepped back, to signal the end of the conversation. "I'll contact Max Hasden and see if he has anything in his notes."

Annie nodded and set off across the town green, an abstracted look on her face.

CHAPTER TWENTY-NINE

When Joe had been starting out as a young officer, he had once asked a veteran officer in his hometown for advice as he struggled to put together what he knew about an act of vandalism that led to assault. The information seemed to swim together like different colors of ink in a glass of water, losing individuality and creating only a murkiness. He had expected each piece to give him a part of a puzzle, that the image would have sharp angles and features, like a jigsaw puzzle half finished sitting on a card table. But he'd been wrong.

"The whole thing has to be clear," the other man said. "Don't go jumping to a conclusion because a few pieces make sense. All the pieces have to fit. If you have a few left over after you've come to a conclusion, then your conclusion is wrong. Every piece has to make sense. Every piece has to take its place."

Joe had listened, taken the advice to heart, and learned to live with murkiness, until the entire picture came into focus, like twisting a manual camera lens to get a clear image. He reassured himself now with that memory as he tried to sort through the odd bits of information about Deb and Randall, Cecily and Leo, the Lady Mistral and plastic wood, and all those boats sitting in a harbor unguarded, often unlocked and unlockable. He sifted through earlier conversations at the Mellingham Community Center as he drove up the steep hill to a large parking lot.

The Four Square Fitness Center offered just about every activity that could be done indoors, expanding through the years to accommodate rock climbing and other sports. Joe still thought of it as a place to swim, play tennis or racquetball, or take physical fitness classes. Gwen sometimes returned from the Center with news of a new exercise regimen, and she and Jennie would be lost for the evening in a discussion of merits and comparisons of yoga, pilates, and a few other things Joe had no idea about.

Joe walked past the check-in office and onto the main floor. To his left was a glass wall shielding the swimming pool, with about a dozen youngsters finishing a lesson at the far end and a few women standing at the near end preparing to enter the water. To his right was the first of a series of fitness rooms, and along the far wall, straight ahead, was a café that looked out onto a garden and woods. Beyond that, he knew, was the highway. With the windows closed, anyone would have thought the Center was deep in a forest. With the windows open, the same person's nerves might be jangled with the sound of incessant traffic. A young blonde woman, a whistle tied onto the end of a lanyard dangling around her neck, approached him.

"Hello, Chief. May I help you?" Peg said. "Are you here to check on the registration for Jennie, or is it Philip this year?"

"Neither one," Joe said.

"Oh, okay," Peg said, nonplussed. "Because I was going to say that I'm pretty sure Jennie is all set for swimming." Joe knew the high school used the pool for swimming classes, and Jennie had been taking lessons since she entered middle school.

"I've come about something else," he said. "Do you have a place where we can talk?"

Peg's smile faded and she looked uncomfortable; she led him back to the check-in office, where a young woman now sat behind the desk with a telephone to her ear. Joe could hear her making incoherent noises and nodding while she listened to the person on the line. Peg motioned to her office; the receptionist nodded, glanced at Joe, and returned to her phone duty.

The room, though small, offered an enviable view of the woods beyond the parking lot, where flowering shrubs had been planted, perhaps to soften the harshness of the macadam. Peg took a seat behind her desk and Joe settled in a chair in front of it.

"I must have spoken out of turn at the community center," Peg began, looking as guilty as any toddler Joe had ever seen. "I shouldn't have commented on Cecily."

"You didn't cross any boundaries, Peg." Joe tried to reassure her, lest she try to rewrite the history of the last few months. "I'd like to be clear on a few details."

Peg swiveled in her chair, trying to get comfortable, and looked at the mess on her desk, a computer that sat on a stack of old calendars, a rolled-up yoga mat, and clipboards with various sheets untidily clipped. "Well, whatever I can do to help, of course." Joe almost felt sorry for her, looking like a caged rabbit facing a hungry lion.

"I'd like the dates when Deb began teaching Cecily to swim," he said.

"Oh." Peg frowned as though this wasn't at all what she expected. She relaxed, gave Joe another look to make sure she heard him correctly, and then turned on her computer. She clicked and scrolled and scanned. "Hmmm. Here it is. She came in in late May, Deb I mean, and asked me if there were really quiet times at the pool and could she stay a little late if someone was still here in the office."

"You mentioned that," Joe said as he wrote down the dates. "That's unusual, isn't it?"

Peg relapsed into her guilty toddler look. "Well, I suppose." She looked around for an escape but there was none. Joe repeated his question. "Yes, but Deb Connolly wasn't just anyone. Oh dear, that sounds terrible."

"Why don't you explain that," Joe said. "Take your time."

"It's not hard to explain, Chief. As beautiful and as idyllic as Mellingham seems, there are a lot of families who can barely afford to live here—or anywhere, when it comes to that. Deb and Randall made an anonymous donation for a program to provide sports activities for low-income children in the area. We have almost an unlimited number of annual memberships for kids in town that can't afford sports any other way. This is quite separate from anything they do for the school programs." She paused and stared at him. "Oh, shit. Sorry! Our program may be coming to an end. I didn't even think about it."

"The donation is made annually?"

Peg nodded and sat forward, to peer at the computer. She clicked and scanned. "Oh, damn. The passes run out in December. We'll have to notify everyone." She rested her fingers on the keyboard and sighed. "Damn. It's such a good program." She slouched in her chair and gazed at Joe. "I don't suppose you want to donate about fifty thousand dollars."

Joe managed not to laugh, but he couldn't suppress a smile.

"I didn't think so," Peg said. She glanced wistfully at the computer screen.

"Perhaps there's a provision in Deb and Randall's estate," Joe said. He advised her to write to them and let the letter be forwarded. "And her friends might want to help."

"Oh, that's an idea."

"Cecily Harris, for example," Joe continued. "She might be grateful to Deb for helping her. You said she learned fast."

"Did she ever!" Peg said, cheering at the thought. "It was like she was meant to be in the water. Deb was very proud of her."

"Was Cecily ashamed of not being able to swim?" Joe asked. "You mentioned that Deb asked for times when the pool was empty, or nearly so."

The idea seemed new to her. "I did say that, didn't I?" She learned forward and rested her arms on the desk, clasping her hands in front of her. She had the smooth polished skin of the active young woman, tanned and supple and taut. Her fingers were bare of rings, and her watch was a simple waterproof one with a black cloth band. She was pared down and straightforward, unable or untrained in concealing uncomfortable truths. It was easy to see, Joe thought, why Gwen liked and trusted her.

"Yes, you did."

Peg laughed. "Let's see. I remember Deb came in on a Tuesday afternoon, a quiet time, and asked about helping a friend learn to swim."

"Did Mrs. Connolly give you a reason for wanting privacy for the swimming lessons?"

"I guess, now that you ask, she said her friend was self-conscious about needing lessons and she was the one who wanted privacy. I didn't know who Cecily was until near the end."

"You weren't introduced to her at the first lesson?"

"Oh, no." Peg was adamant and bounced her clasped hands on the desktop. "On the first class I talked to Deb about who else was there just so she would know if she saw the custodian or someone else like that. I didn't see Cecily then. And later, when I was locking up, Cecily was doing something with her bag. It seemed like that every time—either she hadn't arrived, or had already left or was doing something so I couldn't talk to her. A couple of times I thought Deb was going to introduce us, but it never happened. I just never got to meet her while she was taking lessons. I never even really got much of a look at her till the end."

"Did you meet her then, informally, I mean?"

"On their last evening," Peg said. "I overheard Deb telling Cecily that she was just as good a swimmer as she, Deb, was. Well, when I heard that I had to go out and congratulate her. I mean, it's so important to give positive reinforcement, especially when someone has overcome a deep fear. And people who don't learn to swim as children often have a hard time of it. So I went straight out. I was really so glad that I had let Deb stay late. It made me uncomfortable at first—I was worrying about the owners and their worries about liability and all that—but it really paid off."

Joe recognized the hobby horse being trotted out of the stable, and interrupted before Peg could saddle up and gallop off on her favorite ride. "How did Cecily react to that? Was she pleased with the compliment?"

Peg frowned as she thought back. "Actually, I think I embarrassed her. She thanked me but she went right back to packing up her bag." The hobbyhorse's reins fell to the ground. "I felt bad for putting her on the spot. She seems very shy. I can imagine if she didn't want anyone to know she couldn't swim, especially around here, it's embarrassing. But Deb thanked me—she was always thoughtful—and off they went."

"Other than Mrs. Harris's shyness, did you ever get any other idea why either one wanted to keep the lessons quiet?"

Peg blushed a deep red. "Oh dear."

"That sounds like you have something to tell me."

"I suppose I have to tell you."

"Yes, Peg, you do."

She shook her head. "People tell me all sorts of things. You get close to people you see every day working out, and they start to feel like they can trust you. It's like being a therapist sometimes. When I was a personal trainer I used to hear the most personal things, and sometimes I felt so awkward, but you get used to it. Once—"

Joe knew it was time to grab the reins again. "What did she tell you?"

"Nothing, she didn't tell me anything directly. I mean it wasn't like a confession or anything. I didn't mean that. But I overheard her talking to Deb one night. They were leaving, crossing the parking lot, and they stopped. They'd parked in different parts of the lot and they stopped to finish their conversation. The windows here in the office were open." She paused to look at them, perhaps to make sure they were still there. "It was in the summer, and you know in the summer, in the evening, voices carry."

"Tell me what you heard?" Joe hoped he didn't have to prompt her through every word.

Peg took a deep breath, exhaled, and leaned forward. She gave Joe a questioning look, as if to reassure herself that he was who he was and she was preparing herself to speak. "Well, Deb said that when she could at last swim, she should tell Leo," Peg said. "But Cecily said no, she didn't think she could do that. She sort of squirmed and Deb tried to encourage her but then Cecily was adamant and said no again. She said she was afraid Leo'd just come up with something else to frighten her."

Joe waited.

"I can hear her even now," Peg said. Her tone of voice changed, and Joe recognized the mimic repeating what she'd heard. " 'Leo said if I gave him any trouble, all he had to do was push me overboard. Sailing accidents happened all the time. He pretended it was a joke, but I know he was angry.' " She swallowed hard. "I just cringed when I heard that."

"Do you remember Deb's response?"

Peg nodded. "She offered to introduce Cecily to a counselor who worked in domestic violence but Cecily said no, so she offered to drive her to a woman's shelter if she ever wanted that kind of help, but Cecily said no again, she just wanted to know how to swim. That was enough."

Joe waited, letting her think back.

"It was funny, though. She could swim but she was still afraid of the water," Peg said.

"Did you hear her say that?"

Peg shook her head. "No, I saw her taking a kind of test with Deb on their last day. They were running through all the things Deb had taught her about swimming and safety and stuff. Deb had told me she was going to do something like this earlier, so when she said the lessons were winding up, I figured the last one would be the test, a chance for Cecily to put it all together and feel good about the whole thing. Anyway, Cecily arrived before Deb, and no one else was around. I was in the office and I heard someone coming in, so I came out just for a second, to make sure it was Cecily or Deb there and not someone else. I wanted to wish Cecily luck, but she was at the far end of the pool on the diving board. No one else was around, and I don't think she saw me watching her.

"I was about to go back into my office, figuring I could talk to her later, when I saw her dive in. That dive was so graceful, so perfect—almost professional. I was really impressed. But when it came time for the test, when Deb showed up to grade her in a sense, she fell apart. She just fell apart under pressure. She had a lot of trouble diving. She's still frightened of the water," Peg said, leaning back in her chair. "It may be years before she gets over what happened out on the water with Deb, and until she gets over that she'll never really feel confident with swimming or anything else like that."

CHAPTER THIRTY

Mellingham was a quiet town, and like most New England towns had evolved to accommodate the changing population. The changes weren't always obvious but were noticeable. The inner cove embraced small boats, and when the railroad came to town and the trestle closed a gap, larger boats were consigned to another part of the harbor. As the population changed, working boats were replaced by pleasure boats. Pastureland turned into tracts for housing with vegetable gardens, and barns became furniture factories. Stores carrying notions for families pushed out feed stores and hardware, and the Harbor Bar and Grill offered alcoholic drinks in a respectable setting.

The bar had limped along for almost eighty years until a new owner changed the name, renovated the interior, upgraded the food, and offered local brews along with the usual wine and spirits. The long-surviving Nan's Cafe at the tip of the cove, not far from the police station, had been the last vestige of a town long gone, of a history its current residents had no inkling of. Now called the Dockside Bar and Grill, with sunny windows and a nautical theme, the bar and grill catered to a younger crowd.

Joe could see the back of the Dockside from his office window, and occasionally wondered what it had been before it became the local dive years ago. He guessed it had once been part of a small working port, based as it was on the edge of an old wharf, but that must have been many decades ago, in the eighteenth century. The building had survived hurricanes, flooding, mild New England earthquakes, and town protests. Joe knew the names of those who had once patronized it in its previous incarnation, most of whom were dead or in nursing homes. He was thinking about the local watering holes as he studied the preliminary autopsy report for Randall Connolly and a few notes added by the EMTs, he recalled that Randall was known around town as an abstemious host and guest. Which made the notes all the more concerning. He shoved the file back in the cabinet and headed for the door.

The Blue Lobster Restaurant, located along the railroad tracks by the small park and the tip of the inner harbor, drew mostly an upscale crowd and a few tourists. Occasionally, guest sailors rowed in from the harbor for dinner, but otherwise the patrons were well known even if they only showed up once or twice a month. Joe knew both bartenders, Ted and Ernie. As chief, he made a point of meeting anyone in town who served alcohol and might end up calling the department. At four-thirty in the afternoon, however, the staff was busy setting up and the only arguments, if there were any, would be between employees. Joe walked through the long narrow room to the back.

The restaurant occupied the first floor of a two-story structure originally built as a marine supply and repair shop, finding its customers on the other side of the train tracks in the harbor. Turning the building into a restaurant meant lining the waterside wall with windows, a few tables, and a bar opposite, where a long mirror gave a reflected view of the water and park. The rear of the building held offices and a small kitchen. The restaurant didn't produce anything in the way of fancy food but the meals were respectable. The second story contained an apartment, usually rented to one of the bartenders, and a small storage area.

"Hey, Chief." The bartender at this hour was Ted, a young man who looked like the typical surfer but, as Joe knew, was a serious young man working his way through an environmental studies course at a local university. He had confided to Joe that he set a goal of graduating with a degree and no debt, and was on track to do so. He greeted the chief with a smile that transformed him, and Joe guessed that was one of the reasons for his success in life so far.

The only other person in the room, a young woman setting tables, hurried back to the kitchen, and Joe turned to Ted, getting down to business at once by asking him when was the last time Randall Connolly had been in for any reason—dinner, drinks, meeting a friend and going elsewhere—any reason. Ted rested the tray of glasses he'd been carrying onto the edge of the bar and half-closed his eyes.

"I'm glad you came in," Ted said. "I've been thinking about that and I wasn't sure if . . ."

"It sounds like the last night you saw Randall Connolly has been bothering you. Can you tell me why? When was the last time you saw him?"

"I've thought about that because at first I wasn't sure, well, I didn't want for it to be that night, but it was," he said. "It was the night he died, or technically I guess it was the night before. I guess he died in the early hours of Sunday morning."

"Are you sure about that?"

"Yes sir, very sure."

"Because?"

"I remember." He slid the tray onto the back counter and turned to lean on the bar, studying Joe for a moment. "Mr. Connolly was here that night and he sat at the bar and he was drinking."

"That sounds like you were concerned."

"He had a lot to drink, which isn't like him."

"Do you remember how much?"

Ted paused, glancing from Joe to the rest of the room. "I think it's all right if I show you. You know the owner pretty well. And besides, there's no reason not to show you." With that tantalizing comment, Ted led the way into the kitchen area and then into an office. After resting his hand on the file cabinet for a moment, he pulled open a drawer and rummaged in the files. "This is it." He dropped a bulky file on the desk and opened it. "The receipts for that night are in there alphabetically by customer. Take a look." He glanced at Joe. "I liked Mr. Connolly. He always said to call him Randall but I really liked him. I called him Mr. Connolly. He seemed to deserve that kind of respectful treatment."

"You said you were concerned," Joe said.

"Yes, I wondered about him that night, but I thought he was okay. I knew about Deb—we all did—so I was cutting him some slack. If he wasn't here I figured he'd be home alone drinking—depressed and all. Drinking alone is never good, so I kept an eye on him and I didn't say anything. Now I wish I'd been more cautious. Anyway, take a look."

Joe thanked him and reached for the file.

"Just put it back when you're done. I gotta get back out there."

Joe picked up the stacks of clipped bills. The charge slips were in alphabetical order by last name and Randall Connolly's collection was on top. Joe pulled out Randall's packet. The man had consumed eight drinks, which Joe estimated was seven more than his usual.

He picked up the other packets, and folded through them. Deeper into the pile he came to the charge sheets for Leo Harris, a much thicker packet covering almost three months. Joe leafed through them. Leo, it would appear, was a heavy drinker and a light eater. And judging from a quick glance at the other charge sheets he was Randall's only companion on the last night of the man's life.

The office window faced the driveway to the building next door, which had once been a private home and was now a coffee shop on one side and the office of an electrician on the other. Above were apartments. A car came into view, its tires grinding on the gravel as it turned into a parking space in the rear. Joe could see a sliver of blue sky, the same kind of sky Deb and Cecily must have enjoyed when they set sail on that fateful afternoon.

Randall had been stoic throughout the visit by the police officers, and Joe thought him more courteous than he needed to be until he recognized the stress the man was under. He was barely holding it together. Joe glimpsed a trickle of blood flowing down the other man's little finger as his fingernails dug into his palm. And when Randall reached out to take the sheet of contact numbers, he left a red-pink smear on one page where his thumb had held it.

The following morning Randall called the police station to tell Joe and anyone else there that he had hired a couple of boats to continue the search. If they didn't find Deb's body, then she might have surfaced and floated away, unconscious or injured but at least alive. He gave no thought to death by hypothermia or drowning and talked only about the skill and experience of the searchers.

Joe had not expected him to be so desperate, and went round to the house to talk to him but he was gone, out on one of the search boats, exhausting himself to get through the pain of losing his wife. Coming into the Blue Lobster later that night to drink was more of the same, desperation hiding grief.

Joe replaced the charge sheets and refiled the packet. Ted was arranging bottles in front of the long mirror when Joe returned to the main room. He sat on a stool and waited for Ted to take a break. "Were you on duty that night, when Randall was here?"

"I was." Again, Ted leaned on the bar, placing his feet back as though he were tired, and leaned in, his arms stretched, his head forward. "A rough night. I was surprised to see him here, Randall, I mean. Leo comes in a lot, usually with someone he's doing business with. But not Randall. And he could, easily enough. They live just over there." He stood up and nodded towards the window, and Joe knew what he meant. Across the tracks, the park, and the marshy inlet sat the spit of land where the Connolly house sat, its three stories of shingles almost a beacon, if the owners had had the ego to put up a lamp on the roof.

"How did Leo and Randall leave?" Joe asked. "Were they driving?"

Ted winced and gave a quick shake of his head. "No way. They walked, I'm pretty sure. I saw them going along the park after they left, so unless they parked in the lot over there they were walking."

"Makes sense," Joe said. "It's not even half a mile." He paused, and swung back to face the bar. "They were here for almost the entire evening, according to the bar bills. They're time stamped, and the timings cover the hours almost up to closing time. Any idea what they were talking about?"

Ted shut his eyes, gathering his thoughts. "It sounded like Randall was in here because he was unwilling to be home alone, you know, with Deb just gone. That's what I thought at first. But I don't think that was it."

"What gave you that impression?"

"He talked about being out on a search boat," Ted said. "He looked like he'd been on the water all day—worn and tired and covered in salt. Sunburnt. You know the look."

"Did he sound like he really expected Deb to be found?" Joe had noticed at the outset that Randall struggled with the news of Deb's disappearance over the side of the Lady Mistral, but he hadn't considered it unreasonable. But the news that he was continuing a search on the second day changed things. "Did he say he thought she was still alive?"

Ted's expression softened. "I thought he did, but later I thought he knows she's gone. He knows. He just doesn't want to give up. They were great people, Chief. Really nice. Thoughtful. Kind." He took a deep breath. "Anyway, every time Leo said something about whatever, Randall went back to the searchers. He said he was going out the next day too, Sunday. And then he'd sort of deflate, just sag."

"What about Mr. Harris, Leo? I didn't know they were such good friends."

Ted shook his head. "I don't know if they are or not. Any time money came up, Randall didn't seem interested in the topic and went back to the search boats. I didn't really get what they were saying most of the time. Leo kept his voice low and Randall didn't say much else except all that about the searchers. Leo kept ordering drinks and Randall seemed kind of out of it, like he wasn't really listening to Leo." He tried to smile. "I thought Randall was depressed and Leo was trying to cheer him up. I didn't try to hear—I wanted to give them their space."

"So they left when?" Joe asked, torn between appreciating Ted's tactful behavior and wishing the young man had been the nosy sort.

"Just before closing."

"Did either one say where he was going? Did Randall say he was going home? Or Leo?"

"I didn't hear them say anything, but I'm pretty sure Randall went straight home because I saw his lights come on."

Joe swung around to look through the panel of windows. "You can see them from here, at night?"

"Oh yeah. Especially in the winter." Ted rested his arms on the bar and looked across to the windows. "I saw them go on. I was kind of relieved, you know? Even though they were walking I thought about getting them a taxi, for Randall. Leo seemed fine. He can hold his liquor. If I'd thought Randall was driving, I would have stepped in and called a cab."

"What time did you close that night?"

"About one—it was Saturday, but even though it was a weekend, we're not really a party place and most of our regulars are thinking about the next day, going out sailing or tennis or something like that. They want to get up and out in the morning. The diners are long gone by then. Maybe a few people stay to watch a game from the other coast, if one's on," he said, nodding to the television mounted over the bar in the center of the long expanse of a mirror. "There's not much doing after the dinner hour summer or winter even on a weekend." Ted glanced around the dining room, recalling the rituals of the restaurant.

"Were the lights still on at Randall's when you left?"

Ted placed both hands on the counter edge and leaned forward, and Joe wondered if he felt like a caged animal halfway through the evening, running back and forth along what was basically a run for a puppy. "That's the thing, Chief. I live upstairs. There's a studio apartment up there, and I live there for most of the year."

"So you must have a pretty good view of what goes on at the other side of the harbor," Joe said. "Do you remember anything else about that night?"

"Not really."

"That sounds tentative, Ted."

"It's probably nothing."

"Let me decide that."

"It sounds like I'm spying on folks," Ted said, pulling a face.

"I know you well enough to know that's not true," Joe said. "Tell me what you saw or heard."

"Something woke me up in the middle of the night and I looked out, thinking maybe someone was trying to steal a boat or something. I saw lights on across the marsh—Randall's lights. Not much else was lit up—it must have been close to three a.m. I felt bad seeing lights on in his place at that hour, figuring he was pretty depressed over Deb and all. It was getting to be a drizzly night too. Depressing. Plus he'd had an awful lot to drink, which wasn't like him.

"But I was looking for what had woken me up. I didn't see anything in the harbor or the park, so I guessed maybe some train workers had gone by on the tracks with one of their rail carts, or maybe moving a line of train cars. I forgot about it and went back to sleep." He closed his eyes for a moment, and Joe knew what he was thinking—he'd heard the gunshot that killed Randall.

The first dinner guests arrived, and the waitress seated them by a window. It was early, but the evening was perfect. Ted took an order for wine, poured the glasses and set them on a tray. He slid the charge slip into a slot by the cash register. Finished, he returned to Joe still seated at the end of the counter.

"You said you can see quite a distance from your studio upstairs," Joe said.

Ted nodded. "I can see across the harbor to the shore and a few of the houses over there, and I can see to the outer harbor and the bay. I can see out to the islands." He grinned. "I have a great view for all the fireworks—three nights running. You know just about every town around here does fireworks for something. So what did you want to know?"

"Did you ever look out and see people walking along the shore path late at night?"

"You mean like Coralee's sailor?" He smiled.

"You've heard about that?"

He laughed. "Everyone knows about that. It's how we measure her decline." He waved to a customer and hurried off to mix a drink. After a moment he returned.

"That sounded pretty insensitive, that bit about her decline. I didn't mean it quite like that. Sometimes when Babs brings her into town, they stop here for lunch. Coralee talks about seeing the sailor, or something else. If she mentions the sailor looking for his gal, it's not a good day for her." He lowered his voice and grew serious. "I didn't mean any disrespect to her."

"I'm sure you didn't."

"We all love the old gal," Ted said.

"How often did she say she saw the sailor?"

Ted looked confused. "I dunno."

"How about a week ago? Two weeks? Three weeks? Did you see her then?"

"I ran into her and Babs in the grocery store a while back. Not so long after Deb and Randall were both . . . well. Anyway, Coralee said the sailor was lost trying to find his ladylove. Quaint expression, isn't it? Anyway, he walks the path pining for her. Pining. Quaint, huh?"

"Do you ever see anyone walking the path?"

Ted laughed. "Oh sure, but no one who could be mistaken for one of Lafayette's men. Annie Beckwith, for instance."

"Really? When was that?"

"This week on the shore path. A couple times," Ted said. "I was getting ready for work."

"How could you tell who it was?" Joe turned slightly to the row of windows. "It's quite a distance."

Ted pulled his mouth to one side, glanced down the bar. "It's boring sometimes. I have a pair of binoculars. I'm usually looking at the boats, the races, that kind of thing." He shrugged.

"Who else have you seen on the path?"

"Just the people who live along it," Ted said. "Annie Beckwith, Babs, Mr. Manderson, the Harrises." He continued to name families whose land ran down to the shore.

"And what else have you seen late at night? Anything that seemed the least out of the ordinary?" He leaned closer, watching Ted think back over the last few days and weeks. He was good looking, personable, and bright but not suspicious. Although after this experience, Joe wondered if that would continue to be true.

"We have some paddle boarders," he said. "Usually they paddle around the inner harbor in the early hours, but I've seen them once late at night."

"Did you see them in the last few days?"

Ted shook his head. "Last week, maybe? It's probably not a good idea to be out at that hour, just in case something did happen, but it must be fun, to have the harbor to yourself. There were no thefts from any of the boats reported, so it seems innocent enough. I figured it was someone from a boat visiting from another club, maybe coming back in from dinner in town. They couldn't exactly call the launch and if they didn't have a dinghy with them, they'd be stuck."

Joe didn't mention that he had a few names of paddle boarders who liked going out late at night. "Where exactly did you see them?" Since the very beginning, Joe hadn't been able to figure out how someone could have gotten out to the Lady Mistral without someone on land or water noticing, but a paddle boarder late at night was practically invisible.

"I saw them going around the boats, just weaving in and out."

"Them? How many?"

"Two."

"Could you tell if it was the same people?"

He shook his head. "I didn't think anything of it. I figured there were people who wanted to go out then. Hell, people walk their dogs at three in the morning. I hear them going into the park and down the docks, walking up and down the streets. Sometimes I think I'm the only one who's trying to sleep around here."

"On the night Randall and Leo were here," Joe said, thinking back, "how did Leo get home? Did he leave a car at Randall's and drive from there? I'm wondering if you saw or heard a car. Though," he said, turning to the window again, "maybe that's too far."

"He didn't drive," Ted said at once. "He walked. He took the shore path."

"And you know that how?"

"I saw him." He stood up straight, looking over Joe's head to the window. "I saw him walk with Randall up to the deck and he saw Randall safely inside. Then he walked down to the shore path."

"He didn't walk up to the road?"

Ted pulled a face and shook his head. "He grew up in that house, Chief. The shore path is part of his back yard. That's how those folks feel about that area—it's their space. Leo walked home along the water."

"Ted," Joe said with an amused look, "it sounds like that part of the quiet little town of Mellingham has a very busy night life."

Ted chuckled. "Yeah. Paddleboarding. Walking the dog. Drinking all hours. Ghosts looking for lost loves. It's a real busy neighborhood."

CHAPTER THIRTY-ONE

The sliding glass doors in the atrium behind the Silva house let in the warm morning air, but since it wasn't yet seven o'clock, neither Joe nor Gwen was uncomfortable. Later in the day, however, it would be too hot to sit on the enclosed brick terrace without turning on the AC, which Joe knew Gwen would refuse to do. "This is New England," she always said, as though New Englanders were not allowed to enjoy a comfortably cool interior during the summer months.

Joe placed his now empty breakfast plate onto a serving table behind him and returned to his coffee and newspaper. He watched Gwen bent over her sewing for another minute before he capitulated.

"What are you working on?" He crumpled the paper in his lap as he leaned closer. "What is that?" He was used to seeing Gwen doing handwork. He knew she loved embroidery, cut work, and other forms of decorative sewing, but he didn't recognize this piece. It looked like mending, but was too small for anyone in their household to wear.

"Don't you recognize it?" Gwen turned the navy blue fabric over and held it up. Joe pushed aside a small bowl of fruit and leaned in even closer. "New glasses perhaps?"

"I don't need new glasses. I just need an explanation." He leaned back in his chair and stared at his wife. Her Cheshire cat smile lasted only a minute.

"That's the town seal." She draped the small cloth across her lap and continued stitching.

"And?" Joe waited.

Gwen glanced at him. "I'm making a flag for Philip's boat. He wants something for the stern."

"Well, well, well." Joe held up the paper, gave it a shake, and returned to reading.

"Hinkie told him he could put it on the top of the mast, but I guess Philip wants it where he can see it better for a while at least. Then I guess he'll want another one, bigger next time, to put atop the mast." She worked the fabric quietly. "Next he'll probably want a special jersey with the boat's name embroidered on it."

"You mean you've started work on that already?"

"I think he wants to wear it to the next PFLAG meeting," Gwen said.

"He told you that?"

"Not in so many words, but he asked about the next meeting and were we all going, and would it be anything like last year's picnic." Gwen paused to look at Joe, waiting for his reaction. Ever since it became clear two years ago that Philip was gay, the family had joined PFLAG and attended meetings every other month, sometimes more often, and Philip had made several good friends. If sailing was going to be a big part of his life, he'd want some way to show that.

"And you're going to make t-shirts for him?" Joe asked.

"I could have some printed, couldn't I? Would you wear one?"

"Of course, if you want." Since becoming a stepfather he had surprised himself with the things he was willing, even eager to do. He couldn't remember ever asking his father to wear something embroidered or decorated in some way to promote one of his children's activities, but he had no doubt his father had done other things without quibbling. And Joe would too, much to his own amusement. "If you want."

Gwen tilted her head and winked at him. "Just trying to keep our teenagers out of trouble." She reached for the spool of thread and began to rethread the needle. "So what great crime will you be solving today?" She looked over and her smile immediately faded. "Oh. What's up?"

Joe had spent much of the previous evening sorting through what he had learned, and what he had learned led him straight back to one big question. Who shot Randall? He was no longer willing to accept the man's death was a suicide, regardless of what the state police had concluded. The entire scenario seemed too pat, the questions too conveniently answered, the motives and behaviors too obvious. It was entirely possible, Joe admitted, that a man recently widowed, home alone late at night after drinking too much, would pull out a gun and shoot himself. But in this instance, the facts didn't fit the death.

The day after Deb's disappearance overboard Randall had been distraught. His sudden appearance at the Eaton house to arrange for the use of their lower garden for a memorial was a man going through the motions, not a desperate man jumping at the opportunity to steal a gun. His swerve to begin a search for his wife in the waters off Mellingham was certainly an act of desperation but not despair. His conviction on the night of his death that Deb might still be found clinging to flotsam somewhere at sea was not the sign of a man about to kill himself. He wasn't depressed; he was determined.

Ted's testimony that he saw Randall arrive safely home and Leo depart, and then saw Randall moving around on the first floor of his house while Leo made his way down the shore path, could not be discounted. And Ted's being awakened later in the early morning hours without discovering why suggested something more critical had happened then. He had seen no paddle boarders that night, no dog walkers or cars.

If nothing else, Ted's testimony gave Joe a more precise timeline, and the time of death it suggested fit snugly with the estimate provided by the preliminary medical report.

"Joe?" He looked up at Gwen's voice. "You disappeared there for a minute. I didn't realize you were working on something major. Guess I haven't been paying attention." She frowned, hunched over her sewing, her coffee going cold and the butter on her English muffin coagulated.

"A few unanswered questions now seem to have answers." Joe smiled and folded up the newspaper. "Philip has really taken to sailing, hasn't he?"

"He loves it, really loves it." Gwen smiled and fluffed up the little flag. "He tells everyone about it. He wants to know when you're going out with him again."

Joe stood up and dropped the newspaper onto the chair. "Soon, at least before I'm too old and stiff to get into that little thing. I hope he's ready to move up next summer because I may not be able to get myself into that Penguin by then."

"I won't tell him that just yet," Gwen said. "He's too excited as it is."

CHAPTER THIRTY-TWO

The Whipple family lived on a quiet side street not far from the sprawling high school. Joe parked under an aging red maple, its brittle branches threatening to collapse on the top of his squad car. He wasn't surprised to see a yellow slash on the trunk, marking the tree for removal in the coming weeks, before the hurricane season took it down free of charge.

The tidy red house sat back from the street, with two paths leading to two front doors, one on the right for the family, Joe surmised by the mailbox, and the second on the left, leading to a small office in what was once a garage. Joe headed for the office.

Alex Whipple cleared off a chair for Joe in a crowded office and then took his place behind a desk stacked high with three-ring binders and manila folders. He was a tall man with thinning white hair and the clear eyes of someone who spent time on the sea, perhaps before his life behind a desk. Despite working in a home office, he wore a shirt and tie, the tie having been loosened and the top shirt button undone. His sleeves were rolled up and his fingers stained with ink.

"Is this business?" Alex Whipple asked cheerfully.

"Not at all," Joe said.

"Damn," he said with a grin. "Always happy to have more business.

"Actually, it's your son Aaron I want to talk to you about."

Alex's face fell, but he looked confused rather than worried. "Has he done something?"

"No. I'm hoping he can help me with some information." Joe was quick to reassure the father.

"Of course he can, I hope." Alex swiveled in his chair and gave a shout. A moment later Aaron, a younger version of his father, stood in the door with a large pad of drawing paper in his hand. His father stared at the pad of paper, and Aaron slipped it behind him. "He's supposed to be working, but honestly he's always drawing. Machinery. He likes to draw machinery." Alex turned back to his son, with affectionate resignation. "Chief Silva wants to ask you something."

"Yes sir." Aaron stared at the chief, and Joe waited.

"I can wait outside," Alex said, taking the hint and standing up.

"I can assure you this is strictly for information," Joe said as the older man left the room.

"It's about paddle boarding at night, isn't it?" Aaron said, after his father closed the door.

"Go ahead and sit," Joe said.

"Dad doesn't always know," Aaron admitted. He looked so hangdog that Joe felt sorry for him, but he was here for information that he was guessing only Aaron might have.

"Do you go out alone late at night?"

"Mostly." Aaron shifted on the chair. "Dad sleeps like a dead man, so does Mom, and I don't get to do much in the summer because I'm working. He wants me to learn the business so I can take it over when I'm grown."

Joe nodded. He knew how that went. "What are you drawing?"

"You know what Dad does? He fulfills orders for the Pentagon, but some of the stuff they want is so dumb—I mean it works but not very well." He folded the pad open and handed it to Joe, pointing to a drawing that, Aaron insisted, would work far better than the equipment now available. "Dad thinks it's a waste of time."

"Looks interesting," Joe said. And it did. He could see the future successful industrial designer in the drawings. He handed back the pad. "I want to ask about the nights when you were out paddle boarding. Did you see anything unusual? Anyone else out on the water?"

Aaron shook his head. "It's pretty quiet, even with all the lights from the yacht club and some of the houses. It's almost like daylight at three in the morning. Weird."

"No one else out in a dinghy or another paddle board?"

Aaron continued to shake his head. "But once I thought I saw a swimmer." He leaned forward, eager to have something to offer the chief of police.

"When was that?"

"Hmm. A while ago, maybe three or four weeks ago. Maybe more."

"And where was this?"

"Oh, out in the harbor. Out by the yacht club. I figured it was rats."

"Can you describe exactly what you saw, or think you saw?"

Aaron shrugged. "It was so quiet—it's almost perfect at that hour. You can hear all the water and everything. I guess I was maybe out near the bigger sailboats and I saw a little wake, like the kind I leave but different. So I thought, yuk, rats swimming across the harbor. They come out, you know, looking for scraps when someone has a cookout on the beach, so I figured that was it. But I didn't want to get close to them so I turned around and came back in."

"What about the shore? Do you ever see anyone along the coast? There's a shore path that runs the length of the peninsula, from the street down to the Harris house."

"You mean like that ghost Mrs. Eaton is always talking about?" He grinned. "That is so cool. But I've never seen it. Sometimes you can see light reflecting on the path, on the rocks and such, glass, whatever, but I've never noticed anyone out there."

Joe thanked him and tried another tack, but the boy was certain he'd never seen anyone walking along the shore late at night.

"Where do you launch from?" Joe asked.

"The beach sometimes, the little one next to the yacht club, or the little dock by the gazebo. It's public."

"Yes, I know." Joe smiled. "Do you often see lights on at that hour?"

The teenager shook his head. "I like going from that spot because it's more private," Aaron said, looking guilty. "I'm not in any trouble, am I? I mean, I know it's late, and I'm sneaking out of the house," he began, leaving the statement to find its own end.

"You're not in any trouble," Joe said. "I was glad to see you wearing a life vest the other day. I hope you wear one at night."

"I do, I do. I'm very careful."

"But I think you should tell your dad when you go out," Joe said. "And I think you should invite him to go with you." Once again, Joe found himself looking at someone who was convinced he had at least three heads, maybe more.

"Oh, sure."

"No, Aaron. I mean it. You have to tell your dad."

Aaron's face fell and he looked around the room, but there was no escape. "Yes sir."

And Joe knew he would.

CHAPTER THIRTY-THREE

Joe followed up his visit to the Whipple family with a call to Annie Beckwith. The weekend was fast approaching and he wanted to wind up the questions surrounding Deb and Randall's deaths before witnesses' memories grew hazy and faded, or, even worse, lies became truth. His phone call to Annie Beckwith had been greeted with suppressed anticipation until he outlined what he was looking for, and then his request was met with silence, a long silence. Joe thought he was pretty good at interpreting silences, and this one seemed to him to suggest surprise not unwelcomed. He waited. She invited him to drop by and take a look at something she'd found.

"Your phone call was so unexpected you had me thinking you were a mind reader," Annie Beckwith said as she led the way into the house. The kitchen island was covered with envelopes and documents sorted into various piles. After the obligatory offer of something to drink, which Joe declined, Annie hopped up onto a stool and shifted a stack of letters towards the chief.

He reached for the pile and lifted the top sheet, a letter addressed to Randall from his attorney, Max Hasden. He scanned it and read the next one on the pile. "Are there more of these?"

"All those letters and emails are about the same thing, some investment that Leo has going," Annie said.

"But from the sounds of this, your sister and brother-in-law weren't involved," Joe said. "Is that correct?"

"You're right," she said. "I was getting ready to throw out some of these old files and Max said I should sort through them so I knew what I was getting rid of." She pulled a wry smile. "He's watching out for me, I guess, but the idea of having to save all this paper." She shook her head and continued to smile. "So when I sorted them I found I had this one big pile on a non-investment. That didn't make any sense. So I played the sleuth and put them in chronological order and the first one is right there, on top."

Joe reread the date and glanced at the three short paragraphs. "So Randall was inquiring about an investment on behalf of his neighbors, Carl and Edith Manderson." He began to read through the letters and emails, turning over each one and stacking them neatly on his right. Annie watched, leaning on the polished stone countertop.

"Curious, isn't it?" she said when he'd finished. He flipped the stack of paper over so the top one was once again the first in chronological order.

"Why don't you give me your overview of the matter," he said.

"Oh, Chief Silva, my viewpoint on investment matters is worth less than an empty cup of coffee, but if you insist, I'm glad to give you an opinion." She sat up straighter on the stool, brushing her hands down the front of her blue and white striped jersey, as though dusting off crumbs from her breakfast. She had rolled up her khakis to her knees. "Have you ever noticed that the less we human beings know about something, the readier we are to hold forth?"

Joe smiled but asked her to continue.

"Okay, so here's my take on the whole thing." Annie closed her eyes and took a deep breath, the student about to recite her lesson. "Deb and Randall were very conservative investors, careful and steady. And quiet, really quiet. They mostly liked hanging out with people but I never knew them to talk about investments at parties, at least when I was around. I know they liked Carl and Edie because I met them here a few times last summer and the year before, I think." She frowned trying to work out the dates.

"Go on," Joe said.

"Anyway, it looks like Carl asked Randall about a certain investment he was in with Leo and asked his opinion about it and Randall said he didn't know about it but offered to look into it," Annie said, coming to a halt. "And then he asked Max about it." She screwed up her face and wrinkled her nose. She gave her head a little shake, as though trying to rid herself of an unpleasant smell. She looked about four years old.

Joe waited. "Yes?"

"Well, it just goes to show how little I know about these things," Annie said. "I mean, if you don't understand an investment, would you ask a lawyer or would you ask someone in finance? I mean, Randall and Deb had a broker, someone they'd had for years, and they liked him. I only met him once. He wasn't like Max, who's practically a member of the family, but he was okay. They trusted him."

"But they didn't talk to him," Joe summarized. "They called Max and talked to him."

"And then last month, I think it was, Max forwards him this email from an intern in his office, not a paralegal but some kid who's working there for the summer." Annie sat up and pressed her hands to the side of her face, pushing her hair back and giving him a confused look. "I don't get it. I read that email a hundred times and I have no idea why he sent it. What on earth is it about?"

Joe pulled the email out of the stack and scanned it again. He was beginning to understand what it might be about, the rows of figures and dates and cryptic letters began to look a lot like the stock reports in the newspaper, which he never read. He noticed them only on his way to the sports section.

"Did you find any other ongoing correspondence with Max on a different topic?" Joe asked.

"A different topic?" Annie reached out to touch the stack of letters in front of Joe and then pulled back. "Well, yes. A few of them."

"A brief summary?"

"Okay," she said, turning to the other stacks on the countertop. "There's one on the sailing program for the high school." She smiled. "You know, chief, it's like I've been given a chance to get to know my sister all over again. I had no idea of some of the things she and Randall got up to. They gave anonymously a huge amount of money to keep the sailing program going for free for all the students. That is amazing. I had no idea she cared so much about sailing—I thought I was the one in our family." She slid a stack of emails and letters across the counter towards him.

Joe knew about the sailing program and the ongoing issues about funding for sports programs. The townspeople had been delighted and moved when the anonymous donation came into the office, delivered as an electronic deposit in an account set up exclusively for the program. The accounting went to an attorney in Boston, and he forwarded the thank you notes from the students to the donors, whoever they were. There was rampant speculation in the town about who the donors might be, but Joe had never heard Deb and Randall Connolly's names among the suspected philanthropists.

"In this one, where he's just starting to talk about the donation," Joe said, tapping a printout of an email, "Max Hasden writes, 'per our conversation.' Do you have any idea what that was about?"

Annie reached for the printout and read the message aloud. She shook her head. "No idea. Max and Randall talked all the time but when it came to business, Randall liked to have paper. I asked Deb once if it meant he didn't really trust Max, and when she stopped laughing, she said no, it was Max's idea. He loves paper, or emails or any form of the printed word that he can go back to. So, yeah, I suppose it was unusual for them to talk. But they talked all the time, just not officially, I guess." She leaned back. "Do you think it means something?"

"I don't know yet," Joe said. "But I think I'll give Mr. Hasden a call." With Annie Beckwith's permission he gathered up the documents. "And now I have another request."

CHAPTER THIRTY-FOUR

Joe crossed the neat lawn to the unruly hedge that divided the Connolly, now Beckwith, property from the next. Annie turned and watched him following her, and then pushed through the narrow opening between a scraggly honeysuckle and yew. It looked to Joe as though the owners had planted and abandoned a variety of plants, gaining the tight wall of green that guaranteed privacy.

On the other side of the plantings Joe followed Annie onto a narrow path in which the grass had not yet been killed by walkers but only flattened. The path dipped along the marsh and rocks, turning among the trees and shrubbery. Joe came around a turn, where the lane opened to a lawn falling down from a house with a broad terrace. He recognized the Eaton estate.

"Oh, how fun!" The words came from an elderly woman on the arm of a younger one. Babs Eaton held her mother-in-law as she walked alongside a narrow garden paralleling the path. The yard was open almost to the shore, giving the house magnificent views of the harbor as well as the small town on the other side. "Have you come to visit?" Mrs. Eaton alternately pulled and pushed Babs to move closer to Joe and Annie.

"We're taking a walk along the shore path," Annie said. She stepped onto the lawn, and Joe noted the change in tone. She was politely entering someone else's home without an invitation, and was careful to explain herself. "Chief Silva has never been along here before, so I thought I'd show it to him."

167

Babs glanced at her, then Joe, and he guessed she wasn't deceived.

"You have a beautiful day for it," Babs said. She turned to her mother-in-law to introduce the chief and Mrs. Eaton reached out and wrapped her arthritic hand onto his forearm. She pulled him to her and pressed her face close to his.

He could smell her talcum powder and a hint of perfume, just enough to be pleasant. Her cotton dress was perhaps fifty years old, a classic for others and a rather ordinary summer outfit for her, perhaps a favorite. The splashes of muted color, repeated in the cloth belt, picked up the color of her cheeks. Her skin was remarkably smooth, and her white hair soft and delicate, like an infant's. She wore just a touch of lip gloss, and Joe guessed Babs had suggested she abandon the unruly tube of lipstick for the easier to handle lip gloss, as his sisters had persuaded their mother to do.

"I know what you're doing here," Mrs. Eaton said. She glanced at her daughter-in-law, just over her shoulder, and inched her way closer to Joe.

"You don't think I'm taking a walk?"

She shook her head. "It's the wrong time of day." Mrs. Eaton whispered into Joe's ear, careful to turn her face away from Annie and her daughter, to prevent them from hearing her.

"The wrong time?" Joe repeated.

"He only comes at night." She pulled his arm closer to her and leaned heavily on it. She stabbed the cane in her left hand into the ground and twisted it in a circle to emphasize her point. "Too much light."

"Too much? It's a lovely day," Joe said.

"He only comes at night," she said. "They plan to elope in the dark, before anyone notices she is gone."

"Ah," Joe said and smiled. "The man who returns in hopes of finding his lady love."

"He shines with love, shimmering like a figure of gold in the moonlight," she said. "I do hope they make it. I do love a happy ending. I keep my fingers crossed for them." Her smile faded and she studied him. "You're not on the father's side, are you? You won't interfere, will you?"

"I won't interfere in true love, Mrs. Eaton. I can assure you of that." He leaned toward her as he spoke and she gave him a conspiratorial smile in return. Satisfied, she pushed away from him without letting go of his forearm. She might be unsteady on her feet but she was still strong.

"How nice to see you again, Deborah." Mrs. Eaton turned abruptly to Annie.

"I'm Annie, Deb's sister."

"Of course you are." Mrs. Eaton covered her confusion with a stiff smile and blinked a few times.

"I think I'm getting tired, Mother," Babs said.

"Yes, I'm not surprised," Mrs. Eaton said. "You've done a lot today. We should go back."

Joe paused to watch the two women as they made their way up the hill to the house.

"Babs is really good with her," Annie said. "It must be hard."

When Joe didn't reply, Annie turned and walked on along the shore. The path ran barely one or two feet from the marsh in most spots, land that was flooded much of the day, and often malodorous during periods of the summer. But the path could just as easily take a turn and cut through boulders and over gravel fill where animals had pulled the land away.

Occasionally Joe and Annie passed animal scat and tiny footprints, but in general this part of the shore had been left to grow wild and neglected, possibly a practice meant to keep people from walking what had once been public pathways open to those wanting to fish or fowl in the area, as the old colonial documents described it. As life changed, landowners became less interested in preserving tradition and honoring a right of way across their land. Knowledge of the shore path and its purpose died with the change of ownership, and people like Annie Beckwith, Joe suspected, would come to be regarded as an annoyance with their knowledge of local history and lore. That day was still in the future, however, after all the old families who remembered and maintained their sections were gone.

They passed a number of houses facing the water, some buried behind trees and others robustly and even aggressively jutting into the sky. Annie wandered ahead, occasionally commenting on certain features of the path—the stumps of an old dock left to rot in the marsh, the iron ring in a boulder dating to the previous century, the trash that washed up from a passing boat, the ducks that sometimes hid among the overhanging branches. When he came to the signs of an old stone pathway leading from the water to a yard off to his left, he paused to take his bearings. Through the trees he could see the gazebo and small beach next to the yacht club.

Joe could hear Annie talking to him as she got farther and farther ahead of him, leaving him to squat down for a better look at the path and the break in the trees and the slab of stone among the rocks. He pulled on a latex glove and reached down into the muck by the old flat stone. He slipped the piece of white plastic into a bag and stood up.

"I thought I'd lost you," Annie said, reappearing in front of him. "What's that?" She nodded to the plastic bag but he slipped it into his pocket before she could get a closer look.

"How much farther does this go?"

She studied him for a moment before answering. "Not far. It ends in about a hundred feet, at Leo Harris's yard."

"Does it pick up on the other side?"

"Sort of. You can take a path down to the beach and cross to the rest of the peninsula," Annie said, turning back to look at the rest of the path. "But that part has stone walls and stuff, so we usually took the road when we went there."

"Does anyone else use this path regularly? Or is it just you?"

"No one thinks about it anymore," Annie said. "With a few exceptions the people who live along here are new and they wouldn't think about dropping in for a visit with their neighbors. Deb and I knew everyone, and our parents did too, so we went to visit friends, or just explore." She lifted her head and smiled at the trees around her. "We were just playing. It was loads of fun. Lots of kids our age around then. A few families from back then still live here. I suppose they walk along here sometimes but I never see them. Mostly people drive."

"I wonder how long it will be before it's completely overgrown," Joe said.

"I shouldn't admit this," Annie said, looking around as though someone might be lurking in the bushes, waiting to hear what she said, "but I plan to walk this path regularly. I love walking along here and stopping to wave to people. Weird, isn't it?"

CHAPTER THIRTY-FIVE

The lower level of the Mellingham Police Station held two small cells with small windows near the ceiling, giving a clear view of various shoes passing by. A pedestrian would have to fall to hands and knees and get his cheek almost to the pavement to see inside. This was the result in part of the size and location of the windows and in part of the brightly patterned curtains hanging stiffly on either side.

The grandmother of a previous police chief had taken to spending afternoons in the cell when her household of children and grandchildren became too much for her. She decorated the cots with small handmade quilts and throw pillows and hung a single shelf bookcase from the cross beams. The cells were absurd in the eyes of any other professionals, but since they were so little used for their intended purpose, no one got around to cleaning them out. Mindy Dodge, the newest recruit to the Mellingham Police Department, found them useful. She claimed this was the only place where she had enough room to spread out her papers and get a good look at things.

"My mother wanted me to be an accountant," Mindy said. Joe stood behind her, silently, for several minutes, while he watched Mindy work.

He had returned from his meeting with Annie Beckwith and immediately given the correspondence between Max and Randall to Mindy. And now he waited. As good as Mindy was at her job, and as important an addition to the team as she was proving to be, she had one quirk that Joe fervently hoped she'd

grow out of. She talked out loud while she was figuring out
where to go with a problem, rambling along until her
comprehension kicked in, and then she was dead silent and
unreachable until she'd come to a certain level of understanding.
Both states came dangerously close to irritating Joe.

"She thought I had a good brain for it. My dad thought
so too." She continued to shuffle papers and Joe continued to
watch, refusing to let his toes start tapping. He even stared down
at his black shoe, just in case his foot started off without him.

"Does that mean you're finding something interesting?"
Joe leaned against the newel post in an effort to appear calm and
unhurried.

The police station had originally been a fire station, built
in the late 1880s, and it had been built to last. That was one of
the complaints of the members of his department. The damn
building wouldn't fall down so they could demand a new one.
Even in a giant earthquake, this structure would stand. In the
small cells, the white stonewalls were refurbished every other
year, and the stone floor buffed and polished. Even with heavy
truck traffic passing by, the building never trembled or shook.
Joe sometimes wondered what his former colleagues would think
of his current digs.

"Well, it means that I understand what I'm looking at
even if it's not what I thought I'd be looking at." Mindy had
short brown hair, ordinary brown and ordinary waves, but she
had one long curly lock that she pulled to her mouth and sucked
on when she became absorbed in something. She was tugging on
it now at the corner of her mouth. She reminded Joe of a second-
grader facing a lesson in addition.

"I'm in for a surprise, am I?" Joe had expected some
push back when he hired Mindy, even though he considered his
department relatively free of prejudices. But, as he well knew,
people could surprise you. He had expected her competence to
carry her and was pleasantly surprised that her natural ease with
people disarmed the other officers. Her refusal to act like
anything but what she was, a twenty-six-year-old woman,
gradually brought around everyone until she had an entire
department of fans. As he told Gwen after Mindy's first day on
the job, "She's the future. She and Ken. Others will come and

go, but she and Ken will go the distance." He still believed that, now more than ever.

"A sort of surprise, sir."

"How soon before you're willing to spell it out?"

Her dark eyebrows arching upward, Mindy swiveled her chair so she was facing Joe. "I'm going over everything a second and third time." She glanced at the little piles of paper, looking like the tops of icebergs on the blue-washed cement floor. "I expected to find the usual in some kind of investment scam, pressing for more investments, refusing to disclose costs, that kind of thing."

"But?"

"But it looks like Randall Connolly asked about investing with Leo Harris, on the suggestion of Carl Manderson, and Leo Harris put him off. Mr. Harris said the fund was closed, but Mr. Connolly found out otherwise." She glanced over her shoulder at a stack of papers and then back at Joe. "His correspondence with Max Hasden on this is very discreet, but you can tell the two men were suspicious."

"So instead of Randall feeling cheated by Leo, as Mr. Manderson does, he was rebuffed. And that made him curious." Joe walked closer to the files. "Okay. Keep at it. When it's clearer, I'll put in a call to Mr. Hasden. I'd like to hear first hand what he thought about this."

"I have a few more stacks to sort through, but so far it's all consistent," Mindy said. "And that email he sent with the figures from his intern, well, I think that clinches things. But I have to double check to be sure."

"What's your sense of the relationship between the two men, Harris and Connolly?"

"Presumed friends," Mindy said. "They act like they're friends because they know each other and live in the same neighborhood, probably socialize together at parties and such, but they wouldn't choose to be together otherwise. Not the same type at all." Mindy shook her head and her short curls bounced.

Joe mentioned his walk along the shore path with Annie Beckwith.

"Are you thinking someone swam out to the Lady Mistral and tampered with the vang system?" Mindy cocked her head and stared up at him. "You'd have to be a pretty good swimmer for that, carrying tools and all. You'd probably have to make more than one trip at least."

"The houses along that path have proximity," Joe said.

"But I can't see Leo Harris doing something like that," she said. "Have you talked to him lately?"

Joe stepped away from the stacks of paper and turned his attention to Mindy. "Meaning?"

"He wheezes," she said. "Sounds like he has advanced lung trouble. Emphysema or asthma or something."

"How did you find that out?"

"I stopped him on the sidewalk just after he'd parked his car, and told him he couldn't park there." She adopted the serious expression he imagined her using as she approached the large man. "He said he couldn't find anything closer to the post office and he was only going in for a minute. I told him I had to give him a warning."

"How did he take that?"

"He got tense and didn't say anything, and that's when I noticed it. He started coughing, and then that stopped. But his breathing was worse, so I tried to ease up a bit, and he sort of backed off."

"And that's when you noticed his wheezing?"

Mindy nodded. "Each breath was a struggle. I thought he must have a handicapped placard but he didn't. I suggested he look into one if he wanted to be able to use the handicapped parking places."

"How'd he take that?" Joe knew that not everyone was flattered to be offered the opportunity to apply for a handicapped placard.

"He waved it off," she said, but he looked conflicted. "Pride, sir, is highly overrated."

Joe smiled at that. Mindy was the office philosopher. "I haven't seen an application come through," he said, adding Mindy's information to his picture of Leo Harris.

"I only mention it because if you're looking at him for swimming out to the Lady Mistral, well, I don't know, sir." She lowered her chin and shook her head slowly. "I can't see him swimming in the harbor or even safely in a swimming pool. He'd have buoyancy but I can't see him having the lung power for going any distance. And I don't think he could row out either. Sir?" Mindy looked up expecting to hear a response from the chief.

"Right," Joe said, backing away.

"I thought I'd head out for lunch as soon as I come to a stopping point," Mindy said, turning around.

But Joe had already turned to the stairs and grabbed the newel post, taking the steps two at a time. The tiniest piece of information, he thought as he reached the top of the stairs, can change everything.

CHAPTER THIRTY-SIX

Joe knew Babs Eaton would help in any way she could, but he had come to her home with the kind of question he couldn't ask outright without tipping his hand, and he wasn't ready to do that. She had to guess he was narrowing his focus in particular after meeting him on the shore path earlier in the morning and now finding him on her doorstep.

The evidence pointed him in an unexpected direction, one that shouldn't have startled him but did. He wondered if that was a sign he was getting soft, or getting ready to retire. Odd, he thought, how the elements of a good life didn't fall into line as they should. He was the father of teenagers wondering if it was time to retire instead of enjoying them and feeling younger for having them around. He heard footsteps and dragged his thoughts back to the business at hand.

"Of course I'm glad to help," Babs said as she led him into the living room. He knew she was trying to hide her curiosity, but she went through the usual hostess steps, something akin to nervous tics in this part of the town. He declined a chair and noted once again the beauty of the setting, and the ugliness that had lived hidden behind the perfect view for many years.

"You mentioned a party when Em would have cleaned the entire downstairs and the study, and not gone back to it for a month or so," Joe said. Babs tipped her head towards him as though hard of hearing, but he recognized this as her mannerism of acute listening. Before she could say anything, he heard a cheery greeting and Coralee shuffled into the room.

"I thought I saw someone arrive," Coralee said, approaching with two outstretched hands and a wide smile. She was wearing the same dress as when Joe had seen her earlier that morning. "How lovely of you to drop by, Mr. Silva. We don't see you nearly often enough. How was your sail yesterday?" she said. "Didn't I see you going out yesterday? I saw you on the dock at the marina. Such a lovely view from the balcony. Did you have good air?"

Joe assured Coralee he had good air and a good sail, and didn't try to correct her sense of time.

"And is that your boy?" Coralee looked pleased to hear about Philip. When Joe finished answering, she said, "I must introduce him to some of our neighbors. He'll have a bright future. He's a very good sailor, and you know how important that is. All the best people sail."

Joe thanked her and stepped back as Babs tried to redirect her mother-in-law to the terrace.

"The senator's coming to visit his old pal, you know," Coralee said, turning back to Joe. "They're Leo's neighbors, down at the end. Lots of important people about. I'll just make a note of your boy's name and set things up. An opportunity not to be missed."

"That explains all those black cars and the men in blue," Joe said.

"Oh, yes, they're everywhere," Coralee said. A young girl in a white blouse and black skirt appeared and slipped her arm around Coralee. The old woman turned back to whisper to Joe. "Her husband died recently. They live next door." She gave the young maid a sad smile, before turning to Joe again. "She misses him. No matter what sort of husband he is, we miss them when they're gone." The maid led her away.

"We invited Annie Beckwith to lunch the other day, and Coralee has mixed her up with Deb. I'm sure you noticed that this morning. They look a lot alike, as you would expect from sisters." Babs delivered this explanation but her glance swept the room and she ended up talking to the piano in the corner. "And now she's mixed up the maid with Deb." She took a deep breath and turned to Joe. "You wanted to know something about a party?"

"Your annual party," Joe said. "Tell me about it."

Babs blinked at him for a moment, taking in the request. "Of course. Well, it was the standard guest list." She recited the names of the guests. Joe knew them all, but only four lived on Brewster Street, within walking distance, and were also members of the yacht club. "I see you know them all, at least by name."

"I've met most of them through town business," he agreed.

"A congenial group for the most part." She turned a clear-eyed, somber eye on Joe. "There wasn't anything in the evening that would have warned me about what was going to happen later."

"Tell me about the party."

"It was a cocktail party because that's the simplest. I wasn't going to have an annual party this year because of Coralee, but Betty Winslow approached me and asked if I'd be willing to help with a fundraising effort for the school sailing program. There's a big anonymous donor but the money doesn't cover everything, so we raise extra if we can."

"Have you done this before?"

Babs nodded. "At first I wasn't sure, but then Coralee started asking about when the party was—she's used to having the garden ready for it and, so, when things started blooming it reminded her. Anyway, I thought the idea of combining the two might work out for both of us."

"And Betty Winslow was agreeable," Joe said.

"She was," Babs said, nodding and smiling. "Coralee likes to entertain but with her the way she is, well, it's a bit awkward. But I thought this kind of arrangement would work. Actually, she did well that night. Very well. I was happy for her because I think she knew she was doing well and not fading in and out, the way people with dementia do. I think she was enjoying being whole, all here, you might say. I was very happy for her."

"Who drew up the guest list?"

"Betty and I did it together, along with suggestions from Coralee and some of the others. We wanted it to be something of a neighborhood party as well as a fundraiser."

Joe nodded. "How did the fundraiser part work?"

"People were asked to bring a donation, and there was a basket on a table in the front hall, near the door, so they could just drop it in. Cash or check. We wanted people to have a good time but also to donate. We had information on the sailing program for students, and Lincoln left some information on the Mellingham Yacht Club and its support of local programs."

"Did he deliver it, or did someone pick it up?"

"He dropped it off the afternoon of the party," Babs said.

"Did you speak to him?" Joe asked.

"No, but I saw him leaving in his car. I found the brochures on the table in the hall."

"And the party worked out well?"

"We raised a couple thousand dollars." Babs paused. "But that's not what you're looking for, is it?" She took a deep breath and stared down the hallway to the front door. "You want to know about the gun." The veneer of the perfect daughter-in-law fell away, and Joe looked into the eyes of a woman who had lived a hard life, and made her peace with it.

"Walk me through the evening."

"The guests arrived, and it was all very informal. They could pretty much wander through the downstairs, and that includes the kitchen and my husband's den. But I didn't notice anyone wandering off. No one had an argument with Randall or Deb. No one was caught having sex in one of the bedrooms upstairs. No one was smoking grass or snorting cocaine. No one was caught stealing the silver and no one was trying to hustle any of the other guests. Well, except Leo."

"Tell me about Mr. Harris," Joe said.

"There's not much to tell," Babs said, resting her hand on the back of a chair. "But I think I'll sit down, if you don't mind."

Joe kicked himself for not noticing how tired she was becoming. Her hand and fingers were twisted, and she'd never recovered physically from the injuries she'd received on the night her husband died. That was obvious. He helped her to the sofa and sat opposite her, wondering what life would be like in a few years, an elderly woman with dementia and a younger woman with permanent physical disabilities.

"So, Leo. Well, Leo has been trying to get everyone around here to invest in some new thing he's got going—he brings it up constantly, at least he did. I haven't said more than two words to him in a while. He got Carl Manderson to invest, and some others I don't know."

"How about Randall Connolly?"

"No, not Randall. Leo said he was working on someone else whose name I forget. I don't know why he was telling Carl all this except that Carl seemed to need reassurance. He didn't make his money through investments, and I get the feeling he isn't sure about this kind of world. I did overhear him tell Leo he wasn't sure about what was happening with the investment so he was going to get some advice. Maybe ask Randall."

"Why Randall Connolly? Did he say?"

"He didn't say, but they're neighbors and I think Deb and Randall got along with Carl and Edie." She shrugged. "But I wasn't really listening."

"Where were they talking?"

"I knew you were going to ask something like that," Babs said. "Look, the doors to those rooms weren't locked. Anyone could have gone in looking for the powder room. The key's always in the cabinet door. There's nothing to stop anyone from taking anything in there. I know I should have gotten rid of everything after John . . . but I didn't want to change anything that could undermine Coralee. Her grip on reality is tenuous at best."

"What about Cecily?"

"I did notice her," Babs said. "I was worried she'd be uncomfortable because I knew she hadn't made a lot of friends here and I felt kind of sorry for her. I saw Cecily and Deb off in a corner for a minute, as though they were having a private conversation. But they separated as soon as Leo came back into the living room. He was getting loud. He'd been talking to Carl and came in and started telling some story to whoever was standing nearest the door, and Cecily and Deb almost jumped apart. Maybe they were just through talking, but I noticed it and it stuck with me."

"Is that the only time you saw them together?"

Babs shook her head. "That evening, yes. I've seen them chatting at other parties too. They seemed to be friends." She paused. "I was awfully sorry about what happened to Deb and how it happened. It just seemed so sad and so awful. They were friends, I think, as unlikely a pair as we get around here. But friends, I think."

"Did you invest in Mr. Harris's business?"

"No." If she was startled by the change in questioning, she didn't show it. "No, he never approached us. I don't have a lot of money of my own, but Coralee certainly does even if I manage it for her. So if he wanted her to invest, he'd have to come to me. And he never has."

Joe considered this. It was the answer he expected, but he was only half certain what to do with it.

"It's odd when you think about it," Babs continued, thinking through the idea on her own. She could see her mother-in-law on the terrace, where the young maid was listening to her and looking wherever she pointed.

"Odd? Why do you say odd?"

"This neighborhood is a mix of old Yankees and newcomers," Babs said, resting her hands in her lap. She seemed to have recovered her strength and balance. She occasionally limped, Joe knew, and he had been glad to see her walk fluidly down the hall on his arrival. But then he had begun to wear her out. She seemed better now and he was relieved. He didn't like questioning people when they were struggling with a physical problem. He didn't trust what they said when they were coping with pain. "The thing with Leo is that for this new investment, he's only approaching the newcomers, none of the older families. It seems he's even avoiding us."

CHAPTER THIRTY-SEVEN

The B&M Cafe sat opposite what had once been a train station, built in the late 1800s to welcome the summer residents to their little cottages along the shore, those forty-room mansions that sat on bluffs and looked out towards Spain, or Portugal, if you had known to look at a map. The cafe was tiny, with just enough room for a deli counter and bakery shelf, and a few tables and chairs along the windows. In good weather, what had once been a display area for gardening equipment and snow-blowers was taken up with cast-iron cafe tables and chairs. Joe liked their sandwiches, and he often stopped for lunch. He parked opposite the cafe and crossed the street.

"Hey, Joe!" Hinkie Trask's cousin, Bogie, now in his thirties, called out a greeting as he carried a tray of pastries behind the counter. "The usual?" Joe nodded and Bogie called over to the young man on the counter. "Maybe you can hurry up your staff there. She can't make up her mind."

Joe glanced behind him and spotted Mindy sitting at a table under an open window looking acutely uncomfortable one minute and distracted the next. She barely looked up from her menu. Even though she caught his eye, she didn't seem to recognize him.

"Women!" Bogie said.

"That'll get you into trouble," Joe said.

"Not married yet." He wiggled his eyebrows and walked away to wait on another customer. In another moment Joe's sandwich slid across the deli counter, wrapped and taped. He ordered an iced tea and paid cash. With the sandwich in one hand and the cold drink in the other, he turned to leave but instead walked over to Mindy's table. She nodded to the other chair and he paused, then deposited his lunch on the table, quietly pulled out a chair, and sat down. Just outside the open window three women sharing a table were working their way through lunch. Mindy shifted her shoulders just enough to indicate to Joe that he should notice them.

"I don't want to talk about her," one woman said, "it's too depressing. She should leave him."

"That's just letting him get away with it, Gina. I told her to call the police, take him to court, and wave to him while he walked into prison." Joe didn't recognize the woman called Gina but he knew the woman sitting almost opposite her. Betty Winslow was Leo Harris's second wife and Babs Eaton's partner in the fundraising party.

Gina and the other woman gasped.

"I can't believe you told her that," the third woman said.

"Well, I did. I would have offered her my husband's services, but he's off divorce work now," Betty said. "He thinks it's too depressing."

"He's got that right," the third one said. "When I first opened my office I got dozens of divorcees. You wouldn't think women today would need so much feminist consciousness raising, but it exhausted me. I had to move away from that for a while. So what did she say?"

After listening to her talk about her legal work, Joe recognized the speaker as a local attorney, Pietra Locono.

"She said she didn't want to think ill of him," Betty said. "I told her the richest people can become mean and stingy over divorce, and I gave her Linda as an example. Not by name, of course." Betty poked at her salad. "I love anchovies."

"How is Linda?" Pietra asked.

"Struggling," Betty said, then lowered her voice. "Leo has missed at least two of his last four alimony payments and she's afraid he's just going to quit paying, and she can't really afford to come up here and take him to court. He's been so erratic paying her over the last year or so."

"Spending all his money on Cecily probably," Gina said.

"He asked my husband to invest in something that promised a high return," Betty said, "but since Dave remembers the acrimonious divorce he decided not to. We may be passing up some big returns but the less I have to think about Leo the happier I'll be."

"I thought your divorce was amicable," Pietra said.

"No parting with Leo is amicable," Betty said.

"What do you think of his current wife, Cecily?" Gina asked.

"Typical for someone aging like Leo." Betty stopped and shut her lips, then leaned forward. "I know I'm sounding so waspy, but I'm not really. I'm relieved to be out of that marriage, even after all these years. As for Cecily, I think he wants someone he can control. But he's probably alienating Cecily just as does everyone else."

"I don't think I ever knew Linda," Pietra said.

"She lives in Florida year round," Gina said.

"You stayed in this area. Are you from around here?" Pietra asked Betty.

"The other side of Boston. I stayed because I like it, and I met Dave, my husband, during the divorce. We like it here, so why should we move just because my ex-husband is a jerk?"

The little café was filling up with middle-aged women taking a break from afternoon duties or shopping, young mothers taking a breather before picking up their kids from the afternoon sports classes, men in suits holding business lunches, and the occasional tradesman stopping to chat with a customer. The chatter grew louder though no one was shouting.

"Leo complained about everything when it came to money, especially property taxes," Betty said. "He even said once the town was trying to force him to sell by raising his property taxes, as though it were all about him. I never took it too seriously," Betty said. "I knew he hated paying out anything that wasn't solely his choice, like buying a new car or something like that, but I always thought he had the money to pay."

"I haven't seen him at the club all summer, or out on the water once. Is he not sailing anymore?" Gina looked at both women.

Betty's eyes widened and her mouth opened, but she shut it at once. She looked down at her teacup, poured more tea, and added sugar and cream, stirring slowly. "I did not know that."

"His boat isn't in the water either," Gina said.

"That's very strange," Betty said. "Maggie's Pride is more like a family heirloom. It was a family boat, like yours."

"Ours wasn't as old as his," Gina said. "Right now the one we have is only twenty years old and a pretty ordinary day sailer. We sold our 210 ages ago."

"I remember. It bothered Leo," Betty said. "He used to talk about the fleet all the time—the class of 210s here when he was a teen, the races. I got the feeling he had a sort of obsession with beating the others in every race, but then Deb and Randall Connolly were the only ones left and they didn't race. So that was that. There were two or three other 210s that came through for a while in the summer a few years back but they were sold or dry-docked. One crashed on the rocks in a hurricane a few years ago."

"One of our neighbors is complaining about an investment he made with Leo, Carl Manderson." Gina slid back in her chair, leaving the other half of her vegetarian wrap on her plate. "He's been complaining to anyone who would listen. I think he even went to the police. I saw him coming out of the station a while back."

Betty put down her tea. "That's interesting, because Leo was always very close about his finances. He wouldn't tell anyone what he was doing with his money." Again she paused and lowered her voice, as if that would somehow change the tone of what she had to say. "And then I came to suspect it was because he didn't have nearly as much money as he wanted people to think he had."

"I don't get it," Pietra said.

"People think if you live in a good neighborhood but don't talk about money at all that you must have a lot, especially if it's old money. The less you say, the more you have. Leo knew that. He played the game," Betty said.

"You mean he doesn't have a lot of money? You are so cynical."

"I don't know how much he has now. I just know he has less than he wants others to think he has." Betty smiled and leaned back. "I used it in the divorce proceedings. I asked for what I wanted, and we told his lawyer that if I didn't get that I'd ask for a detailed accounting. Leo hated that."

"So, no alimony?"

"Never." Betty was adamant. "He offered but I pushed for a settlement because if he ever really ran out of money, I'd be out of luck. I didn't know I'd remarry, and I wanted something. He wasn't an easy man to be married to."

"At least you got what you wanted."

"It took a while, but he came up with it—in installments." Betty made a face. "I'm glad I wasn't living nearby then. He might have killed me he was so angry."

CHAPTER THIRTY-EIGHT

Annie Beckwith spotted Chief Joe Silva and Mindy Dodge crossing the sidewalk outside the B&M Cafe. When Mindy nodded a few times while listening to the chief and then turned smartly on her heel and headed to the center of town, Annie threw her grocery bags in the car and sprinted across the parking lot. She reached the chief just as he was about to climb into his car. He closed the door and led Annie to the sidewalk.

"I know you came back to the neighborhood again after our walk this morning," Annie began. She shook her head when he invited her to follow him back to the office. "I'm just wondering if that means something has changed in the investigation."

"The pieces are coming together, but we don't have everything yet." He could tell she was frustrated and trying to contain herself, which he appreciated. It couldn't be easy for her to watch the police investigating a death that had already been ruled a suicide. "Have you thought anymore about why Deb wanted to talk to you?"

"I'm pretty sure it was something different from the usual, like a problem with the boat or something to do with Randall," Annie said, struggling to shift her focus.

"What did Deb say exactly?"

"Exactly? I've been racking my brain about that ever since I left Cecily at the Mellingham Yacht Club. I keep thinking there must have been something Deb told me, but there wasn't. Whatever she wanted to talk about, it was different, something serious, but she didn't actually tell me what it was. You know how when something really serious happens to people who are often emotional, they get quiet and matter-of-fact? It was like that. I don't mean that Deb was someone who got emotional, only that she was not her usual self, the way she always talked with me." She waved her right hand, clenching and unclenching her hand, as though trying to grip the thought before her. "She wasn't emotional but she was light-hearted. And she was never alarmist. But now she was quiet and restrained. It was important whatever it was."

"Did you ask Randall about the phone call?"

Annie shook her head and winced. "I didn't," she said, barely in a whisper.

"She called you just a few days earlier?"

"She'd been out at the yacht club the week before, something to do with the mooring," Annie said. "I was out the first time she called and she asked me to call back but it wasn't until the next day, Friday, a whole week before the accident. We talked but she said she wanted to talk to me in person. And then she was sailing with Cecily."

"Do you remember her exact words?"

"Not really," Annie said, "but I remember she said we still had time."

"She said that?" Joe repeated, taking a half-step toward her.

"Yeah, I thought she meant something about the mooring that I had to do because it's in my name as well as hers. We both sign off on things."

"Did she mention the mooring?"

"Yes, so I just assumed that's what it was."

Joe looked past Annie to the harbor beyond. He could just see the tips of a few masts and the sun sparkling on the water. A car drove into the parking lot at the grocery store and filled his sight, and the harbor disappeared behind a shiny green SUV.

"It's possible that your sister's death had nothing to do with her phone call to you," Joe said.

"Really? You think so?" Joe could see at once that the idea brought her enormous relief, as though by not calling back right away or driving straight out, she had contributed to her sister's death. "Really?"

"Really," Joe said. He gave her arm a gentle touch and saw relief flooding her. "We have a few more test results coming in, as I mentioned. I hope we'll know something soon."

"If you do, will you call me?" Annie gripped the strap of her bag as though ready to rip it in two. "My street is going to be patrolled and crowded, and you may not be able to get out to talk to me, so call me and I'll come right in." She paused, blushed. "You know that don't you?" Joe nodded. "I sound pathetic, don't I? Yes, I do. I know I do, but Chief Silva, I have to know. It's eating away at me."

"I can't give you confidential information," Joe said. "But I'll keep you up to date, and no one in my department will forget that finding Deb and Randall's killer is our top priority."

Her gratitude was unmistakable. He was afraid she'd burst into tears. But at least she didn't notice his slip: Deb and Randall, the way things were shaping up, had died at the hand of one and the same person.

CHAPTER THIRTY-NINE

In one of his earliest cases, Joe Silva had been working with a detective on the murder of a teenage girl. Early morning dog walkers found her body on a beach south of Boston. She was identified within hours, and the detective thought it would be an easy case to solve. Joe didn't understand why the man thought this, but kept his reservations to himself. The family, parents in their late thirties and grandparents, huddled in an office and listened to the detective.

The detective believed in keeping families up to date on "their" case, as he called it. But as the weeks dragged on, and leads petered out, like paths through the sand dunes to a broad, ocean-swept beach, Joe watched each member of the family change in a different way. The father grew silent and morose, as though personally responsible for the failure to identify the killer. The grandfather became aggressive and tracked down poker buddies who might be able to apply some pressure to get more resources onto the case; he asked everyone he knew about who they knew in local government. The grandmother became angry whenever she failed to hear what she wanted to hear, and pressed the detective again and again, forcing him to repeat and rephrase. But the mother was the surprise. One day she came to the station alone and asked to speak to the detective.

"Every time I come here I die a little more," she said. "I'm almost forty years old and I've lost my only child. My husband moved out a week ago. He moved out. You didn't know that, did you? No, of course not. He put his clothes and some of his things in the back of his car and he got into the car and he backed out of the driveway and he never looked at me. He just drove away."

Joe remembered how she closed her eyes, as though resting, exhausted by what she'd told him and trying to keep herself from collapsing and weeping. He expected her to start complaining about all the false leads, the endless report of witnesses who saw a smidgen of the day, and the forensic tests that failed to produce enough information to be useful. He expected her to complain that the department wasn't doing enough. But he was wrong.

"I know you're trying to help us. I know that," she said. "But I don't want to know every detail about what happened to her. She was my little girl. If I have to know what happened— and I suppose someday I will, I'll have to sit in court and listen—but until then, I don't want to know. I want to know she died quickly, painlessly. I don't want my last thoughts of my little girl to be of her in pain. Maybe someday I'll be stronger. But I'm not now, not yet."

She walked out of the station and Joe didn't see her again until almost two years later when the young man who had murdered her child was arrested for another crime against another young girl who had the good fortune to survive. But he never forgot her words. "Every time I come here I die a little more."

Mellingham was a small town, and Annie Beckwith's friends would help her cope, but they would be next to helpless if she slid back into the early stages of grief every time she spoke to the chief of police. She wanted to know he would do everything he could and not forget her and her sister and her sister's husband. Unless a family told him differently, he adopted the hands-off approach with the family. He didn't pick at the wound and he didn't make promises.

Joe pulled into his parking space behind the station and gave himself time to savor the view of the small cove. Across the way million-dollar homes looked back at him. This would be the last quiet time he'd have for a while. The senator had arrived with his important guests, and Mrs. Priestly had called the station at least four times during the night, wondering about who was

really walking through her garden and didn't she have the right
to have a familiar face patrolling her grounds. And it was only
Friday morning. Joe wondered where Mr. Priestly had
disappeared to, but guessed he had learned over the years to lie
low with his guests and wait out the storm. Only two more days
of this, he told himself, two more days. But until that was over,
he had other, more immediate problems to deal with.

      Joe heard the squad car pull in next to him. Dupoulis
lifted an envelope from the seat and waved it at him. It was time.

CHAPTER FORTY

From his office window Chief Joe Silva could just glimpse Cecily Harris holding the car key over her shoulder as she locked the car. He saw the lights flicker once on the late-model green jaguar. A moment later he heard her light step on the stairs, and rose to meet her in his office doorway. It occurred to him as she looked around the outer office of the station that she hadn't changed from the first time he saw her.

She had been standing perplexed in front of the deli counter at the small grocery store that supplied tasty but overpriced choices for those who liked to eat but not cook. Her green eyes scanned the shelves, moving from stuffed clams to crab cakes to fillets of haddock and cod, and on down the line. She might still be there if the counterman hadn't leaned over and said, "Mr. Harris is especially fond of this." Joe forgot what he'd offered, but Cecily nodded and pulled back from the glass-enclosed case and watched the counterman slide open the glass door and lift out a large ceramic bowl. The day had been warm, and she stuck out her lower lip and blew the wayward curl off her forehead. It had been a warm summer then and it was a warm summer now. Her curls were still falling onto her forehead.

"What did I forget to sign?"

Joe led her into a small room beside his office. Before he could answer this, her cell phone pinged and she pulled it out of her small purse and glanced at it, frowned and then paused to read a text. Her eyes widened and then narrowed. She gripped the phone, wrapping her fingers tightly around it, turning the digits white.

"This isn't about signing anything, is it?" The steely thread of her voice, a tone he never would have associated with her, carried awareness and a hint of a threat. "That's from Leo." She waved the phone at him. "He says the police are there at the house right now, your men, they're searching the place, the garage and a shed. They have a search warrant. A search warrant! What exactly is this about?" He offered her a chair. With a shake of her head she refused to sit down.

"I'd like some clarification about some of the details of your sail with Mrs. Connolly," Joe said.

"Details? What details?"

"Some questions have arisen."

"I've answered everyone's questions about that. Yours, the state police, the coast guard. I've been over this again and again." She still gripped the cell in her hand, pressing it to her side.

"This is about something we found on the Lady Mistral," Joe said. "We just want some clarification. You may want to sit down."

"I don't want to sit down." Joe always thought the moment of revelation and reckoning was easy to spot—the moment when the suspect knew what was coming, the inevitability of it all but refused to accept it and doggedly kept to the script she'd originally written, the role she'd adopted and wouldn't give up without a fight, and maybe not even then. "Why are you searching our house?"

"We're not searching the house."

"Okay, the garage, same thing."

"We think the vang was tampered with," Joe said. "Did Mrs. Connolly comment on that?" He could see the calculating in her eyes, trying to guess what she could or should say, how much he knew and what he knew. He imagined she was trying to determine if he was interested in her or in getting to Leo through her. The line of possibilities never failed to flash across someone's consciousness, and he waited to see her expression change. She was ready to tip her toe in the water.

"I already told everyone." She risked a glance at her cell. "I don't really know much about sailing. That was obvious to everyone, maybe not to you, but to everyone else in our part of town. I don't understand anything about the details of sailing so it's pointless to ask me."

"Mrs. Connolly was teaching you to swim, wasn't she?"

Cecily's head tipped back, as though physically struck by the change in subject. She took a deep breath. "I felt I should know how to swim. Living on the water and all."

"Was she a good teacher?"

Mindy popped her head in the door and offered coffee. This little token seemed to tell Cecily she could relax, that no one was after her; the police were after someone else, probably Leo. She thanked Mindy, and took her bearings a second time. She might not have noticed how long it took her before she pulled out a chair to sit down. Joe sat opposite, but turned to the side, as though this were an ordinary casual conversation. She flicked off an invisible speck of dust from her light pink silk slacks, and Joe wondered where she had been headed before being drawn to the police station.

"Mrs. Connolly mentioned to Peg at the Four Square Fitness Center that she wanted to be able to teach you off hours," Joe said.

"Peg said that? Well, yes, she did. She obliged, Peg. She was very nice about it," Cecily said, still feeling her way forward. She thanked Mindy for the coffee and placed the cup in front of her.

"Was there a reason for that?"

Once again, Joe watched her calculate what to say. Her brief burst of confidence faded.

"Well, sort of." Cecily lifted the cup and took a sip. "I didn't want anyone to know I couldn't swim."

"Any particular reason?"

"I didn't want anyone to make fun of me."

"Around here? You think someone would do that?" Joe rested his hand around the cup but didn't touch it. "I'm surprised."

"Well, I really don't like saying this, Chief." She composed herself and offering a sad smile. "But I felt I had to, to protect myself. It sounds awful, and no one else knows, but Leo once said it would be easy to get rid of me. All he had to do was push me overboard." She managed to look prim and disapproving while also appearing injured. But she also spoke more confidently. "Maybe he was joking, the way men do, but it scared me. Just enough, to want to do something about it. He could get angry if things didn't go his way."

"Angry enough to try to sabotage someone else's boat?"

She was a good actress, he thought, but not good enough. Mindy knocked on the door and stepped out into the hall, leaving the door ajar. Joe followed. She held out her cell, Joe read the short message, and he returned to the small room.

"Mrs. Harris?"

She had relaxed her grip on her phone but still held it in her hand. When it pinged this time, she didn't immediately look at it, maintaining the look of innocence and presumed sympathy from the chief. It took her a moment before she understood that the card Joe took from his shirt pocket and read aloud to her wasn't just a note

"You don't understand," she said, turning white. "Deb and I were friends. You can't be serious!" But he was. She swore at him and Mindy's eyebrows went up at the introduction of a few phrases new to her.

Joe led Cecily down the stairs to the cells, wondering how she'd feel about the interior decoration. It seemed appropriate to him that on the day he finally got to use his jail cell, what began as a gorgeous summer day should turn gray and damp.

CHAPTER FORTY-ONE

Joe pulled up in front of the sliding glass doors of the hospital and left his SUV along the sidewalk. The young man in the blue jersey with the hospital logo nodded to him as he headed inside. He was halfway to the Emergency Room when Ann Rose came through the doorway and swerved towards him.

"Oh, Chief, aren't you wonderful!" She smiled up at him, shaking her head at the wonder of seeing him here. "You didn't have to come."

Joe greeted her without admitting he had no idea why he didn't have to come.

"Chandra is just fine." She propped her hands on her hips and smiled even more broadly. "Your boy is just terrific."

"I'm glad to hear you say so, Mrs. Rose. Perhaps you can fill me in." He looked over her head to see Dupoulis coming through the doors to the treatment area beyond. The report had said only that his sergeant had called for an ambulance for Mr. Harris, and he was accompanying it to the hospital. The shock of a search with a warrant was apparently too much for him and he collapsed in an angry gasping heap on the lawn.

"It's ironic when you think about it," Ann Rose said. "We went down to that beach because we thought it would be safer for the baby. Chandra always liked that beach, and it was low tide."

"Safer? Which beach is that?" Joe said. Dupoulis was talking to the receptionist while waiting for Joe, which suggested

198

there was no need to hurry. A good thing, he thought, because it was almost impossible to hurry along someone like Ann Rose.

She named the beach, just over the line in the next town. "And Chandra was having a great time, and the baby and I were having a great time. You know what the little ones are like with all that sand. And then I didn't see Chandra. But, really, she's over eighteen, well, just barely. And then, there she was, with Philip on his boat, sailing up to the beach. He brought his little boat right up onto the sand."

"On the beach?" Joe frowned, wondering if she really meant Philip. The beach was much farther down the coast than Philip and Joe had explored.

"It has a centerboard, doesn't it?" Ann said, smiling. "Just pull it right up and you can go right up onto the sand."

"Yes, yes, you can pull up the centerboard." Joe still wasn't sure what happened.

"That's how he got so close to the rocks," Ann explained.

The fragments were beginning to come together, Joe thought. This sounded like a typical summer day turned into an awkward and embarrassing moment. "So, did Chandra get caught out in the water on some rocks when the tide started coming in?"

"Yes, didn't I say?" Ann took a step back and lay her open hands across her chest. "Oh, yes, she went out exploring and was sitting on a rock, enjoying the sun, and all of a sudden realized she couldn't get back in. She doesn't swim, you know."

"I didn't know."

"So she tried coming back and slipped—all that seaweed on the rocks—and did something to her ankle," Ann said, pulling a face. "I think she got scared."

"And that's when she waved down Philip?" Joe guessed.

"He saw her. He said he could see she was in trouble and he sailed right in," Ann said. "He's a wonderful boy. You are so fortunate, you and Gwen. But then you know that, don't you?"

"We're very proud of him," Joe said. "Is Chandra all right?"

"Just fine. Only a bad sprain, nothing broken," Ann said. "I'm just on my way to get the car. I left the baby with her dad at home, so I'm playing taxi driver as well as grandmother." She started to walk to the main entrance, then stopped. "I can't imagine what young women do when they have two or three children and they're all falling down and getting hurt and everything else." She sighed. "The children I mean. I can't imagine coping with all that. I'm having trouble just being a foster granny." She waved her hand in front of her face, as if ready to faint.

"I'm sure you're coping very well," Joe said.

"Even better now that there are no fireworks tonight," she said. "I know you aren't the only one making that decision, but I'm so pleased."

"It was a matter of consensus," Joe said, about the last-minute decision from the Board of Health. He had found the decision to cancel the fireworks display on his desk later in the morning, and he'd almost forgotten about it in the press of work from the search and arrest. He was glad that was one headache he no longer had to deal with. The Priestlys would just have to find another way to entertain their guests.

"Well, I have to get her home for supper. And don't worry about Philip. He said he was sailing straight back. Thank you so much, Chief."

Joe saw her off and headed into the Emergency Room. Dupoulis stepped away from the registration desk and the two men walked to the back door, to the treatment rooms.

"He collapsed during the search, sir," Ken said. The sergeant was a kind man who had been born and raised in Mellingham. He knew almost everyone, and his relationships changed as he aged, but the families on the peninsula had remained mostly strangers, known by name and by sight but nothing more. "Mindy told me he had trouble breathing when I called for an ambulance, so we did what we could while we waited for the EMTs. They think he's going to be okay."

Joe asked a few more questions, and when he was satisfied that Leo Harris would survive, he returned to the original purpose.

"Yes sir. Exactly what you suspected. Tools. A few things. And some had what looks like residue of plastic wood," Ken said. "It's all bagged and tagged, sir."

Joe could tell the case of Deb and Randall's deaths weighed on him. Ken was a dedicated officer, but he had come into the department expecting to help rather than arrest, and any time he had to undertake the latter rather than the former his disappointment in his fellow human beings was palpable.

The two men walked to the front entrance of the hospital and stepped out onto the sidewalk. The afternoon weather had been iffy, with a gradual drop in temperature and a graying of the skies. It would be foggy soon.

"Is there something else, sir?" Ken asked.

"I just ran into Ann Rose," Joe began. "She was here with her foster daughter. You may remember Chandra Stine. She's Chandra Oliver now. Mrs. Rose and Chandra and her little baby were playing at the beach opposite the islands and Philip was there. Apparently he helped Chandra get back to shore after injuring her ankle while climbing on some rocks." He paused to look up at the sky.

"Oh," Ken said, also looking up. "You don't think he's planning on sailing back, do you?"

"That's what he told Mrs. Rose."

"In the pea soup we're getting?"

"He won't realize what it's like until it's full on him." Joe could already feel the cold damp seeping through his shirt.

"Does he have a cell with him?"

Joe shook his head. "He doesn't take it with him. Afraid it'll get wet and ruined with salt water."

"Still, he should be okay," Ken said. "The bay is full of those guys watching over the Priestlys' guests, the senator and that guy from the Gulf."

"That's what I'm worried about," Joe said. "They won't know who Philip is. I'd better get on to them." He headed for his car.

CHAPTER FORTY-TWO

Philip waved to the family on the beach as his Penguin sailboat, now christened *Explorer,* headed out to open water. He'd never sailed so far down the coast before, nor had he navigated onto the shore before, despite having a centerboard that he could pull up, which allowed him to sail right onto the beach. His stepfather had taken him into the bay and sailed the boat between two islands during an early lesson and Philip discovered the flexibility that came with a small boat, but he hadn't tried to land then. He couldn't wait to get home and tell Pae what he had done. He knew it was late in the day, later than he'd ever been out sailing, but he hoped Joe wouldn't be upset after hearing about his afternoon adventure. He took one last look as Chandra gathered up her things, and then turned back to face the bow.

Dead ahead was a small island, and to his right the harbor of another town. He had sailed farther down the coast than he meant to, but he knew where he was. He came about and headed north, to Mellingham.

The water was a little choppy and he thought his best course was to sail along the coast, hugging the shore and keeping an eye out for hazards. He began to tack between island and coast, zigzagging through the water. He had sailed out of the harbor, across Mellingham Bay, and between two islands, where he could pass even at low tide if he raised his centerboard. He had spent most of the afternoon sailing around the island, and loved discovering the small inlets obscured from the mainland by overhanging trees and shrubbery. But it was late now, and he had no time for exploring.

The breeze was light and he passed the first of several small rock islands. He watched the waves break before they reached the visible outcropping and remembered Joe telling him that breakers this far out meant more rocks out of sight. His little boat had a shallow draft but could still be damaged if he sailed too close to shore or hazards. He tacked farther out. The wind freshened and the sailboat picked up speed.

There were no races out of the Mellingham Yacht Club today, apparently in honor of the senator's visit, though Philip didn't quite understand why a visit from an elected official should affect the sailing races. Only one other boat tacked across the horizon and Philip felt a wave of camaraderie for it and relief at no long being alone on the water. It was too far away to identify its class, but just knowing it was there gave him a sense of reassurance. Philip felt the wind shift—the day was ending and the evening setting in. The wind seemed to be against him now, coming out of the north rather than west or south, but he watched the shore, the waves running in, and people leaving the beaches.

The lateness of the hour reminded him to remain alert. Every few minutes, Philip turned and scanned the horizon. As he sailed deeper into the bay he looked farther out to sea, past islands and hazards. He saw two things. One, the fog was rolling in thick and heavy and fast. He could see it sliding towards him, licking up the air and ocean, another layer of water, cold and dark. In front of it came the other sailboat, and this time it had speed. He could hear the small motor called on only when air failed even though the skipper hadn't lowered the mainsail. The dark boat was heading towards the coast. He saw a flicker of yellow and guessed the skipper had come prepared with foul weather gear, ready for the damp in a yellow slicker. He would certainly make the harbor before Philip.

The fog worried him. If he couldn't see the coast, he couldn't avoid hazards. By the time he felt a rock wrecking the boat it would be too late. He stared back at the island on his starboard and the shore to his port, and tried to decide which tack would be safer. He knew the island well enough to estimate where he was and what was beside him, but he didn't know the near part of the shore well. If he made it to the island, he could hug that shore and then cross Mellingham Bay. The end of the peninsula swung out from an arc of beach that faced the bay, sitting at the mouth of a long shallow sandy bottom thick with grass and clear of rocks. If he crossed the bay but misjudged the channel and ran aground on the sandy bottom leading up to the beach, that wouldn't be dangerous. He could wait out the fog. Besides, he'd have the clanger from the channel marker to guide him.

Philip came about, turned to the island and set a course before the fog could surround him. He tried to judge the passage of his boat by watching spume and the occasional flotsam slipping past. He listened for waves lapping or, worse, crashing nearby. But the sound around him failed, all except the waves lapping at the bow. He no longer heard the sailboat with its motor quietly passing. He listened hard, but still heard nothing. He wondered if the other skipper had dropped anchor, worried about moving through the fog.

Philip eased his sail and kept his eye on the little that he could see, approaching waves and patches of thicker fog. It would be dark soon, and then everything would be impenetrable. He caught a glimpse of the tip of the island and adjusted his course. He wasn't far off his intent, and gained courage from that. He hadn't wanted to admit that he was worried, but now that he saw his course had been correct, he felt enormous relief. And a little elated. He could tell Pae all about it. He calculated the distance to Hidden Rock, the hazard Joe had taught him about on their first sail into the bay. He would sail between that and the island and then tack across the bay. He felt a little thrill at being a real sailor, able to handle the vagaries of the sea. He imagined Pae listening to his tale of the afternoon's adventure—first, rescuing Chandra and then sailing home through hazardous conditions.

At each moment of fog shifting, Philip adjusted his sail and course. He passed safely between the island and the hazard, albeit slowly. Once beyond the rocks he felt a change in the air. He was heading into Mellingham Bay where it folded into open ocean, away from the safety of the shore, or at least the familiarity of the island. He would have less to guide him once out on open water, but he knew this part of the bay. He closed onto his course, reciting all the little details Pae had talked about.

As he felt the wind change, and his sails grow tauter, the fog began to thin. To his surprise, he spotted the other sailboat, but this time he thought he recognized it as one that had crossed his bow farther out some time earlier. The sail was close hauled though there was little enough wind, and he heard the motor sputtering to life. The skipper turned the bow until the boat was coming straight at him. On this course the dark sailboat would plow right into him. He stood up and yelled and waved. He could see a flash of yellow as the skipper adjusted the tiller but held to his course; the skipper hadn't seen him. He yelled again. If the skipper didn't see him, he'd have to come about and try to avoid the other boat, but behind him was Hidden Rock. If the fog came back in, he'd be sailing blind again and could be forced right onto it.

He pulled out his horn and tooted. Waited. Tooted again. The dark sailboat came about. It was as though the skipper misunderstood the call, had taken it as a call to come rather than as a warning to fall off. In the fragmenting fog he followed the boat's progress, glimpse by glimpse. The other boat was again heading straight for him, as though oriented by his warning sound. He stared hard at the boat, but couldn't recognize it. It wasn't Hinkie or any of his other friends. The mainsail had no identifying information on it—no symbol, no number, nothing to tell him its class and who might own it. Even the little boats junior sailors learned in had class symbols and numbers. Hinkie had been firm about learning how to read them.

Philip came about just as the fog lowered itself again, settling deep and hard on the water. Without thinking, he came about again, and headed toward the peninsula. The thought flashed through his mind that the other sailor would only have seen him come about once and head toward Hidden Rock. He wouldn't have seen Philip come about the second time. He crossed his fingers and hoped he'd guessed correctly. If the fog lasted and his luck held, the two sailboats would pass like the proverbial ships in the night—oblivious of each other.

Philip had no idea how long it would take him to cross Mellingham Bay in this weather. For several minutes he raced the fog and the other boat, if his slow speed could be considered racing. The fog swallowed up his immediate surroundings, but the wind remained a steady five knots. If he miscalculated he would crash into the island at the end of the peninsula and miss the long shallow bottom leading up to the beach. Well, he thought, at least I can swim.

The only thing Philip knew for certain about sailing in fog was a comment Joe had made, that sounds aren't reliable in such weather. Philip didn't understand what that meant but the comment came back to him as he listened hard for the clang of the channel marker. He knew it sounded as the marker bounced in the waves, but when he heard something that sounded like it, it came from his starboard, not his port, side. That would mean he had sailed inland, towards the shore, and not the island or the end of the peninsula. Well, if he crashed into the shore, he could tie up the boat and walk home.

He listened again. He heard the puttering of the motor but again he couldn't tell where it was coming from. He thought he heard waves that sounded sharper, as though hitting rock, but that would mean he was heading to the island and not the peninsula, perhaps even out to sea. And then he heard the motor again, closer. The fog thinned and he glanced over his shoulder. There, coming at him again, was the sailboat, its motor puttering toward him. The sail luffed and concealed the skipper, but Philip knew it didn't matter who it was. For the first time since leaving Chandra Stine on the beach, Philip admitted he was scared. Something was very wrong.

Ahead he could see what looked like the outline of the island. If his guess was correct, he was indeed headed out to sea. He came about and headed closer to shore. It was a risk, but he had to move away from that following sailboat. The skipper seemed to think he was someone to go after, and Philip had only one advantage—the fog. With luck, he could use the centerboard to help him sail closer inland, escaping his pursuer, but unless he knew where he was, sailing close to shore was reckless. The dank gray cloud thickened, and the motor grew softer, idling. He had sailed out of sight of the other skipper. He waited. In the quiet Philip realized how cold he was, and damp. His clothes were so damp he thought he could wring them out.

After a while he could see the spindrift of waves along the rocky island. The waves seemed noisier too, as rows of them hammered the shore. He didn't remember that, but on his first turn around the island he'd been caught up in the wind and the view. But if the sounds told him anything, they meant, if he calculated correctly, he was approaching the channel between the island and the mainland, the one that turned into a causeway at low tide. The tide was half way in by now, Philip estimated, and with his centerboard up he could sail straight through. He'd clear the mostly sandy bottom by a good foot or so. He could only hope the boat behind him couldn't do the same.

Weighing the dangers of crashing on the rocks or running aground against passing safely through the channel and then finding a way onto dry land, Philip tacked closer to what he thought was the shore. He held the tiller tight against his side. The wind seemed to ease, and he listened to the waves slap at the boat, heard the halyards slap at the mast. If the other boat was nearby, the skipper might hear that too. He pushed the tiller and let the sail luff, trying to shift the little boat to silence the halyards.

Philip thought about the water patrols he'd seen earlier in the day. If one was still around and he could catch their attention, he would have help making it to shore. He'd be safe. He thought about using his horn, but that would give the skipper following him all but an exact location, practically an invitation to come after him. Besides, the patrol boats were probably busy guarding the Priestly house and their guests. Philip felt the annual twinge of resentment. Every year parts of the coast and some streets were closed off as a security precaution and the residents grumbled. Philip was one of those who thought the Priestlys were just showing off.

The fog began to thin again and Philip felt a frisson of anticipation. If he was closing in on the causeway that led to the Priestly house, the guards would see him, he thought. Awright! He gave a little bounce and felt the boat rock precariously, warning him to settle down.

Patches of sky cleared and he picked out the rising moon through a tunnel of gray. He waited for a little more wind. He hauled in the sail, and began to scull his way for Sutter's Point. He couldn't yet see the other boat but he knew it was there. He could hear the motor idling farther out, and something else, as though the engine were echoing. The fog shrank away from the land and he saw the waves lashing among the rocks at the outer tip of the island. He was so close he could almost touch the rocks and the pines hanging over the water.

He was halfway down the coast of the island when he heard it—the sound of a motor speeding up. He tightened the sheet and prayed he had enough of a head start to make it to Sutter's Point and the causeway. But just in case, he pulled out the box of flares Joe had tucked in the bow as part of the emergency kit. The fog drifted across the bay, rising and falling, thickening and thinning. He turned the flare over in his hands, trying to recall Joe's instructions.

Philip stayed as long as he could on this tack, until he heard the warning sound of small waves on rock. He was close to the causeway now and had sailed along the shore as close as he dared. He listened for a change in the sound to tell him he was nearing the channel. He heard the puttering of the motor but couldn't tell where it was, only that it was getting louder, as though closer.

To make it into the channel, as safe as it might be for him, he had to have enough room to jibe. The flare rolled up against the centerboard housing and he reached for it. He had to take the chance because he had to see where he really was. He'd been wrong so many times. He pointed the flare and pulled. The little red casing blew out and light flew upward a few feet. The flare seemed to explode a second time before it fizzled and fell into the water. Still, it gave enough light for him to see the bow of a sailboat. It was within fifty feet, and on a course to ram him. At the helm stood a middle-aged man. Philip gaped at him, wondering who he was, and then he began to see he was familiar. Philip had seen him before, sailing out of the harbor with a woman of his own age in a day sailor. This day sailor.

Philip recognized him from the first time he and Pae and gone out. They had had waved to each other. Steve somebody. And his wife had a funny name, something like a nickname.

"What is he doing? Twice he's tried to ram me and twice he's fallen away," thought Philip.

Steve Farrell pulled the tiller and the boat fell away. But Philip had seen enough. Steve must have known who this kid in the boat was, and when he and the other man could see each other, in the brief flash of light from the fizzling flare, Steve didn't call out. Something was very wrong, and Philip knew he was right to have been scared. And then he heard something snap, a sound like a snap. He gasped and looked up at the mast, but it was still there, still intact. Whatever it was, he'd have to live with it till he made it to shore—if he did.

Philip tacked into the narrow channel, and came about suddenly. He sailed over a hazard on the outside of the opening, then leaned forward and pulled up the centerboard. The little boat coasted through, and Philip felt a spurt of joy. He did it! He really did it! Giddy with his success, he turned the bow toward land. He could pull the boat up on the sand between the rocks and leave it there till day light. It didn't matter. At least he could get away now. The Priestly house was just beyond the trees. He could be there in a matter of minutes. He'd have a lot of explaining to do, but he didn't care. It would be safer than trying to elude the crazy man behind him.

Philip turned around to take one last look, enjoy one moment longer his outwitting of the other boat, but he didn't see what he expected.

To his surprise, the other boat followed. Philip's heart sank but he gulped for air and tried to calm himself. He knew this area, he knew this channel, he was right about the draft and the depth. He was right—he was convinced of it. Just be patient, he told himself. He waited, drifting on the tide, coming closer and closer to the rocks. Waiting. Then he heard it. The sound of a boat bottom scraping on the sand and rocks. The motor coughed and died but instead of the quiet sound of a wooden paddle against the rocks, Steve Farrell pushing the boat back into deeper water, he heard another motor and voices on a bullhorn. He couldn't tell where they were coming from. Above him he heard the whirring of helicopter blades and a bright light shone down. He heard the sharp voice of his stepfather. But it didn't quite sound angry. And then he heard a gunshot.

CHAPTER FORTY-THREE

Chief Joe Silva made his way down through the boulders and into the water. His shoes sank into the sandy bottom but from here he could see the bow of Philip's boat. He waded out up to his knees and grabbed the bow line just as Philip peered under the sail.

"Pae?"

"Come on, Philip, give me a hand here."

Philip jumped into the water and guided the little boat by the gunwales through a break among the rocks, where he helped Joe lift it out of the water and slide onto the scrub. Before the boat was even secured Joe wrapped his arms around the young teenager and held him, muttering in Portuguese. He hadn't realized he felt it his first language until the events of the evening had stripped away everything he used to guard his feelings.

"I'm okay, Pae." Philip said as he pulled back. "Really. I'm sorry if I made trouble—"

But Joe wouldn't let him say anything. He gripped him by the shoulders and lifted him off the ground and handed him up to a man standing behind him.

"Got him," the man said as another two men came forward to pull in the sailboat. "Evidence," one of them said when Joe glanced at them. He turned back to the small white motorboat and its crew closing in on the other sailboat. The fog dulled the voices coming from both boats, but anyone could guess at the events.

Joe watched the men work. This wasn't his gig anymore, and it had ceased to be his concern after the initial approval for the Priestlys to have fireworks had been rescinded at the last minute. But when Philip had failed to arrive back from his afternoon sail, Joe couldn't be put off.

CHAPTER FORTY-FOUR

Joe left Philip wrapped in a thick blanket in the harbor master's office, located on the lower level of Town Hall, while he went to unlock the back door of the building. He could see Gwen crossing the parking lot, trying not to break into a run and trying not to burst into tears, and failing at both. He opened the door in time for her to run straight through it.

"Where is he?" she said.

He turned to Tango's office and heard Philip call out, "I'm over here, Mom."

After Philip extricated himself from his mother's embrace, he gave her the hangdog expression he'd had since he walked through the door. "I'm really sorry."

"What happened?" Gwen said, looking from Joe to Philip to Tango, after reassuring herself her son was alive and well.

"Philip's a hero," Tango said with a grin.

"I am? What for?" Philip stared at the harbormaster. Startled by this announcement, he sat up straight in his chair and brushed the damp hair off his forehead.

"That's a long story," Joe said.

"Will someone please tell me what happened?" Gwen alternated between staring into Philip's face to reassure herself, kneading his shoulder, and looking to Joe for an answer.

"It seems the senator brought a very important person to the Priestlys' home with him this year, and that made the visit the perfect target for some people," Joe said.

"Our harbor guests have another side to them," Tango said. "And it's a doozy." He shook his head and leaned back in his old wooden chair.

"Who?" Gwen said, looking confused.

"Steve and Bunny Farrell," Joe said. "They were contracted to kill the senator's guest, and decided that Sutter Island, out there in the bay, was the perfect spot for a sniper, so they planted one there. Bunny Farrell."

"A sniper?" Philip's eyes grew wide.

"Bunny?" Gwen's eyes grew large and she looked about ready to scold both men for making a joke of the incident.

"Farrell was right about that," Tango said. "It is a good spot."

"She was an ace," Joe told Gwen. "Ex-military. Private contractor now, or was."

"Bunny?" Philip repeated, wrinkling his nose. He looked exactly like Joe knew he would, embarrassed and disappointed that the great villain he had thwarted was called Bunny. It sort of took the wind out of his sails. How could he tell the story of his great adventure if the sniper was called Bunny? "Bunny?"

"The sniper," Joe said, trying to regain control of the conversation so he could get this over with before he had to deal with a collapsing wife, "was supposed to shoot the target when the fireworks started, but she didn't know they'd been canceled at the last minute. Philip's flare went off, and the sniper took that as a signal."

"It didn't go off very well," Philip said, as if by now he had finally realized his role and wished he'd done a better job. Joe brushed the boy's damp hair from his forehead and then rested his hand on Gwen's shoulder.

"It went off well enough," Joe said.

"It made more noise than light," Philip said. "I thought something had snapped on the mast."

"That wasn't just any noise. That was the sniper."

Philips's mouth opened and his eyes grew wide. He swallowed hard. "Did he—?"

"No, he didn't," Joe said. "There was a second shot and that came from someone in the helicopter zeroing in on her." Joe couldn't tell if Gwen was furious or relieved or too confused to know which. "Bunny wasn't in a position to target anyone on the causeway."

Gwen closed her eyes for a moment, wobbly with relief.

"The security forces moved in early when we figured out what was going to happen." Joe didn't want to admit that knowing Philip was out alone on the water in that pea soup drove him to head straight for the Priestly house and barge in on the security details.

"How did you know?" Gwen asked.

Joe's expression softened as he looked down on Philip, still wrapped in his blanket but no longer shivering. What he wanted to say was he knew because he knew Philip and how he would judge the water and the weather, because he trusted Philip to take a familiar course, because he knew Philip had common sense.

"Joe?" Gwen rested a hand on his arm.

"Well, you just know these things," Tango said, and Joe silently thanked him for the rescue.

"We knew before the flare went off something was up and we had the senator and his guest inside and a dummy outside. Security wanted to know where the sniper was before he panicked and started shooting at anything in sight. Let him see his target and take his best shot. Or her best shot."

"Bunny?" Philip repeated to himself in a whisper.

"And the shot from the sniper told you her location on the island?" Gwen said.

When Joe saw Gwen's expression, he hurried on. "We had no way to reach Philip and we weren't even sure how close to shore he was or where he was."

"And you got the sniper?" Philip asked. The evening had turned into an adventure for him, despite some of the details about the sniper.

"We did," Joe said, "thanks in part to you. The Coast Guard is bringing in her body now."

"What was Steve Farrell doing chasing me?" Philip said. "I thought you were friends."

"You were dangerously in the way," Tango said. "The plan seems to have been to pick the sniper up in a sailboat and toss the rifle overboard. If anyone came along asking if they'd seen anything, they'd just be a middle-aged couple out for a sail who got caught in the fog. Just like you. But no one else was expected to be out sailing because of the security arrangements. The fog was a bonus. But you showed up. That made you a problem."

"Is that why he kept coming at me?"

Gwen began to rub his back, still too distressed to think clearly or calmly.

"It sounds like he was trying to get you to sail along the shore or head inland or sail around the outer islands, because you wouldn't have been a problem then, but you kept heading out to sea," Joe said. "If you got out past Sutter Island and the fog lifted, you'd see Steve Farrell picking up Bunny."

"How was she supposed to get out to his boat?" Gwen asked.

"She had a small paddle board," Tango said. "Man, those things go everywhere."

"I guess I should be glad of the fog. I couldn't tell where the channel marker was," Philip said. "I thought it was on the starboard but it couldn't have been if I was heading out of the bay."

"You can't be sure of sound in fog," Joe said. "Even experienced skippers have trouble then."

"Gee, I was almost lucky he was there, even if he had been trying to ram me," Philip said. "I was never sure where I was."

"I'd hardly call that lucky," Gwen said, her expression fierce.

"I don't know if you were lucky or not," Tango said, "but, young man, you sure can sail." Tango stuck out his hand and after a startled glance at Joe, Philip scrambled to his feet and shook hands with the harbormaster.

CHAPTER FORTY-FIVE

The following morning, Saturday, Joe set out to tie up a few loose ends and get ready for a much-needed vacation, even if that meant only a few days spent cleaning up the garage and taking a day trip to Maine with his family. First on his agenda was a visit to Annie Beckwith, to explain the arrest of Cecily Harris.

When Joe saw the weathered cedar deck chairs on Annie Beckwith's deck facing the town park and inner harbor, he was afraid if he sat down he'd never get up. And then he wondered if he'd be able to talk about the dark business he had come for. Annie Beckwith seemed to understand this and the two of them spent a few minutes watching a small lobster boat maneuver its way around a cluster of skiffs tied up at the end of the town dock, and make its way out to sea.

"It's hard to watch this," Annie said, "as I do almost every morning, and not think about how fishing is one of the most dangerous occupations in the world. It's too beautiful to be dangerous."

"So is farming," Joe said, "but that job's also sometimes ranked as the most dangerous. Fishing and farming and mining."

Annie glanced again at the water. "The state police cars are still up at the Priestly house, and I've heard Ellen is furious but she doesn't know who she's mad at." She dipped her head toward Joe. "There are so many rumors flying around. I guess some of them have to do with my sister and her husband."

Joe pushed himself up in his chair. He was getting too comfortable. "A lot of things came together and we're still sorting some of it out, but we know how your sister and her husband fit in."

Annie's face fell, and Joe felt he'd started off badly.

"I don't mean they were involved in anything questionable," he added quickly.

"That's a relief." She took a deep breath and smiled. "So what happened with Leo and Cecily? Were they involved with whatever happened at the Priestly house? Someone said there was shooting and a crash or something?"

Joe suspected that the farther he got from the Priestly house the more confusing the rumors would be, but wherever he went, he knew they'd be wrong, inaccurate, and slightly or egregiously inflated.

"We arrested Cecily for the murder of your sister and Randall Connolly." Joe paused and waited for Annie to take this in.

"But— She couldn't have. Cecily?" She couldn't seem to think of what to say next, though Joe waited a good while.

"The evidence is pretty strong. If you remember your sister's last call to you," Joe said, "she said she'd just come in from her Friday sail with Cecily and there was something she wanted to talk to you about. She called you on her cell."

Annie agreed. "That's right. She had just come in from sailing with Cecily and she said she couldn't talk right then. She wanted me to come out and talk to her and Randall. She said it wasn't urgent but it was important. I said I'd come next Friday. And then she said someone was coming and she had to get off." Annie frowned, staring at the deck. "That was the week before she died."

"Cecily heard her," Joe said, "and thought she was talking about the investment Leo'd been shopping around."

"But he didn't want Randall to invest," Annie said.

"Exactly, because Randall would have recognized at once what we now know it was—a ponzi scheme. Leo was offering it to newcomers who seemed vulnerable to trying to buy their way into an exclusive group. Carl Manderson, for one."

"Oh, poor Carl." Annie winced and leaned away. "He and Edie are nice but they're so unhappy here."

"Well, Leo targeted the Mandersons and some others, and Cecily was worried Randall had figured it out," Joe said.

"But Leo would never . . . would he?"

"I can't say if he would or wouldn't," Joe said, "but physically he couldn't. But Cecily could."

"She was that strong?" Annie stared at him. "But she'd only just learned to swim."

"Cecily is a very good swimmer," Joe said. "That business about needing swimming lessons was a ruse. She wanted to get close to your sister, as a way to help Leo, so in May she asked Deb for lessons and pretended to be afraid of the water and unable to swim or dive. But that was a lie. She got close to Deb as a way of protecting Leo, to head off any opposition and make sure Leo's plans worked. She knew what was going on financially. He would be broke if he didn't keep this scheme going, and Cecily was ready to help, whether Leo wanted it or not. I'm not sure he even knew about it. She swam out to the Lady Mistral, rebuilt part of the vang system, and set up your sister for her accident on the water. She's very strong, and we know now she had no trouble swimming out with the tools she needed, probably on a paddleboard or a small float.

"We don't know if she did anything more than knock your sister overboard and make it look like an accident, and we'll probably never know unless Cecily chooses to tell us. I doubt she expected your sister to use the vang while both were on the boat but Cecily probably couldn't stop her. This is all speculation, of course, but she rigged up the vang for a deadly accident. It cleared her and could have killed your sister whenever she took the boat out."

"Cecily? It's hard to get used to her like that." Annie fell back in her chair and stared at the water. She repeated the name, barely able to get out the syllables.

"As hard as it is to believe, Cecily gave herself away without realizing it. When she made her statement, she described Deb as standing up in the cockpit while she crawled out on deck to get the loose jib line."

"Deb would never stand up in a boat in a squall. She knew better than that," Annie said quickly. "Oh."

"Exactly." Joe wondered even now if anyone who didn't sail or know the water would understand how revealing Cecily's first statement had been.

"I can hardly believe it. And what about Leo?"

"The information we have on him goes to the appropriate authority," Joe said. "That's out of my hands."

"And that's what Deb was calling me about?"

"No, I don't think so," Joe said. "No, we think she saw something that upset her while she and Cecily were out sailing the day she called you. Cecily mentioned that near the end of the sail, Deb sailed back and forth across the mouth of Mellingham Bay, which meant back and forth in front of the head of Sutter Island. We think she may have noticed signs of recent activity on the island that disturbed her, something beyond a couple of kids sailing close in to explore. If you recall, it was late in the day and everyone else was in. Lincoln was only waiting for your sister to return so he could close up. The yacht club was almost empty, and Deb felt worried enough to call you right away to make sure you came out so you could all talk about what she thought she saw."

"She wouldn't have wanted to stir things up if it was nothing," Annie said. "We always talked over things like that, something we weren't sure about."

"She might have worried it had something to do with the senator's visit," Joe said. "The annual summer visits at the Priestlys were becoming more and more contentious, and Deb wouldn't have wanted to look the other way if she thought someone was mounting a protest on the island. I doubt she suspected anything like a sniper."

"No, she didn't sound worried like that," Annie said, frowning. "So she didn't mention to Cecily anything about Sutter Island?"

"If she had," Joe said, wishing he could avoid it, "Cecily might have taken a different tack. But she felt something had changed in Deb and assumed the worst, for her and Leo, that is."

"But what about Randall?"

"Do you recall Coralee Eaton's revived obsession with the sailor returning for his sweetheart?" Joe asked. "Cecily came down that night along the path and shot Randall, leaving the gun behind to make it look like suicide. She was careful to wipe off her fingerprints and put Randall's hand on the gun."

"When did she get the gun?"

"It could have been anytime that weekend," Joe said. "The Eatons never lock their doors, and the gun cabinet is in that small room just inside the front door. Anyone could have come in and taken it. It just happened to be Cecily. Randall came by to ask about a service on the lawn, and Lincoln came by to leave information on a fundraiser for a youth sailing program. The Eaton house was a busy place that weekend. Cecily walked by the house often. It was nothing for her to walk in and take the gun out of the cabinet and walk away without anyone noticing."

Annie slumped in her deck chair. She drew her hands to her chest, as if to comfort herself but perhaps also to stop them from trembling. "That seems as outrageous as all the rumors flying around." Her breath was ragged. "Some of them have been unbelievable. I heard one that your son, Philip, had something to do with catching a sniper."

"That one's true," Joe said, hoping he could keep the unprofessional note of pride out of his voice.

CHAPTER FORTY-SIX

Joe Silva's early morning visit invigorated Annie Beckwith. Less than an hour later, she stood on the deck of her sister and brother-in-law's house, and tried to accept that the mystery of Deb and Randall's deaths was solved, and the world was settling down, but life would be different now. She wasn't going back to her tiny studio apartment in Watertown, and she wasn't going to worry about bills ever again. She cradled a coffee mug in her hands trying to understand her new reality as she stared out across the water.

All she could think was that every cliche she had ever heard about the ocean and its beauty was true. And she didn't care. She was literally bursting with the beauty of it all. She was a homeowner with a cottage on the water, something she had never expected. And the idea of being responsible for all of it focused her attention on scenery she had merely admired, without ever thinking about how it got to be so lovely.

From the spot on the deck, dressed in old dungarees and a striped blue and white jersey, Annie assessed how much work the yard needed. No one had cut the lawn in weeks, and it showed. The grass might be browning in the dry summer sun but it was still growing in the shade. Something that looked like a flower was slowly being strangled by something that also looked like a flower, though not as attractive. Should she pull up one or the other or both? Perhaps she should go back inside and rifle through Randall's files for a lawn service.

The morning had come on coolish, the way late summer mornings can be. On the water a few lobster boats had set out, their skippers sporting sweaters and caps. It might warm up a bit later, but this was going to be one of the cool days.

It felt strange to have Cecily in jail for Deb and Randall's deaths and Steve Farrell carted off for an assassination attempt, Bunny Farrell's body in the morgue, and Leo in the hospital with a heart attack facing prosecution for investment fraud. Annie knew she should be celebrating but instead she felt like she'd lost something, had something taken from her, until she realized the something had been her sense of how the world, at least her part of it, worked. The people on the peninsula, where she'd grown up, weren't supposed to be murderers and frauds. But they were.

Annie glanced down at her empty mug and put it on the edge of the deck. She picked up her gardening gloves. If this was her home now, perhaps she should make it her home—bury the dead, honor their memories, and get on with life.

She walked down to the marsh and turned around, staring up at the small three-storied cottage, its graying shingles and white trim contrasting politely with the blue door and black-painted iron elbows for hanging plants. The gardens needed work. She turned back to the marsh. And a dock would be nice. She smiled.

"You're having a good morning."

Annie turned at the sound of a woman's voice. Through the shrubbery she caught sight of Babs Eaton, a bunch of sea roses in a trug hanging from her right wrist and a small pair of clippers in her left hand. "You're out early." Annie walked toward her.

Babs smiled. "Early morning is one of the few times I don't have to watch over Coralee. She sleeps late." She wore a sun hat tipped back on her head, though it was far too early to need it. "I saw the chief's car driving in. I hope that means good news."

"Definitely news!" Annie nodded. "Interested in a cup of coffee?"

A few minutes later both women sat on the deck with mugs of coffee in their hands, enjoying the view of a small harbor waking up. The glassy sleeping water began to ripple as the breeze searched it out, and the sounds of engines puttering to life cluttered the air.

"It must be a relief to have it all over now," Babs said. "I never would have suspected Cecily and Leo of anything nefarious."

"Me neither," Annie said. "I still find it hard to believe."

"Ellen Priestly is beside herself. She doesn't know if she should be insulted that someone would have the temerity to shoot at her guests or be frightened that it actually happened." Babs pressed her lips together. "I shouldn't laugh. It's unkind."

"She doesn't elicit a lot of sympathy," Annie said. "But at least everyone out there is okay."

"Most of the security people have left, thank God," Babs said, lifting the mug to her lips. "Coralee has so many stories of why they're out there that we'll be hearing about it for years."

"I still can't get over how simple it all was," Annie said. "The chief explained what happened and it's hard to believe that both Deb and Randall died because of a chance sighting while out sailing and then something overheard at the yacht club. Cecily overheard her calling me and then saying she couldn't talk."

"I feel terrible that Cecily could have taken the gun from our house," Babs said. "I was thinking a man took it, but she was there too. Funny, how women can be invisible, even to other women." She raised the coffee mug but didn't drink. "I'm going to have to persuade Coralee to get rid of those weapons."

"You could put up plastic replicas," Annie suggested, "if you think she's liable to have a hard time with that. She won't know."

"I'll always feel guilty," Babs said.

"You shouldn't," Annie said. "Cecily was a woman on a mission. If she hadn't taken a weapon from your house she would have found another way."

"I suppose so." But Babs didn't sound convinced.

"She certainly moved fast," Annie said, "getting out to the Lady Mistral, booby-trapping the vang, and then making sure Deb went overboard." She paused. "We'll never know if the

boom knocked her overboard or Cecily did. But she managed to
make the whole thing look like a terrible accident."

"And we all felt so sorry for her," Babs said.

"And then shooting Randall. I suppose when Leo came
home and she saw how drunk he was and heard he'd spent the
evening with Randall, it was easy to head down here and—"
Annie stopped to stare at the opening in the bushes leading to the
path. It suddenly looked ugly and dangerous. She couldn't bring
herself to finish the sentence.

Babs reached across from her deck chair and rested her
twisted hand on Annie's forearm.

"Anyway, Cecily in her foul weather gear or swimming
outfit was probably the shimmering pirate Coralee saw on the
path at night," Annie said.

The two women reclined on chaise longues, their legs
stretched out, ankles crossed. One of Annie's sandals dangled
from a large toe.

"I think Chief Silva was on to more of what was
happening than I gave him credit for also," Annie said. "He's a
really good policeman."

"I guess," Babs said after a pause.

Annie smiled as she sat up, putting her feet on the deck
so she was facing the other woman. She reached for the plate of
scones and cut one in half. She was suddenly very hungry for
more than food, for the honesty and trust she'd had with her
sister and the place in a small town she'd known as a child, for a
world where people in positions of authority exercised judgment
as well as power. "The last few weeks have shown me more than
how my hometown has changed." She rested her forearms on her
legs. "I mean, I feel lucky to be here, to live in a town with a
chief like Joe Silva."

Annie thought about the way Chief Silva had accepted
the word from the state investigators, that Deb had died by
accidental drowning and Randall had died by his own hand,
distraught over his wife's death. But he had gone about his
investigation quietly, tactfully, pulling together the odd bits that
others ignored or didn't understand. He had sensed something
was wrong and held on. "We're lucky he's our chief." The
minute she said it, she regretted it. She'd been talking only about

herself, but now she understood what it meant to others, to Babs and Coralee as well.

Babs sat up and put her mug on a small table near the head of the two chaises. "I don't usually encounter anyone at this hour of the morning. I like the quiet time, time to myself." She slid to the edge of the chaise, ready to stand up.

"I'm sorry," Annie said, regretting her tactlessness. "I owe you an apology."

"For what?"

"For a while I thought maybe you had shot Randall."

Babs stared at her, breaking into an incredulous smile. "Me? Whatever for?"

Annie laughed. "I don't know. I never got that far in my speculations. I started thinking that if you had access to a gun, you could have done it." She tipped her head down and closed her eyes. "I'm sorry. I wasn't thinking. I mean, I realized that you couldn't have done it. I mean, physically." She swallowed and tried to smile. "Coralee is lucky to have you."

Babs looked around the grounds, the grass dipping down to the marsh where it turned into the poor cousin of the old salt marsh grass that farmers harvested. "She has dementia, Annie. Lots of people do and their relatives take care of them." Babs stared hard at Annie.

"But she never forgets how much she loves you. She probably even understands how much she owes you, in a strange way."

Babs looked away at the marsh, the grass that looked dead or dying, its straw-like stalks bent over to the water.

"I didn't mean to insinuate anything," Annie said. "I was just crazed after both Deb and Randall died." She couldn't help glancing at Babs's twisted fingers and palm, her nearly useless right hand.

"I know where you're going," Babs said. "Because I shot my husband I could have shot someone else."

"I don't believe you shot your husband," Annie said.

"Really? You know more than the police?" Babs began to shy back but she looked curious, and Annie decided to risk it.

"I don't believe you shot your husband because you couldn't have. He smashed your hand weeks before. You couldn't have picked up and fired a gun if your life depended on it. But it's none of my business."

"You're right about that," Babs said, massaging her right hand with her left. "How did you come to that conclusion?"

"If you listen carefully to Coralee, she makes sense, but most of that is lost in her ramblings. She adores you. It's so obvious. But your husband's behavior towards you must have frightened her beyond reason. It pushed your mother-in-law over the edge. She adores you. She'd do anything for you. Maybe she knew what John was like. Maybe he was like his father and she couldn't stand seeing it happen all over again. She saw what he was doing to you physically that night and she knew you might not survive, so she picked up the gun and stopped him. One bullet. No one will ever know what was in her mind. Maybe she meant to stop him but not kill him but that's not what happened. An old woman killing her only child. Whatever she meant, she chose you over him."

Babs grabbed Annie's hands with her left hand and pulled her close. "I did it. I signed a confession, I went to prison, I did it."

"Coralee is lucky to have you," Annie said, looking down at her wrist. "But you couldn't fire a gun to save your life. You can't even hold one. I've seen you try to cut flowers with those clippers. Your right hand is useless and your left hand is so weak it's pathetic. But no one's going to question a woman holding a gun when she's covered in blood and a witness backs up her story. And that witness is the dead man's mother."

"Her grasp of reality is tenuous," Babs said. "But on certain things her memory is perfect in its lucidity. She's never said anything like what you've suggested. And she never will."

"I'm sure you're right." Annie looked down as Babs released her wrist. "You're very good to her, and I think she still understands how things came to be as they are. She saved your life and you saved hers."

Babs closed her eyes and leaned away, pulling her hands to her waist. Annie wondered if her damaged right hand was a source of constant pain. "She's an old woman. She'd never survive prison, not even for a day."

Babs had learned the art of complete and utter stillness. She reminded Annie of the Buddhist monks who could control their heartbeat or breathing or pulse or some other feature that western medicine considered automatic and beyond conscious manipulation. Babs had mastered something similar.

"I didn't mean to say anything," Annie said. "I only meant to apologize for ever suspecting you."

Babs laughed, and the sound was easy and light.

"Yes, I know, it was absurd. Apology accepted?" Annie said.

"Of course." Babs shook her head, still smiling.

"Why did you come back to Mellingham, if I may ask?"

"When I was released, Coralee was there waiting for me. I can't tell you how wonderful it felt—to see her standing there by the car, leaning on the hood to keep her balance." Babs looked wistful. "She no longer had a chauffeur and she was supposed to stop driving. It must have taken her hours to get there, twenty miles an hour on all the old back roads—she was afraid of driving on the highway. She waited at the entrance and then she brought me back here." Babs looked over at the old house peaking over the treetops. "Coralee treats me like her daughter. I have no regrets."

"You're fortunate," Annie said. "Not many people can say they have no regrets."

-End-

ABOUT THE AUTHOR

Susan writes the Mellingham series featuring Chief Joe Silva, who was introduced in *Murder in Mellingham* (1993). *Come About for Murder* is the seventh entry in the series.

Susan Oleksiw also writes the Anita Ray series featuring an Indian-American photographer living in South India at her aunt's tourist hotel. In the first book, *Under the Eye of Kali* (2010), a guest disappears and another falls unconscious. In the fourth book, *When Krishna Calls* (2016), Anita and Auntie Meena face the loss of their hotel and everything they care about.

Susan's short stories have appeared in *Alfred Hitchcock Mystery Magazine* and numerous anthologies. In addition, she published *A Reader's Guide to the Classic British Mystery* (G.K. Hall, 1988), and served as co-editor for *The Oxford Companion to Crime and Mystery Writing* (1999).

www.ingramcontent.com/pod-product-compliance
Lightning Source LLC
Chambersburg PA
CBHW061140170626
46809CB00003B/936